The Anchor is The Symbol of Hope

"Always shorten sail before you have to."

BEYOND THE
LONG-EARED MOUNTAINS

DAVID D. HUME

*For Melissa – who put
this together to make up
a real book – Thanks*

David

PublishingWorks, Inc.
Exeter, NH
2008

PublishingWorks, Inc.,
60 Winter Street
Exeter, NH 03833
603-778-9883
For Sales and Orders:
1-800-738-6603 or 603-772-7200

Designed by: Anna Godard
Edited by: Melissa Hayes

LCCN: 2008923758
ISBN: 1-933002-63-8
ISBN-13: 978-1-933002-63-7

Printed in Canada.

For

CHRISTOPHER, ADAM, BENJAMIN,
CHARITY, AMITY and NOAH

who heard much of this tale when we sat around
the fireplace in Salem, Connecticut.

This story is a work of fiction and not based on the lives of anyone in reality, except, for the small priest who is so similar to one inspiring clergyman that I have known in Wilmington, North Carolina. I also acknowledge the fact that my uncle, Cyril Hume, actually wrote the sonnet that so inspired Eli when he discovered it among the forbidden books in the monastery of Theodoric Yorb. (This sonnet, found in Chapter 40, was the last in a cycle of sonnets published in the Centennial Issue of the *Yale Literary Magazine* in 1936.)

CONTENTS

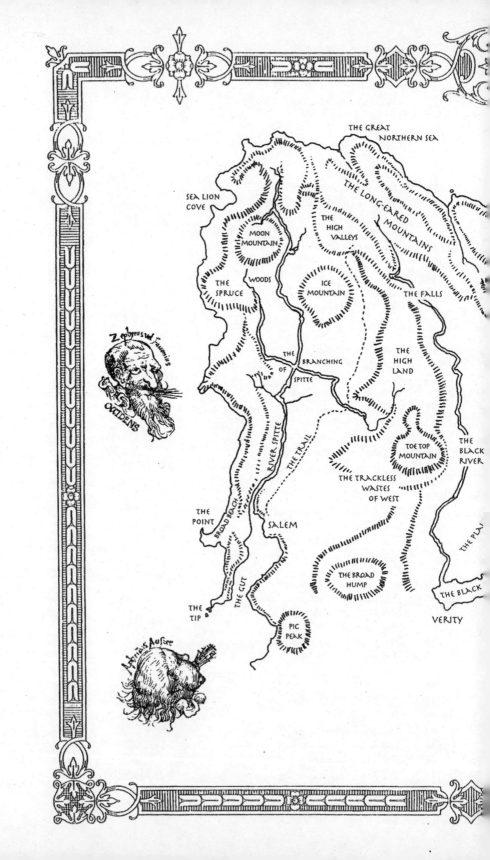

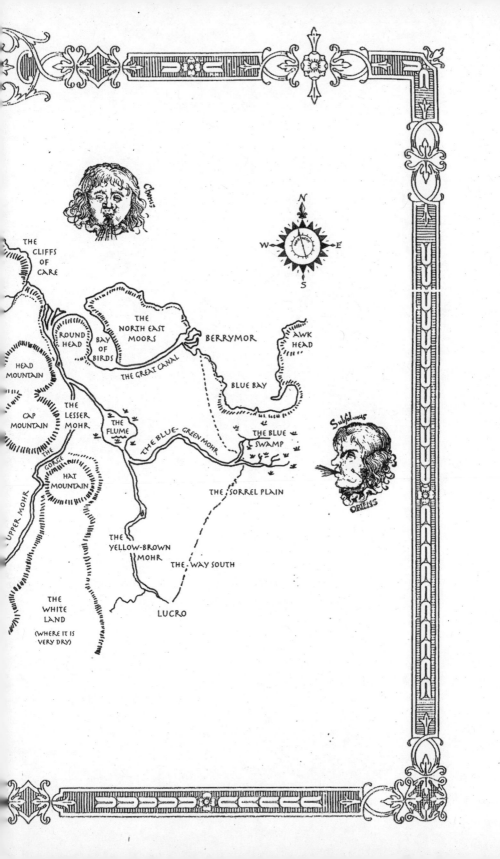

Chorus

THE
CLIFFS
OF
CARE

THE
NORTH EAST
MOORS

ROUND
HEAD

BAY
OF
BIRDS

BERRYMOR

AWK
HEAD

HEAD
MOUNTAIN

THE GREAT CANAL

BLUE BAY

CAP
MOUNTAIN

THE
LESSER
MOHR

THE
FLUME

THE BLUE- GREEN MOHR

THE BLUE
SWAMP

Subfolinus

UPPER MOHR

THE
GORGE

HAT
MOUNTAIN

ORIENS

THE SORREL PLAIN

THE
YELLOW-BROWN
MOHR

THE WAY SOUTH

THE
WHITE
LAND
(WHERE IT IS
VERY DRY)

LUCRO

THE SOUTH WIND

Once, in that time, on a blustery September day, Eli was blown far up the River Spitte against the force of both tide and current. The southeast wind had increased in the afternoon as Eli set out to check the position of the buoys in the little bay of the River Spitte near the town of Salem. Now he did not need to scull the old skiff at all. He had hoisted his simple lug sail and found he was making rapid way upstream with a brave bow wave spreading beside him in the sunny water. The light was clear and the afternoon was pleasant. He reflected that he might have better prepared for a longer adventure if he had shipped an anchor and a lunch. But at just seventeen, he was carefree and sometimes careless of the precautions which older sailors knew about taking on pleasant afternoon cruises.

When he looked aft at the sun-streaked river, he noticed that the whitecaps following his wake were an angry dark green on their undersides, and they seemed to be rising ever higher in the increasing wind. Controlling the skiff was an adventure, and the sensation of surfing along past the unfamiliar shore was exhilarating.

Eli was not the least anxious for his safety; the old skiff was wooden and would float even if swamped and full of water, and he was a strong swimmer. Still, the angry waves behind him looked unfriendly and perhaps even a bit menacing. He tightened his grasp on the steering oar balanced in the notch in the stern transom. Eli, the youngest of a family of sailors and explorers, and the youngest son of Solomon the chart maker, also took comfort in the old sailor's maxim that the wind went down with the sun. As the day was largely done, there would soon be a slacking in the amazing force of the south wind.

The old skiff rolled about in the roughening water and he soon realized that bringing her about with the use of the steering oar was unlikely to work—and actually more likely to capsize her when his clumsy vessel turned across the seaway. So he steered carefully as the western sky turned a luminescent yellow, and then orange and red. Somehow, the wind at his back seemed to take on greater force as the light waned, instead of slacking as he had expected. He finally came upon a cold sunset while the black shadow of the sail still raced forward on his starboard side. It almost seemed to be pulling him forward, toward the north of the country.

He shipped the steering oar and went forward to get the kerosene lantern from the locker at the bow, lighted it, and hung it from a peg on the after side of the mast. But when he came aft again, he stumbled as he stepped over the midships thwart and struck his makeshift tiller with his knee. He hesitated for a moment, startled by the pain. The steering oar wobbled in its chock for an instant and then, as he tried to grasp it, its heavy loom slid through the notch in the stern and it disappeared into the rolling waters of the Spitte.

He rubbed his bruised knee and, lifting the other oar from the bilge, he stood up to steer again. With one oar he could direct his course before the wind, but he could no longer row the heavy boat against the tide if the wind did slacken. Sculling with a single oar would be possible, but slower and harder still. The shore looked dark and rocky now, and Eli knew that the riverbank was rimmed with shoals, and there were tree stumps and other snags in the shadows close to the shore. Farther than this up the river he had not been.

But as dark settled, leaving only a few pink shapes visible among the peaks of the Ice Mountain, Eli could see a glow in the sky ahead. From behind the very distant bulk of the Moon Mountain, the moon itself began to rise.

Moonlight showed him a path in the middle of the river but did little to light the tree-shrouded margin of the water. He could not tell what he might be passing on the dark riverbanks. But he did know that over-hanging limbs could foul his mast and possibly upset his craft. He steered away from the dark shapes of the hills that fringed the river, aiming for the deep water in midstream where the course of the Spitte beckoned him forward, to the north, into the interior of the land, toward the Mountains of the Moon and the Ice Mountain. The wind still blew with a trace of late-summer warmth as it forced him ever farther to the north.

All night long he sailed while the white moon passed his right shoulder and threw his shadow ahead of him on the bilge planking of the boat. All night long he shivered in the cooling wind and searched the shores for a place where he might moor the skiff to a friendly tree. He wondered why he had never thought he might need an anchor before. He was very hungry now and his mouth was dry. He dipped up some river water in his cupped hand but found that it tasted faintly of leaf mold.

While steering between the dark borders of the riverbank, Eli thought of the soundings he might take of the upper river depths. Eli came from a family of explorers and cartographers, and he knew that his father, Solomon, would value the information that could be added to his charts. He sailed on in better spirits through the night. Then, after a long time, there came a high dawn, gray above the murky shapes of the Green Vale to the east. He passed shapes that appeared to be familiar: a dock, a fisherman's shack, a ferry slip with a derrick on it. But all changed in the growing light as the objects began to resolve themselves into the reaching branches of ancient oaks or the whitened skeletons of dead chestnut trees that his tired eyes mistook for signs of human presence. He sailed through a low land of swampy meadows and muddy shores. Straight, black ditches ran off into the Green Vale on either side; far ahead, he could see other hills rising to the north.

His eyes smarted with fatigue and he was overcome with the need to put down the oar and stretch out in the bottom of the boat. But he steered on as the river swung around a broad curve to the west, and he found himself facing a rocky hillside mantled with hemlock and pine trees. *At last*, he thought; *I can tie the boat to a tree if I can just climb far enough up the smooth riverbank to reach one.*

He put his weight on the steering oar and forced the boat alongside a low ledge of granite. And suddenly, just at the level of his hand, he saw an iron ring in the rock. He hooked his feet beneath the midships thwart and reached far enough out to grasp the ring with both hands as the old skiff surged past it. The wind was still in the sail and Eli, his feet well braced, was dragged against the granite of the rock face. He managed to hang on painfully, holding the boat against the force of the wind that pressed him forward. His arm and shoulder scraped against the rock and his back was wrenched sharply as he brought the boat to a stop against the ledge. Slowly the boat came under his control and he was able to thread the end of the painter through the worn metal eye, pulling the two ends of the rope together to wind them in a hitch around the large bow cleat. He dropped the sail and held his injured left arm cradled in his right while he rinsed his wounds with river water, tying up his bleeding shoulder in a bandanna. Before he could do more, fatigue overtook him; he rolled himself in the sail and in an instant, he was sound asleep in the bottom of the boat.

THE RIVER GIRL

Marna had grown up as much on—and in—the water as on the shore that circled the coves and swamps of the upper reaches of the River Spitte and its three tributaries, where she lived with her grandfather, Sennet of the Tower. She was strong, although slight of stature. No longer a little girl, she had grown up from the water sprite who had early learned to swim, paddle, and sail along the pools and sandy beaches at the fringes of the Pine Woods and the Green Vale in the foothills of the Ice Mountain.

Sennet had taught her how to use lines and knots, how to bend an anchor to its rode, how to trim a simple lug sail to make a boat go to windward, and how to unship the rudder when a small boat is brought up on a beach. Passing mariners had taught her other things about larger vessels, and Sennet had added to the ocean lore that made up the bulk of her education.

But Marna had learned about more than just how to handle a boat. She learned to roast pheasant and duck and how to make a delicious soup of the leftovers. She knew how to make salads of the herbs and wild celery that she harvested along the trails in the Green Vale, and how to roast potatoes in the glowing ashes of the fireplace of the Rock Tower.

Sennet was the Keeper of the Tower, and also maintained the few navigational markers that were moored in the river or fastened high up on tree trunks along the shore. The brightly colored markers provided ranges to guide mariners on the upper reaches of the Spitte. They had to be refastened if the winter storms blew them loose from their supports, and often repainted in red and green when, in time, the weather washed away their signals. Some had oil lamps in them that had to be lit at night. Range markers had to be precisely placed both vertically and horizontally so that a pilot on the river could sight the higher above the lower and be led straight and true in a course that would avoid the shoals and bring his vessel into safe, deep water.

Whenever Sennet set out in his skiff to plumb the channels, Marna went with him. As soon as she was big enough, she would pull on the oars to hold the skiff in place against the current while Sennet took soundings with a lead line to find the location of the deep water. The scour of the river's current kept a deep clear passage open for boats, but the channel often shifted after a great storm or after the ice came down the river in the spring, carrying the winter's spoil to the sea in its muddy waters. After her grandfather took soundings in a few places, while they drifted backwards, downstream, he took the oars again and rowed to the next location while showing Marna where to mark the new depths on the chart with a pencil.

Marna was happy in the company of her grandfather in the Tower, which was fortunate, because her parents were always unhappy and restless there. They often seemed to be planning to go somewhere else, and perhaps, to leave her behind. She determined when she was very young that if they did go somewhere else, she would stay and become the Mistress of the Tower, caring for the navigational markers, taking the soundings along the shoals, and assuming the knowledge of the River Spitte that Sennet had gathered over the years.

One day her grandfather said, "I am sending you out on a brief voyage for me. It is a half-day's sail up the Spitte to the Branching and then a short distance along the East Branch to the house of that rascally young glassblower, Lucindar. He lives under the shadow of the Ice Mountain. You must stay a day and a night with Lucindar, and bring back to me three each of the red and green globes I will need for the lighted channel markers, and three amber globes for the range lights. I fear the storms that come around the equinox will shatter some of the marker lights, and I will have to replace those that are broken.

"Be careful of Lucindar while you are there," said her grandfather. "He is said to be an attractive man, but he has no wife, and you are not a child any longer."

So Marna, well prepared for an adventure, set about readying for a voyage. Although her canoe looked fragile, Sennet had built it of thin-sawn white cedar and ribs made of tough juniper, steam-bent. Its inwales were made from slender white spruce, and it was covered with tight-woven canvas impregnated with many coats of dark green paint. Even though the tiny vessel was delicate in design and light in construction, it was a very able boat for an experienced paddler such as Marna.

She packed a basket with three apples, a jar of almonds, two bananas, a tin box of pilot biscuit, three quarts of water, and a wedge of hard cheese. She might have taken more bananas, but she knew they would all ripen on the same day and would spoil if they weren't eaten right away. She also took a clasp knife with more than a dozen blades and tools folded into its red handle. She examined her slender spars and the sail battens and sheet rolled in the diminutive sail. She also shipped aboard a light folding anchor attached to two yards of quarter-inch chain, and sixty feet of five-sixteenths-inch anchor line.

She bid her parents good-bye. They were used to Marna being out on river excursions, and they were distracted by the maps they were studying and the plans they were making for a trip—something about a search for "green stones." Perhaps, thought Marna, they were like the stone her mother wore on a slender chain around her neck. Her father had a faraway look in his eye. And for some reason, Sennet was scowling.

"We will see you when we get back," said her father.

"*If* you get back …" grumbled Sennet.

Marna took the letter Sennet had written to Lucindar and put it in the fold-over pocket of her yellow foul-weather jacket. She tucked her knife in the pocket of her blue denim shorts, picked up the basket and her paddle, and ran swiftly down the trail to the dock, her braids swinging from side to side.

She was ready to begin her journey.

3 MEETING

Eli's skiff was much older than he was, and probably even older than his brother Reuben, who had bequeathed it to him when he went away to act as crew for Old Gormley. The boat might have been older than Gormley, but that was unlikely, since Gormley was even older than Solomon, who was himself very old, and no longer able to explore distant waters. Gormley sailed an old ketch named *Mercy* and made long voyages to far-off ports.

Many parts of Eli's skiff had been replaced over the years. The big cleat in the bow had been salvaged from a larger vessel. She was fifteen feet long and

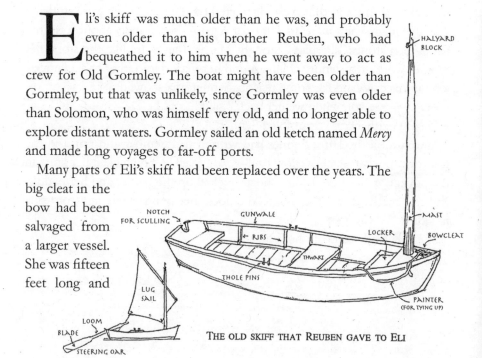

THE OLD SKIFF THAT REUBEN GAVE TO ELI

had heavy thwarts and gunwales with fat round thole pins to act as fulcrums for the long oars. A stout mast partner spanned the bow where a short, thick mast was stepped. A dipping lug sail was lashed there, furled in its own mainsheet. The skiff sailed easily off the wind, but lacked keel or centerboard for going to windward. There was a sculling notch in the stern and the boat was steered when under sail by trailing an oar.

Eli had six older brothers, but Reuben was the closest to him in age, and had stayed at home with him for the longest time. The others had all gone out on quests to help their father with his work, preparing nautical charts. They traveled the seven seas and the six continents in search of the geographical information Solomon provided to navigators all over the western country. Reuben had set out with Old Gormley into the Western Ocean when Eli was still a boy. As the youngest, Eli would stay at home for a few more years. He had rowed, sculled, and sailed the skiff on the Lower Spitte for several years already, but this was the first time he had been so far to the north, nearly as far north as the Branching of Spitte and the Spruce Woods.

Marna had seen such homebuilt boats before, but when she came upon Eli's skiff in the river, she knew that this one was unfamiliar to her. As she approached, she glided easily in her own canoe, for there was still some strength in the southwestern breeze pressing her along the shore. She paddled carefully, with shallow strokes, making broad j's on the starboard side of the canoe, seldom needing to change sides to steer a straight course up the river. Marna knew about the mooring ring fixed in the face of the rock by some long-ago mariner who had traveled on the river many years before Marna—or even Sennet—was born. She had moored to the ring several summers ago, and to make things easier, she'd hung a braided rope ladder from it. This allowed her to climb high enough to reach the tree trunks and roots above the rock face, so she could scramble up the high bank to where there was an overhanging mass of granite, thirty feet above the river. From this point she had first dared to jump in the recent warm weather, flying through the air with her arms flailing like a windmill, until with a great splash, she had plunged into the green water, rising quickly and regaining her canoe in a few quick strokes.

But today she paddled to the moored boat and grasped its gunwale. The skiff contained a pair of black sea boots, a black sweater, some trousers, socks, and a dark blue shirt, all carelessly thrown into the fold of a stained piece of sailcloth. There was no immediate sign of the owner of the clothing.

An empty boat and a pile of clothing meant just one thing: someone must be swimming. Marna turned and looked back down the river the way she had come. She searched both shores, but could see no one in the water.

Suddenly she heard a cry above her.

"*Oh hi-yi!*"

As she turned quickly toward the sound, there came a great splash, and a flying wave of foam struck her full in the face. A head streaming with water appeared in the river beside her canoe. The hair on the head was more brown than black, and was so directly plastered down by the water that Marna could see neither eyes nor nose beneath it. There was, however, a wide smiling mouth that contracted and spouted an arc of water backwards, over the head itself. She then could see the boy's face.

"I'm sorry," he said, shaking hair and water out of the eyes. "I didn't mean to scare you!"

"If you weren't wet already, I'd splash you with this paddle till you drowned!" she sputtered, wiping the water out of her eyes with the back of her hand. "And if you'd been a foot closer, you would have broken your neck on the bow of my canoe, which would have served you right!"

"I'm sorry. I'll go away," the boy said again, and disappeared slowly under the water. Several great bubbles rose to the surface to mark the spot.

The water was untroubled for what seemed a very long time, and Marna began to worry that something terrible had happened. Then he reappeared, right next to her, and a long arm attached itself to the canoe.

"I am most truly sorry, and if you really want me to drown, I will drown myself just as soon as I can if it will make you happy. But in the meantime, could I ask you to turn your back so that I can climb aboard my boat and get into my clothes again? I have come a long way during the night, and I slept so hard on the bottom of my skiff that I had to have a swim to wake myself up, and to see if I could work out the soreness in my shoulder so I could scull the boat. This water is getting cold, and I'm very hungry too, so I hope that you are a kind person and have something to eat in that basket."

"Oh, go and get dressed," said Marna. She spun her light craft about and stared down the river while she heard a splash and knocking of the skiff against the rocks behind her.

"Who are you, anyway?" she said over her shoulder.

"I am Eli, the youngest of Solomon's seven sons," said the boy. "From Salem, down the Spitte, almost all the way to the Gut."

"I've not been there," said Marna as she began to let the current carry her down the river.

"Don't go away," he called, struggling into his trousers. "Wait—you can turn around in a minute."

"Why should I want to turn around?" she said, but as soon as she'd said it, she realized not only that she had done so to make him feel less important, but also, that her course had been *up* the river, and now, that direction was behind her. She circled away from the shore and approached the skiff again, smiling at its occupant. Eli was clad in his black trousers and was pulling on his rubber boots. His left shoulder was bruised black and blue on one side and marked with several deep cuts on the other. He tried to put on his sweater, but bending the shoulder proved very difficult for him, and his left arm remained inside when he was done.

In his turn Eli examined the solitary paddler in the green canoe. The girl's red-brown braids hung down on her shoulders, one in front, one behind. Her slightly arched eyebrows framed large brown eyes. Her bare knees were tanned, and her position in the boat was very straight as she knelt nearly amidships with the paddle in her hands.

"I'm really hungry," said Eli. "I haven't had anything to eat since yesterday morning. Do you know where I could find something for breakfast?"

Marna said nothing, but shipped her paddle and explored the basket. Straightening up again, she tossed a large Winesap apple toward the skiff. Eli caught it in his one available hand, and sat back in the boat, one boot on.

"How nice of you," he said as he took a large popping bite of the firm fruit. "Umm, thank you so much. Do you live near here?"

Marna took a second apple from the basket and took a bite. "What did you do to your shoulder?" she asked.

"It got bunged up when I grabbed for the ring," he said. "And it feels like I cracked one of my ribs, but I think it'll get better."

"If all those cuts don't get infected," she observed. "Look, I do live near here, at the Rock Tower with my grandfather, Sennet, who guards the river just below that bend to the south," she said, pointing her paddle in the direction from which she had come.

"The granddaughter of the Keeper of the Rock Tower? My father told me that Sennet had made soundings of the Upper Spitte. He needs them to publish new, corrected charts."

Marna wasn't paying attention, as she was watching a small steam launch, still quite far away, coming toward them. Its course was not near the rocky shore where Eli was tethered to the iron ring, but well out in the center of the river.

"I think my parents are in that boat," she said. "I wonder if they are finally going to look for that stuff they want, that's supposed to be in the Long-Eared Mountains."

"Have your parents been all the way to the Long-Eared Mountains?" asked Eli, as he finished the apple and prepared to throw it toward the shore.

"Don't throw your garbage in my river," said Marna.

"It's not garbage," said Eli. "It's a perfect package of apple seeds, and I was going to throw it on the land where it might grow to be an apple tree someday."

"Maybe," said Marna. "But it's too rocky there, anyway."

"All right," said Eli. "Do you have anything else to eat? I'm still hungry."

Marna was studying the boat coming up the river. Her parents were aboard, standing and peering forward. For some reason, they were ignoring the two small boats on the shore. The launch passed by them, several hundred yards off, and pressed on up the river. Marna looked away. She rummaged in the basket and produced the pilot biscuit, the cheese, and the almonds, and one of the bananas. Eli crunched a mouthful of nuts, cut a thick slab of the cheese, and started on the biscuits.

"You're very nice," said Eli, "but your parents don't seem very sociable."

"They're not," she said. "All they care about is that green stone they found way up the river a couple of years ago." And as they sat in the two boats, Marna told Eli the curious story of the special green stone and her parents' desire to go looking for its like. She didn't know much about the stone they sought, but her grandfather did. The other vessel had disappeared far up the river by this time, and Marna and Eli sat in their boats for a long time while Eli finished almost all of the food that Marna had brought for her trip to the house of Lucindar, the glassblower.

"Where do you intend to go, Eli?" she asked eventually.

"I don't really know for sure," said Eli. "As long as I'm up here, I should get some soundings for my father's charts. He publishes them in Salem. Maybe I should follow your parents and get a copy of their soundings chart to bring home? Either that, or take the soundings myself all the way to the mountains," he said. "It's a long way down the river to Salem, and I have no supplies. I don't really want to go home yet, with nothing to show for my trip.

"I would like to go farther upriver someday—maybe all the way to the Long-Eared Mountains. But I didn't sleep at all last night and only a little this morning, and I can't do much with my left arm right now. Wherever I go, I need to prepare better than I did for this voyage."

Marna sniffed. "I notice," she said, with a slightly superior air, "that you don't carry an anchor. Perhaps you should have thought of that, along with some food and water. And speaking of provisions, now that we have eaten everything that I had planned for my trip, I guess you should come back to the Rock Tower with me, and start fresh from there."

Marna's words seemed so sure, and her ability in the canoe was so impressive, that Eli was quite willing to follow her lead. So he cast off the skiff from the iron ring and sculled with his right hand on the single oar in the stern chock, despite his painful shoulder. He stood in the stern and followed the green canoe paddled by the girl with the red-brown braids and the yellow jacket. They moved slowly with the current, going downriver against a gentle southerly breeze that scarcely slowed their course.

4 THE ROCK TOWER

Eli made his boat fast to the dock and tried to help Marna lift the canoe to its rack. She said she could do it very well by herself, one end at a time, but she let him heave it up partway with his good arm, to encourage him. Then they started up the hill. They climbed over roots and across small ravines on rough cedar bridges. Squirrels chattered at them, and small brown and white chipmunks darted away as they approached. A woodchuck surveyed them from above for a moment and then hurried clumsily back to the safety of his burrow as the boy and girl reached his ledge.

Marna stopped several times to pick mushrooms from the sloping forest floor. Once she carefully removed a large bracket fungus from the stump of a dead tree.

"We can have mushroom soup for lunch," she said with a knowing smile.

"How do you know they're not poisonous?" asked Eli.

"These are polypora," she answered, turning over one of the mushrooms and displaying its finely waffle-printed underside. "This is usually a pretty good indication that they aren't poisonous. But be careful of the ones with gills on the underside, especially white gills. Some of them are so poisonous that one forkful can kill you."

"I'm not sure I want to try any of them," said Eli.

"Silly—don't be afraid of anything just because it's new. We will have my grandfather look at them before I make them into soup," said Marna. "He knows all the mushrooms very well. It's always best to have someone who really knows mushrooms check them before you eat any—like these bracket fungus. When they have yellow pores on

THE ICE
MOUNTAIN

THE ROCK
TOWER

THE
SPRUCE
WOODS

WHERE MARNA
AND SENNET
LIVED

THE
RIVER

the underside and they're growing off the side of a tree, that means they're healthy, but sometimes they are too old, and then they can be as tough as wood. This one is nice and new and should be fine in the soup. There are also chanterelles and morels that are perfectly delicious. I can always recognize those, but I take them to Grandfather anyway, just to be sure."

The thought of the mushroom soup began to reawaken Eli's appetite, but his sleepless night was wearing on him even more. As they went higher, hunger and sleep fought for control of his attention. By the time they had climbed over the last hemlock roots and entered a clearing, Eli thought he was ready to lie down and sleep wherever he could find a place on level ground.

They approached the Tower by climbing up stone steps to a broad terrace that surrounded the square house, which made up the base of the Tower itself. Three stories high, it was built of rough boulders mortared into walls that seemed to grow out of the hillside. A deep porch of cedar rafters and shingles surrounded the lower story. Above, windows looking in all directions were hooded by slabs of stone that projected like awnings from the surrounding masonry.

They entered through a pair of tall glazed doors, and Eli, his head swimming with fatigue, found himself in a high room, ringed by a balcony that gave on a row of stout oak doors on the inside and a series of windows on the river side. Eli glanced briefly around the great room and his eyes fell upon a long divan padded with rust-colored corduroy cushions, set facing a large fireplace. The need for sleep came over him like a wave and he settled into the cushions without saying a word to Marna. In a minute he was sound asleep, oblivious to the scuttle of squirrels in the rafters above or the soft opening and closing of oaken door latches of portals that turned on wooden hinges.

He did not know how long it was before a voice awakened him from a long and complex dream. He had been dreaming about grasping some-thing and falling away again into consciousness, trying to remember a place and a name but not able to do so. And then he heard the voice singing three tones of a song, or some combination of songs that he knew but could not remember: "Three Blind Mice," or the end of the dirge of "Cock Robin, It was I." *It was I ... It was I*. He found himself where he had fallen asleep, hot from an afternoon sun that streamed in from the windows that faced the river, his face damp and creased from a wrinkle in the cushion. The room smelled most deliciously of mushroom soup. A smiling girl with red-brown braids was looking intently at his face and softly singing a song he did not know.

"Now that Solomon's youngest son is conscious again, I think he is ready to have his wounds dressed." Her voice sounded amused, not annoyed, but her tone was very directive and made Eli sit up quite straight. She turned to a great iron stove in a kitchen that was visible through an open archway at the back of the room. She stirred a bright red enameled pot as she spoke. The yellow oilskin jacket was gone and she wore a dark blue sweater patterned with snowflakes. She shook her head to swing both braids over her shoulders and out of range of the pot.

Marna picked up a large pot of water that had been warming on the stove and brought it to a low table in front of the divan where Eli had slept. He was too surprised to object when she took hold of Eli's sweater and deftly pulled it up and over his head. Then he looked at his own shoulder. In spite of his plunge in the river, the cuts and scratches were obviously still full of dirt and fragments of sand.

Marna uncorked a green bottle of a white soapy liquid, and dipping a washcloth in the hot water, she began to dab gently at the wounds. Her efforts were soothing to Eli's feelings but still painful to his bruised and lacerated arm and side. He decided that he wasn't going to let the girl see him as less able to stand up to her therapy than a Spartan soldier, so he submitted wordlessly to her ministrations. When she was done she put a clean bandage over the cuts and produced a loose linen shirt which she helped him put on. Then she fastened a sling from a soft scarf of purple silk which she knotted around his neck to support his arm, taking the weight off the bruised and lacerated shoulder.

"Now, come," she said when she was done. "Come and have lunch or tea or whatever it is now." As she spoke she produced three large white bowls of steaming soup and brought them to the long trestle table that separated the kitchen from the area that surrounded the fireplace and the divan.

"Grandfather!" she called. "Our wounded guest has awakened, and the soup is ready."

There was a stirring from above and Eli looked up to the high balcony. A man rose from a high stool in front of a brass telescope that commanded the view from one of the tall windows on the upper level.

"Welcome, guest," he said rather solemnly, as he descended from the balcony by a small iron spiral staircase. "Know that you are very welcome to share our food."

He was not a tall man, not quite as tall as Eli. But something in his manner seemed tall and dignified. He wore a dark gray, roughly knit, high-necked sweater, dark trousers, and neat black boots. His hair was white and he had a carefully trimmed white beard, but no mustache. His shoulders were broad, his hands large, and his voice, resonant.

"Come to the table, lad, and tell us something of who you are and how you came to be in the river. My granddaughter tells me she found you leaping and splashing like a bluefish on the rising tide. First, take the edge off your appetite and then give us an account of yourself."

"I am pleased to meet you," said Eli, rising from the divan and bowing very stiffly from the waist. "I have heard of you and your daughter from my father Solomon of Salem on Spitte, who publishes and sells charts to river navigators. But he never told me that you had a granddaughter, or that this was her home. This tower is a wonderful and curious place," said Eli with a smile. "All of my six brothers have left Salem to explore distant places and prepare new charts. As for me, I was taken by a great southern wind in my skiff and driven for a day and a night up the river.

"I came north looking for a beach until I was able to tie my boat to a ring in a rock and sleep for a few minutes. Then I swam to wake myself up, and that's when I met your granddaughter. She most generously gave me something to eat, for which I am very grateful. Then she suggested that I accompany her to the Rock Tower."

"He ate more than half of the provisions I'd packed for a three-day trip," said Marna.

"And where will you go from here?" said Sennet.

"I should gather soundings of the waterways in the north and other geographical information for our chart business," answered Eli, "but I am afraid that my arm will not let me do much for the present. Now that I am so far from Salem, I think I should go farther still, since I am at least halfway to somewhere, and indeed, I've already found myself in a place I knew nothing about when I set out. I would like to learn more."

"Well, I suppose you are young and you must go out and seek something unknown," said Sennet. "For now you may stay with us. Marna's parents have left today, also intent on seeking some knowledge, somewhere, I know not where. They took their corrected charts of the upper river valley with them. I fear they will not find what they seek even with the help of their charts."

Eli spooned up the steaming pink and brown soup with a large silver spoon. It tasted of musty spices and wild herbs. There were thick slabs of brown bread in a basket on the table, an earthenware crock of butter, and a bowl of creamy cottage cheese. Marna placed a pitcher of cider beside her place and set out three heavy glass goblets which she filled to the brim.

"We saw them pass by," Eli said, then stopped, seeing Marna's pained expression.

"They are not long gone, nor perhaps far gone yet, but they intend to go far. Far beyond the Branching of Spitte, beyond the Moon Mountain to the Long-Eared Mountains, where they hope to find something that seems to call them.," said Sennet.

WHAT MARNA KNEW

Eli stayed for many days at the Rock Tower while his shoulder healed and the muscles grew less sore during Marna's therapeutic exercise regimen. For seven golden autumn days, he roamed the woods and fields with Marna, learning the names of mushrooms and field flowers from her. She taught him the difference between the milk snake and the copperhead, which seem so alike in their coloring but are so different in the deadliness of their bites. Once they waded through a field of asters beside a stone wall and an ancient apple tree where they found a morel, a wondrous mushroom that looked like a brain on a stalk, and brought it home to the Tower to flavor their dinner.

Marna led the way on these excursions, and Eli delighted in watching her move like a dancer among the trees and through the fields, her braids swinging, her slender legs seemingly tireless as she climbed stone walls and jumped the bog trots in the swampy lower places.

Marna's chief delights all seemed to begin with the letter M. Mycology is the study of mushrooms, and in this she was becoming expert, but she also loved music and mathematics, and all things maritime. She was skilled on the recorder, a sweet-toned wooden block flute on which she played the music of early musicians with strange names like Josquin Des Prez and Orlando Gibbons. Eli had not heard this music before, but he found it pleasant to learn about anything that Marna wanted to teach him. While she was explaining or playing the recorder, he could look directly at her large, dark eyes and study her face without being the least bit self-conscious about staring at her.

Her fascination with mathematics led her to draw mysterious curves on squared graph paper and then to create formulas that would describe them in the language of algebra. She explained to Eli that the beauty of a curved line was also present in the beauty of the formula that described it. Her large brown eyes grew even larger as she drew the lines that resulted from her calculations.

Eli listened to all that Marna said and he listened to the music she made, but in the evenings he turned to Sennet to ask many questions about what was in the country to the north and east of the Valley of Spitte. He learned that the land was wooded and passable among the uplands between the Trackless Wastes of West and the Long-Eared Mountains. There were also fields that had been cultivated and stone walls that showed where farms had been long ago, although this land was now covered in forest. Beyond the last cleared fields was wilderness, no farms at all until a new slope descended from the Long-Eared Mountains and bore the Black River down into the High Valley. It was said that this river flowed across the High Land to the city of Verity. Sennet said he knew nothing about this place except that it was rumored the people there always lied. But such tales were hard to credit because the man who said his neighbors were liars might have been lying himself.

One morning, after massaging his shoulder, Marna gave Eli's bare back a slap with the flat of her hand.

"There!" she said. "You're cured and ready to be sent back to duty!"

Eli grinned and went back to wearing his black fisherman's sweater. But he did not leave the Tower right away. He listened to all that Sennet said and resolved to go and learn more about these faraway destinations.

"Are Marna's parents going to these places?" he asked. "Why would they go and leave their daughter behind?"

He glanced at Marna and she looked back at him, without emotion. "People have gone to the north and east and beyond the Long-Eared Mountains often in the past, but none has ever come back to tell what they found there, if indeed they found anything at all. As for Marna's parents, perhaps leaving her here was the last good thing they could do."

"I don't understand," Eli said.

"Before Marna was born, another great wind came up the Spitte, and it blew her parents far beyond its branching, to a cold valley. They were able to anchor in a gray backwater and wait for the wind to blow itself out so they could return downriver. But before they came back, something happened to them. When they brought up the anchor from the mud of the riverbank, they found, clinging to one of its flukes, a slender chain. Riveted fast to the chain was a small green stone, shaped like a triangle. The chain was made of steel, but of a type that never rusted or became stained. It was a metal such as they had never seen before, and the links were so fine that you could not insert the point of a needle into them.

"From that day on," he continued, "they were different people. My daughter was already with child, but even after Marna's birth, I think her mind was still on the stone. She searched for more of them, for some distant wealth. She didn't speak of it much, and what with her work as mistress of the Tower, and her roles as wife, mother, and daughter—well, she seemed occupied. But she always remembered that day, when the wind pressed their boat so far up the Spitte and that slender chain fouled the fluke of their anchor."

Sennet paused and Eli leaned in, waiting for more. "Marna's parents took to whispering about the search they planned to make someday, and the riches that must certainly await them in the mountains. They planned how they could then live easily in the south, far away from the rocks and the pine woods here to the north of the Green Vale. Eventually they forsook their simple sailboat and acquired a small steam launch that could drive upstream against the current, even when the wind was not in the south.

"They repeated stories they had heard of the cities of the Sorrel Plain, where there are supposedly towers with red banners and purple roofs that can be seen from a great distance by travelers who attempt to cross the White Land where it is very dry, or by those who approach on the Way South, coming from the Great Northern Sea.

"Now I had heard of such cities both north and south of the Sorrel Plain, although even when I traveled as a young man, I had never been there. Some of these cities are mere ruins of towns that used to be there. Others have been rebuilt on the foundations of older buildings. The greatest of these cities is supposed to be one where there are many merchants—where everything is for sale at all times. Everything has a price. Sometimes prices are raised, and this causes great interest among buyers who then offer more and more for whatever is being offered, until on some days, there are crowds in the marketplace shouting higher and higher prices and great quantities of houses, cattle, carriages, boats, and even household furniture are being exchanged at higher and higher rates, all to the great satisfaction of those who are buying and selling. Some say that they even buy and sell their own children. But not everything can be exchanged in the marketplace, so they also take to buying and selling pieces of pretty paper that represent whole warehouses full of things: farms, oceangoing ships, and the contents of the mines in the South Mountains.

"Perhaps my daughter thought that they could buy more of the green stones there."

"But," said Sennet, "as Marna's parents talked about these strange lands, their desire to go there grew inside them, until at length it grew so large that it was ready to burst from its confines. This went on until I scarcely knew my own daughter. She seemed almost estranged from her own child, and no longer spoke the tender words a mother says to a little girl. Her eyes became as green as the fragment of stone she wore around her neck, and she wore her long black hair bound up in the fine links of the shiny chain. Her cheeks became pale, and the stone hung on her pale breast next to her heart. Her husband became greedy and morose, and his dark and misery-deep eyes sought that stone around his wife's neck more than he ever looked at the smiling face of his daughter.

"And so as she grew, Marna became more and more my helper in the keeping of both the Tower and the River, until the day she went out on that errand for me. That's the day her parents vanished in a moment, without bidding either of us farewell. That was the day Marna found you flying into the river over her head."

Marna didn't exactly blush; her face didn't often work that way. But she looked down at her folded hands while Eli looked at her with a smile.

"Now, no one has ever come back to tell us much about the things they are seeking beyond the mountains, although the old sailor from the River Spitte, Gormley, claims to have been there, and repeats stories about the wonders of the eastern cities. Are such places really there? Are the stories about them true? I do not know. But now my daughter has gone with her husband to seek them. As I said, they did one good thing: They left Marna here with me. I do not think they will make themselves happy in the East, and I think Marna would have found nothing but sorrow there with them." Sennet concluded his narrative and fell silent.

Eli again looked at Marna and tried to read her thoughts from her expression, but found he could not.

"Would you want to go and follow them?" he asked Marna.

"Perhaps to persuade them to come back, and to abandon their search for things that cannot truly make you happy," she said. "There is good work for them to do here instead. But I do not know if I could leave the Tower for so long," she said, turning her eyes to Sennet. The older man was silent.

"Then why should *I* not go and find them?" asked Eli. "I can bring your message to them, and, while I travel, I can also record information for my father's charts.

And I'm sure your parents will change their minds when their search is exhausted."

Marna looked not at Eli but at Sennet. "Part of me wants to go too," she said, "but I don't know if I am able, and I don't know you very well, Eli. Perhaps you could succeed. But are you able to do what you suggest? Can you go and come back again?"

"I trust myself," said Eli. "I think I will be able to do anything given my strength and the use of my wits. And I want to try."

Sennet looked at the two young people solemnly. "You will both be able to go places and do things that you have not yet even dreamt of. But remember—go with the grain when things are confused, and you may find your way through. Sometimes you have to go left to come out right from all the wrong ways you might go, until eventually you will find your way out to see the stars again."

ELI'S SECOND VOYAGE

When Eli set forth from the Tower, Marna helped equip his boat for the trip north. She filled two strong baskets with provisions for his journey: loaves of bread, crocks of pale pink mushroom soup, jars of wild blueberry jam, and delicate smoked fillets of shad that had been netted in the river. The shad is the boniest of all the river fish, but Sennet was an expert shad-boner, and his fillets never had a bone in them. Sennet also gave Eli a flask of old apple brandy, which he might need if frostbitten. He also had a string bag of red onions and squash, some dark and aged vinegar, and a bottle of green olive oil that he had received from an Italian boatman who had passed along the Spitte. Eli had learned which of the plants that grew along the riverbank would make a good salad in the wooden bowl he took aboard. Marna also supplied him with a sizable chunk of hard cheese, pale yellow and fragrant.

He packed everything in a weather-tight locker in the bow of the skiff and prepared to set forth in the early hours, right at dawn. He wanted a long day to get well beyond the Branching of Spitte. Marna cast off Eli's painter as the south breeze caught the old tan sail. He leaned to the sculling oar and looked back at the slender figure standing under the leaning hemlocks, braids divided front and back, holding one hand high in a gesture of farewell. He caught his breath, once again struck by her gracefulness. Far above, at the balcony window, Sennet waved his horny old hand behind the glass windowpanes and smiled over his beard.

The sun was bright and the current chastened. Eli made good headway. The banks of the river were broad and green through the morning, and the current seemed less of a hindrance as the Spitte widened and twisted this way and that among small islands and sandbars. Twice the steering oar scraped bottom as Eli crossed shallows in midstream, but the flat-bottomed boat never went aground.

At length Eli could see a broad stream joining the river from his right, and then another that seemed to open to the left. Ahead the river wound on as before. The four arms of the river seemed to come from the quarter points of the compass and flow together at some unmarked spot in the center of the wide body of water across which he was sailing.

He had reached the Branching of Spitte.

There was a ruffling of the water visible at some distance from the place where the branches came together. Eli was sailing north before a southwest wind, against the flow of the river. He knew that when wind and water flowed in opposite directions, there were often choppy seas ahead, but these swirling and prickling waves were different, something he had never seen before. Streaks of yellow and white foam seemed to be moving in two directions across his course around a dark area of water, as though some sunken snag lurked below the surface. Eli steered to starboard to where the rolling waters of the Southeast Branch joined the flow. But even though the wind carried him forward, the current of the branch still turned his bow to the west, moving the skiff off on a new course across the mouth of the Northern Branch. Here the current pressed him to the south again, against the wind, and he sculled helplessly in the grip of the waters until he found the boat turning again, this time to the north as the full strength of the wind coming up the river caught his sail. Eli's exertions at the steering oar seemed to make little difference to the swift circling of the boat, until at length he found her stem pointed directly at the mass of bubbles and foam at the very center of the whirling waters.

Foam and spray poured over the lee gunwale and a great sucking noise came from below as the skiff lurched into the center of the whirlpool. Eli struggled with his oar, and then Sennet's admonition came back to him: "Go with the grain when things are confused ... you may have to go left to come out right ... go left to go right ... follow where it leads you until you come out to see the stars again."

White water blinded his eyes, and the boat began to turn ever more toward the center of the maelstrom with a rattle and a great cracking of the sail and creaking of the mast. He shut his eyes and put all his weight on the opposite side of the steering oar, trying to turn his little vessel with the current, into the very center of the roaring whirlpool.

His speed increased, and suddenly he was lurching back on an even keel and the rip was behind him, sucking greedily at his stern as he found himself propelled beyond its grasp into the mouth of the Northern Branch. A puff of freshening wind lifted the sail, and the sturdy old skiff spread its broad white bow wave to either side as she forged on to the north.

Now his way was clear, and the river ran ahead with the dark blue of the Spruce Wood crowding one bank and the lofty pale blue of the Ice Mountain raising its distant head on the opposite side. All day long he sailed beneath the shoulder of the great snow-topped mass of rock. At night it hid the moon from his sight, and in the day it hid the sun by mid-afternoon, creating an early twilight on the river. For three days he sailed, often steering by the sight of Cassiopeia among the constellations of northern stars, with the distant mountain forever at his right side, until at length on the third day he realized that its bulk was behind his shoulder as he stood facing the bow. He had passed the Ice Mountain.

Far ahead Eli could see a rounded bulk of gray-green hills and peaks that rose at a great distance from the river. These highlands loomed misty above the river trees in the mornings and formed a neutral background to the pale ochres and reds of the changing leaves on the eastern bank of the Northern Branch. All the colors seemed to turn eventually to pale brown and ruddy buff as he sailed on; only the grasses of the sandbars and the willow branches that dragged in the water where the trees overhung the backwaters remained green. At length, in the flat marshes of the eastern shore, he descried an opening into a pine-girt cove, ruffled blue by the fading wind that had brought him so far from his new friends at the Rock Tower, away in the south behind him.

He sculled the boat slowly and with some difficulty into the cove and up its half-mile length toward rocky banks of hemlocks, which seemed to close it off in a quiet pool beyond a gravelly sandbar. There was a small, two-story stone building at the shoreside of the bar, but its windows were dark, and an open door below showed it to be empty.

He skirted the bar and found that the cove narrowed into a rocky gorge for a space of thirty yards. Beyond that he could see an open valley. Green meadows sloped upward from the marshy edge of the inner cove on three sides, but on the fourth there was a gray wooden bulkhead and dock at which no boats were moored. On a tidy lawn that stretched back from the bulkhead, there stood a neat white building with porches at either end and a row of barrels along its side. A stone chimney gave forth a vertical shaft of blue smoke, for by now the wind had ceased entirely. Eli shipped his sculling oar as he approached the dock and jumped ashore with painter and stern line in his hand to make fast to the floating dock. Then he went back aboard and fetched another length of rope to fashion into crisscrossed spring lines, to keep the heavy skiff from sliding either fore or aft as the tidal current changed direction.

While he was thus employed with securing his craft, a man emerged from the building and approached, ambling with hands in pockets and a peaked cap on the back of his head.

"Good morning," offered Eli.

"Nearly noon," responded the man somberly. "Be afternoon before long."

He was a smallish man, stooped slightly as though he had stood for a long time in the low headroom of a ship's cabin. His boots were laced halfway up his shins, and his faded blue trousers were supported by bright yellow suspenders that he wore over the shoulders of his black-and-white-checkered woolen shirt.

"You fixin' to stay at that dock for a piece?" he added.

"I don't really know yet," said Eli. "Is this as close to the passes between the Moon and Ice Mountains as I can go by water? I am looking for the pass through the mountains to the valleys south of the Long-Eared Mountains. Am I going the right way?"

"You are if there is a right way to go there," mumbled the man as he dourly regarded the hitches with which Eli had made his boat fast to the dock. "But if you'll be venturing toward those mountains, I'll thank you not to leave your boat in the middle of the dock. It'll be long before you get back, if you do, and I'll be needin' that place at the dock for others less foolish."

"Oh, I can move the boat as soon as you wish," said Eli, "but first let me recover from my sculling. May I have a moment to ask you for directions?"

The man mumbled something more about the dock and motioned for Eli to follow him as he turned back toward the door from which he had come.

The porch of the little building supported two aging rocking chairs, painted bright green. The porch rails were gray and the posts were brown. In fact, every part of the building seemed well and newly painted in many shades of strong colors. Inside the walls were paneled in narrow planks of light-grained wood, and all was varnished and smooth. Woven webs holding green glass net floats decorated the window openings. From brown-stained pine rafters there hung coils of rope and loops of black-painted chain. All across the back wall of the building were neat shelves holding rows and rows of metal pails of paint. There were enamels and stains, flat paints and shiny, Venetian Red, Rose Madder, and Alizarin Crimson. There were yellows and blues of all hues and intensities, which proclaimed themselves from the color of the pails arranged on the neat brown shelves.

"Well, hello and good day to you, sir," exclaimed a hearty voice from behind a massive gray-and-white enameled stove in the center of the room. "Come in, sir, come in, I say, and join us for a bite to eat. It has come time to lunch, I believe. Bring him in, Brother Stanley, whoever he may be."

The second man was dressed in exactly the same fashion as the first, except that his suspenders were a bright apple green, and his face was wrinkled with smiling and his eyes crinkled at the corners. Indeed, the smile never left his face while speaking, drinking, or chewing, but remained in a variety of elastic curves, demonstrating every possible contortion of his mouth.

"His boat is tied up at the best position on the dock," said Brother Stanley. "I've told him he'll have to move it if he is to leave it here for long."

"I am Staley," said the second man, producing three bowls of stew from a counter behind the stove and ignoring his brother. "Come, sit yourself down with us and eat."

"I am Eli, least of the sons of Solomon of Salem on the Gut," said Eli. "And I would be grateful for some food if you have enough to spare."

"Always enough, and often too much," said Staley, patting his broad stomach with both hands. "Come, seat yourself, Eli." And without further comment he sat down upon a red stool at the counter. There were seven stools in all, each of a different color. Eli selected a lavender one and took up a large tarnished spoon that was set beside his bowl.

The stew was thick, with a deep brown sauce, and there were bright orange carrots and golden onions floating in it, as well as big chunks of meat, pale parsnips, beet greens, barley, and deep green scallion tops. The two brothers ate with great slurping and chewing sounds that made conversation impossible. Indeed, it seemed that no one was expected to speak another word as long as there was even a drop of sauce left in the bowls. But as soon as they were empty, Stanley rose from the table, gathered up the crockery and spoons, and took them outside where he could be heard rinsing them with a great splashing and clanking of a hand pump.

Eli wondered if the fact that Staley seemed to do the cooking and Stanley the washing up had anything to do with the difference in their

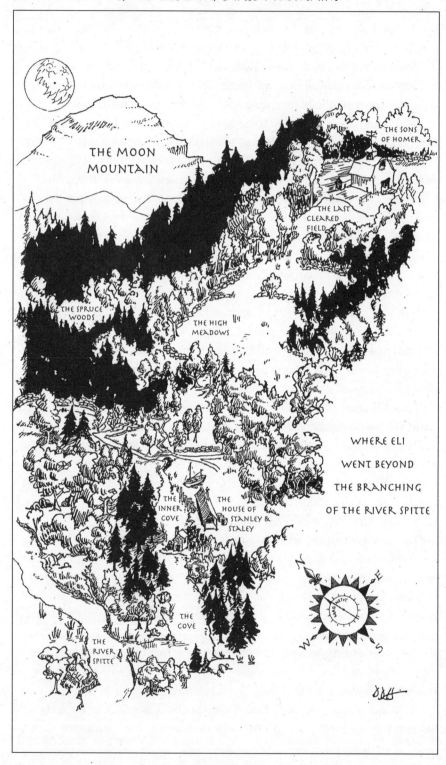

THE MOON
MOUNTAIN

THE SONS
OF HOMER

THE LAST
CLEARED
FIELD

THE SPRUCE
WOODS

THE HIGH
MEADOWS

WHERE ELI
WENT BEYOND
THE BRANCHING
OF THE RIVER SPITTE

THE
INNER
COVE

THE
HOUSE OF
STANLEY &
STALEY

THE
COVE

THE
RIVER
SPITTE

temperaments, for Stanley seemed to be doing an awful lot of grumbling and snorting while drying the crockery.

Once Stanley had returned, Staley said, "So now, tell us what brought you here and where you are going while Stanley and I recover from eating. Great exertion after meals will surely shorten a man's life more than smoking tobacco, which, as you know, is bad enough. Or at least working after eating will decrease a man's enjoyment of life, which is just as important."

Eli began more or less at the beginning of his adventure, from the moment the great wind from the southwest had blown him up the river. Stanley rattled the bowls as he shoved them under the counter while Eli told them about the Rock Tower and Sennet. When he described Marna, he found himself speaking in a manner he'd never before used.

"She is slender and quick, and her hair is a ruddy brown," Eli began. "She paddles a canoe as though she had spent all her life on the river. Her eyes are large and seem wise when they look directly at you … or at me, I guess I mean. And I think there is nothing about her mouth, nose, and chin that anyone could ever want to change …" And then he surprised himself by adding, without thinking about it, "Because she is as beautiful as any girl could ever be."

"Hmph!" said Stanley. "All girls of that age look the same."

But Staley looked up at the ceiling as though he sought the memory of some such face in the dark spaces where the coils of rope and bolts of canvas hung between the rafters.

"I suspect," Staley said, "that such rare beauty as Eli describes may partially be in the eye of the beholder, but might also be the outward sign of character within a young woman who is also possessed of a beautiful soul."

"I have not known her long enough to know much about her soul— at least not yet. But her spirit seems very lively, and she doesn't seem to want life to take her passively down its stream. It seems she needs to paddle strongly against its current. And sometimes she mocks me for my clumsiness."

"If she mocks you," said Stanley, "you're probably wasting your time and energy in thinking too much about her."

"Perhaps not, Brother," replied Staley. "I have heard that young females protect themselves from the conquests of young men by saying things that they do not really mean, but say to keep the males at a safe distance for a time."

Eli told them of Marna's parents and their pursuit of the green stone beyond the Long-Eared Mountains, and how he planned to find them and persuade them to return.

Stanley frowned, and even Staley's smile seemed less sure than before.

"You will never find them—nor will you return—alive," said Stanley gloomily.

"Nonsense, Brother," said Staley. "You will need provisions and equipment for such a trip, Eli," said Staley. "We will equip you with things we have here."

"You do seem to have a lot of equipment here," said Eli. "But who comes to buy it?"

"In our grandfather's time," answered Staley, "there were many people who came up from the Cove and down from the country to buy their paint and supplies from this store. And then for many years there were fewer of them. But our father was a very conservative man and kept the shelves filled with paint, boat hardware, shackles, turnbuckles, nuts, bolts, drift pins, and pump leathers, in case anyone decides to come back again."

"But they never come," said Stanley sadly.

"No, they never come in numbers," admitted Staley. "But once a year or so, the three short Sons of Homer come from the upper hill country, where they keep their goats, to buy a gallon or two of barn red."

"Last year they took a pint of nice chrome yellow too," added Stanley.

"To tell the truth," concluded Staley, "you are the only one who has come up the Cove in the past four and a half months, from last Tuesday."

"Then you have seen nothing of Marna's parents?" Eli asked.

"Nothing," said Stanley.

"But," added Staley, "they might not have come this way. If they took the southeast branch of the Spitte, they might have long since rejoined The Trail and gone around the east side of the Ice Mountain and gone up into the high valley that leads to the Long-Eared Mountains. Although I don't know if there is a trail that leads as far as the distant ears of those mountains. We have never gone that far, and no one has come here from that direction to tell us much about that part of the country."

"But the three short Sons of Homer who live near you," said Eli. "Have they ever been so far?"

"Farther than we have," said Staley. "You could go and ask them. But better tomorrow than today, since it is late and the light fades soon in this season. Besides, it will be nearly time for supper soon. In the meantime, perhaps we could haul your boat up above the highest water mark so that it will not be damaged by the winter ice if you do not return to the Cove very soon."

"Or especially if you don't come back at all," said Stanley. "Then it won't block the middle of the dock forever."

So they worked in the late-afternoon sunshine with two double-sheaved blocks and a stout line fastened to a tree and to the skiff. The boat slid easily up two smooth wooden rails until by nightfall, it stood on chocks and wedges in the field behind the brothers' building, safe from the winter ice for as long as Eli might be gone on his quest into the mountains.

That night the three ate heartily of beans and macaroni with grated yellow cheese and slices of zucchini in the well-painted little building by the shore of the Cove. During the evening's conversation Eli learned much about the land and about the people who came there long ago. There were stories about their long blue and white boats with colored sails and paper lanterns hanging from their booms in the evenings. There was music on the water in those days, and there were tales that people of great wealth came up the last branch of the Spitte in the midst of the Spruce Woods to catch fish for sport and to explore the backwaters in delicate lapstrake boats. The boats were made of thin mahogany so light that a man could carry such a boat around shallows and rapids in the upper reaches of the river.

Eli fell right asleep and dreamt of the high valleys across the mountains and the towns and cities that lay south of them, along the course of other rivers that flowed beyond the High Land toward lakes and rivers whose names he did not yet know. And always in his dreams he kept catching glimpses of someone in a canoe who paddled away from him just as he tried to catch up.

MARNA'S FIRST JOURNEY

In the weeks after Eli's departure, Marna felt that life in the Tower was less filled with novelty as each day succeeded another. She asked Sennet about making another attempt to travel to the home of the glassblower to bring back a seasonal supply of new lenses for the navigational marker lights.

Sennet grumbled that the season of the equinoctial storms was now upon them, but if she was to go at all, now would be the time to make the trip. She prepared carefully for her voyage by canoe, and the hike through the woods that it would entail. She wore stout hiking boots for the times she would have to pull the canoe out on shore and travel on foot. She packed her rucksack with a change of clothing, her recorder, and, in case Lucindar had formal guests in his house, a pair of black Chinese slippers and a short, dark blue dress with a pattern of white snowflakes on it.

On a very early morning not quite three weeks after Eli had started north, she began paddling up the Spitte once again. The sweater and yellow oilskin jacket she wore were comfortable in the cool of the morning. She slipped along close to shore, well out of the steady current in the middle of the Spitte. Cormorants swimming in search of their breakfast submerged at her approach, and once a great blue heron rose awkwardly from his shoreside perch and winged his way laboriously into the air over the river. He crossed the breadth of the water just a few feet in the air and then returned without ever touching down on the farther bank. He finally landed behind Marna, where he found a firm footing in a few inches of water, close to his original takeoff location.

The woods along the shore were black in shadow under the hemlocks, whose twisted roots seemed to writhe over the boulders that lined the riverbank. Twice she saw chipmunks perched on the rocks, but they darted away into the crevices before she came close to them. She hugged the shore in her shallow-draught craft and, at a safe distance, passed the whirlpool that had nearly overwhelmed Eli's boat. Then she turned to starboard and glided up the mild current of the Southeast Branch.

The day was sunny and clear, but overhead Marna noticed parallel racks of cirrus clouds, mare's tails that reached from horizon to horizon. Sennet had called these high clouds "premonitory cirrus," and said they meant foul weather was on the way.

But the trip to the glassblower's house was quick by canoe, and before dark Marna had reached the stones that served as a landing for Lucindar on the bank of the little tributary of his particular Branch of the Spitte. She hauled the light boat out on the shore, inverted it, and, shouldering her rucksack, started up the path to the east. Once or twice she was afraid she might lose her way as the path wound through a tangle of mountain laurel bushes, but she soon came out on a little knoll looking over a country road. Directly across the road was an enormous white pine tree, bigger than any she had ever seen before. Its main upper trunk was missing, shattered by a lightning bolt many years before. New leaders had sprung upward on either side of the tree and now gave the appearance of full-grown trees in their own right. These were immense branches, nearly three feet in diameter at the point where they left the main shaft, curving upward and carrying many side branches to a summit more than a hundred feet over Marna's head. Below the noble tree was a small white house close to the road.

There was a green lawn behind the house and a gray barn beyond that. The barn had several large metal ventilators on its roof, and Marna could hear a humming sound and a whistling like a gentle wind. Up the hill beyond the barn she could see the large green and yellow sphere of a hot air balloon.

Marna deposited her rucksack at the wooden base of a green hand pump at the side of the house and walked toward the barn. The doors were on the far side of the building, and she could not see what was within until she had reached them. What she saw was a row of four brick furnaces, each with a glowing golden-red eye in its door. The draft of the gas flames created the sound she was hearing. Above was a pair of slowly turning fans powered by wind turbines on the roof of the barn.

A man with fierce bright eyes and a large brown mustache was stirring something in one of the furnaces with a long iron rod. Just as she was about to speak to him, he turned toward her with a glowing bright orange mass of soft glass balanced on the end of the iron pipe. Without saying a word, he set the pipe between a pair of small wheels, spinning it slowly in this support as he applied his mouth to the other end of the pipe. Puffing out his cheeks, he filled the vessel with his breath. Then he put his thumb into his mouth and closed off the end of the pipe.

He looked up, smiled under his mustache, and watched the glowing orange mass slowly grow in size as the breath of air inside expanded in the heat of the melted glass. He then thrust the growing sphere into a ring of blue gas flame beside him and then put it into a charred wooden box on the floor, giving it another puff of air.

"Fresnel mold!" he said with some authority. He pronounced the word as though there was no "s" in it.

Beside him, on a scarred and blackened wooden bench, were arranged a line of a dozen or more orange glass globes with a series of sharp ridges circling their upper and lower edges. The middle of each globe swelled outward in a cylindrical lens that reflected the light from the open door.

"And that," he continued, "is a word you won't find in your dictionary."

"Well, I don't have a dictionary here anyway," answered Marna, who was reflecting that whatever a Fresnel was, Lucindar was surely very handsome.

"Fresnel was a Frenchman," he went on with an intense look. "He invented these molded glass collars to magnify the light of a little oil lamp by putting a lens all the way around the flame. That way a small light could be seen from a long way off, and a lighthouse could be seen by ships a great distance from the land. But who are you?"

"I am Marna, granddaughter of Sennet of the Rock Tower," said the girl. "I have come to purchase green and red lenses for navigation lights and some orange lenses for range lights. I am told I can get them from Lucindar the glassblower. I take it you are Lucindar."

"Yes, I am Lucindar, the loneliest man this side of the Trackless Wastes of West. And I have been waiting much too long for someone as young and beautiful as you to come and keep me company. But come, enough of this work for today. Most unusually, I have guests coming to dine with me tonight and I must prepare. Will you help me?" And with a quick motion, he knocked off the neck of the new glass globe and stood it on the bench beside the furnace.

Marna was not sure whether the glassblower wanted help with preparing a dinner for his guests or with his seemingly serious case of loneliness. She

THE HOUSE OF
THE GLASSBLOWER

started to follow him toward the house, but stopped, surprised at the fact he would be abandoning all of this heat and flame.

"Will you leave all this flame burning?" she asked.

"Forever," he replied. "My flame burns perpetually until all the sands of the sea are melted in my furnace. For if the fires go out, it would take many, many days of patient heating to make it into a clear, glowing liquid again. But now I must take down and deflate the balloon, which is what I use to guide people to my shop. It is too breezy to leave it up, even on a tether—." And with that, he strode to the crest of the little hill behind the barn and started pulling on one of the many lines connecting the balloon to the basket. He opened a vent that let the hot air escape, and in short order, he had folded the colored panels of the balloon and weighted them down with flat stones.

Lucindar's guests turned out to be three merchants who came from beyond the hill country to the east of the Broad Hump. They were serious men with bushy black beards and flashing white teeth. They talked of margins and discounts and a variety of things that were unfamiliar to Marna. They discussed the state of things in the cities of the Sorrel Plain and in the markets of Lucro. She had changed into her dress before dinner and was conscious that all four men stared at her a great deal as she moved about in Lucindar's house. Their talk went on while they drank many cups of coffee after eating the platter of potatoes, carrots, onions, tomatoes, garlic, and broad beans which Lucindar had prepared.

"Does she dance?" asked one of the merchants.

"No," said Lucindar. "Not for you. Nor even yet for me."

Actually, Marna did dance almost every day at the Rock Tower. She loved to twirl and leap in the sunshine, but that night, she was glad Lucindar's guests did not know about her favorite exercise. She spent the night in a tiny bedroom up under the eaves of the house, where she carefully locked her door. She wondered about what was outside in the woodland where the merchants had returned after concluding their purchases of colored glass bowls and goblets from Lucindar. For some reason, although she liked the handsome glassblower, she felt uneasy in this house with him. On the other hand, she had a sense that there were perhaps more worrisome things outside in the woods where the traveling merchants had encamped for the night.

The next day dawned warm and still, with just a hint of a heavy breeze from the southeast. Marna recognized the day as one that Sennet would call a "weather breeder," a day in which the pleasant, unseasonable warmth would give way to a change for the worse.

Lucindar was in very good spirits the next day, after concluding his business with the merchants. He selected three sets of the thick glass Fresnel lights Sennet had required: red, green, and orange. He packed them in a basket stuffed with straw to keep them from breaking and, grumbling slightly, accepted the payment Sennet had sent with Marna.

"They should be a bit more this year," he said. "But perhaps you can come back to me again and bring me the difference and stay with me again, and even dance for me."

"Perhaps," said Marna.

However, Marna did not leave the house of the glassblower that day, for a warm rain began pattering about the house by midmorning, and by noon, there was a strong and gusty wind blowing from the northeast. The rain increased and the wind blew at greater velocity in the afternoon. By early evening the trees were swaying and writhing in a tangle of storm-tossed branches, and Lucindar had climbed the field behind the barn to roll up the collapsed balloon and store it in the glass shop.

All that second night the storm roared through the trees and lightning crashed in the woodlands in the surrounding hills. In the middle of the night there was an awesome quiet and the wind ceased entirely. Then it came back again from the southwest, howling stronger than before. Wondering if she would have to flee, Marna hung her cotton flannel nightgown on a peg on the back of the door and dressed quickly in hiking boots and foul-weather jacket, ready to make a quick exit from the house if lightning should happen to strike the giant pine tree outside.

But although the huge tree creaked and groaned in the wind, the great trunk held firm, and by morning there was clear sunshine and a fresh west wind drying the wet woods and fields.

"Come with me," said Lucindar. "On such a clear day, it is time to inflate the smaller balloon and send an observer aloft to see what damage the country has sustained from such a great storm. One as light as you can go up in the small balloon very easily."

Lighting the gas burners over the observer's basket which he brought from the barn, Lucindar soon had the balloon inflated and tugging at its ground lines Marna watched how he regulated the flow of the gas to the burner, shutting it off with the valve overhead and relighting it again with a loud popping sound when he struck sparks from the trigger mechanism.

"Here," he said. "Climb in and regulate the gas flow while I tend to these lines to be sure they are secure. With this western wind, we should be careful that the balloon is securely tethered. Today is no day for a free flight!"

Marna did as she was told, climbing nimbly over the side of the broad gondola.

Once aboard she reached up over her head to adjust the valve. The basket rocked as she shifted her weight and then quite suddenly, it rose swiftly into the air. Marna looked over the side to see where Lucindar had tethered the balloon. But his back was turned and the silent balloon rose above his tangle of ropes, shaking off first one and then another until it was completely free.

Lucindar turned and looked with amazement as the gondola swung to the east.

"The trees! The trees!" he shouted, and Marna looked ahead and saw that she was rapidly approaching a dark and tangled forest that would certainly ensnare the basket high in the branches. She reached up to the gas valve and turned it full open. The blue flame at the open mouth of the balloon swelled, and almost immediately the basket rose a few feet until it passed just beyond the reaching branches and out over the forestland below. Marna looked back and saw Lucindar pounding his fist into his hand and staring after her.

She looked ahead to see if she could spot a cleared field or pasture where she could descend safely by cutting off the heating gas or by pulling the ripcord. But all she saw to the east were the seemingly endless forests of the Trackless Wastes of West and the rocky peak of the Toe Top Mountain projecting above them. She turned around three times in the basket but

The Ash Grove

found nothing that she could do, nothing that would steer the balloon, only the valve that would make it go still higher. She contemplated shutting off the gas entirely and waiting until the cooling air made the balloon settle. But the tangle of trees below looked like a very dangerous place to land, so she contented herself with closing the valve most of the way to see if she could keep her craft at a more-or-less constant altitude as she moved to the east.

And then, because there seemed nothing else to do for the time being, she rummaged in the pocket of her yellow jacket and pulled out her recorder. All was silent in the air, for the balloon moved at the same speed as the wind that carried it along, and there was no whistling or even murmuring in the rigging. Searching her memory, she began to play an air from long ago, "The Ash Grove."

THE SONS OF HOMER

Equipped with a stout canvas rucksack donated by Staley (despite Stanley's grumbles that the stock of the store was being depleted), Eli packed a small provolone cheese and several packages of hard biscuits, along with some cashews and pistachio nuts. He left the flask of apple brandy as a present to the two brothers, who pressed many other gifts on him in return. He took a woolen cap, a warm scarf, and a pair of fleece-lined deerskin gloves. Finally, at the surprising insistence of Stanley, he accepted two small cans of paint because that was what the brothers had most of. Eli really didn't want to carry the paint, but Stanley's feelings would obviously have been hurt if he had refused the offer. So he carefully accepted a can of strong Cadmium Yellow and another smaller one of the richest Cerulean Blue, settling them with a brush and a flask of thinner in the bottom of the rucksack. Then, with everything strapped up and lashed to his back, he bowed to Stanley and Staley and set off up the dirt road that bordered the Cove.

"Farewell, Eli," said Staley. "We will look after your boat while you are gone."

"But what should we do with it if you don't come back?" asked Stanley. "It takes up quite a lot of space in the meadow."

"I will come back for it," said Eli. "The boat will not end her days as a flower container here. But if Marna should come here before I return, give her the boat as a present from me. I received it as a gift, and a good old boat should be passed on as a token of affection to someone else when it can no longer serve its owner."

And with that he turned and waved good-bye, striding swiftly up the path that led through the valley to the woods and fields beyond. His track climbed generally to the north and east of the landing at the Cove. He walked among oaks and maples crowned with red leaves and yellow, brighter even than the pigments in Stanley's pails. He crossed great arching meadows of green stubble grass along the stone walls that dissected the country. Some of the great oaks grew from the stone walls themselves, as though they had been there long before the time of the Wall Builders, whoever they were.

Eli climbed the walls from one meadow to the next and up the broad breast of a high, close-cropped hill that was crowned by a heap of rounded stones and a ruddy clump of sumac bushes. At the crest he paused and looked behind, far, far below, to where he could see the Cove lying bright blue inside its hemlock and meadow-rounded shore. Far beyond the Cove, the distant thread of the North Branch of the Spitte curled away to the south until it was lost behind the distant bulk of the Ice Mountain.

He turned and continued up the gently sloping meadow, the way growing narrower between great oak copses and solitary cedar spires with close packed woods on either side. The grass path dipped once between lower stone walls and became a swampy spot where the ground was sunk in two great ruts between bog tufts, as though many wagons had been drawn through the soft ground long ago. Brambles grew among the ruts, and he picked his way carefully among them and the tall dry mullein stems on the lower slopes of the next narrow meadow. Beyond, to the east, there was a dark border of deeper forest.

Eli realized that he had reached the last cleared field, which was less steep than those that led to it, and seemed to be the summit of the local land. In the far corner of the final field there stood a great gray barn with an overhanging gambrel roof topped with a dark red cupola. Rising above the peak of the cupola was a weathervane in the form of a strutting rooster which shone with gold leaf. The farm seemed almost deserted and a bit run-down, except for this ornament at the top of the barn, and a low shed along one side of the building which was neatly painted barn red with white trim.

Approaching with the feeling that he was at least unexpected, if not unwelcome, Eli came to the open door in the side of the shed and peered into the empty darkness inside. It smelled of sweet hay, dust, and age.

"Halloo!" he called. "Is there anybody home?"

No sound broke the stillness, and Eli was almost ready to search elsewhere when a solemn voice, quite close to him, said in a hoarse whisper,

"Don't speak so loud; you'll frighten her!"

"She doesn't like it at all, and you mustn't startle her," said another voice, this one higher pitched and more cheerful.

"You see," said a third voice, quite firmly, "we are putting this evil-smelling stuff on her feet and she complains about it!"

Eli stepped into the gloomy interior, ready to effect a rescue if there was need of it to save her, whoever *she* was, from the dreadful things being done to her. What he found was three short, stout men intently occupied with a slender form lying in the hay before them. Their hair was gray and long, their beards were full, and their clothing rough and hairy.

The one with the first whispering voice slapped a stopper back into a bottle of black liquid which he held in his hand. "I guess that will hold her for this season," he said.

All three men stepped back from the bed of hay and, with a shake of its neat little horns, a gray and white goat rose from the hay and looked quizzically at Eli.

"You see," said the second, "she needs to have her hooves trimmed."

"And we have to soften them with this evil-smelling stuff," said the third.

All three men wore bright red woolen caps pulled down over their ears.

"Are you the Sons of Homer?" asked Eli.

"We are the three. Through thick and thin we brothers be, and I am Horace," said the first.

"If you are sure you want to know with whom you are visiting," said the second, "I am Hamlet."

"And I, Horatio," said the third emphatically. "And you, sir? Who are you?"

"I am Eli, an explorer and chartmaker. I have come to ask your help to find my way through the forests to a pass that will lead me beyond the Long-Eared Mountains."

"Over the passes to the Long-Eared Mountains? I don't think we should ever go so far as that!" said Hamlet.

"I have only once been as far as the final stone wall," said Horatio. "Perhaps now is the time to learn what lies beyond it."

"Beyond fields and passes, beyond springs and fountains, what lies beyond the Long-Eared Mountains?" mused Horace.

And then, seated on the heaped hay of the great barn, Eli explained to them the story of Marna's parents and their quest for the green stone that they found clinging to the fluke of their anchor. He told them of their restlessness and lack of feeling, and the little men looked uneasy. And he told them of Marna and her braided hair, and they smiled and laughed at him.

"Friend Eli," said Horace, "I think you are set on a quest to win the favor of a young lady more than to make charts or to find her parents."

"But at least we can get you started on the right path," added Horatio. "We often tramp our bounds, the boundaries of our father, Homer. We go in all directions from this barn, and now that many of the leaves have fallen, it is an appropriate season to do so again. You can come much of the way with us, and we could show you the way to the final stone wall."

"Are you sure this is the season to tramp boundaries?" questioned Hamlet.

But the others seemed sure of themselves, and it was speedily agreed that they should set forth on the following day to tramp the farthest bounds of Homer, even beyond the Final Wall that would mark the way to the passes in the Long-Eared Mountains themselves.

The three short men took Eli into the great barn. At the far end of the huge structure there was a large room enclosed by snug board walls and lighted by lanterns hung from pegs in the beams overhead.

"It seems the gleam of lanterns will beam from the beams…," murmured Horace.

They dined on a delicate cheese veined with blue mold which they spread on toasted oaten cakes. Hamlet prepared the cakes by holding them on a long-handled fork over a small fire he kindled in an iron pot. He would toast the cakes and then examine them many times to see if they were properly done, until he was finally satisfied that all four cakes were done, and of the same color.

The cheese tasted as though it had wintered in one of the caves of the Mountains of the Moon, as indeed it nearly had. They washed down bread and cheese with draughts of pale golden ale made in their cellars underneath the barn. When they were finished, the three little men lit corncob pipes and blew clouds of blue smoke up toward the hay wisps that hung through the board ceiling of their room.

Then Horace took down a small harp from a peg on the wall and began to strum chords while he hummed. The other two joined him, and soon the three began to recite an old song of the goat farmers of the hills.

High here in hills
Homer his hall and barns had built
Here where goats of his gathering stayed
His good garner stored food for his ewes
Long since the others had gone.
Gleeful young maidens and their squires attentive

Long used to play in high pastureland.
Where fled the others of valley and river?
Why not returned for play in the pasture?
The others are gone
Long gone away to the vales in the west
Far to the south and the east in their season.
But the goats are a-gamboling when winter will come.
Winter will come and the garner be warm
Goats and goatherds will crowd in together,
Willingly sharing the warmth of the garner.
For sure comes the spring and the ram in the sky.
Then rise the skunk cabbage in fenland and swamp
Scallions and rushes grow from the bog
Fescue and vetch rise in the fields
The goat-herding boys pipe on the hillside
Loud are ravines with echo and song.
Are there no maidens to dance to these pipers?
Will there be fauns in the fields once again?
Will cymbals and tabors of corybant dancers
Waken the memory of people once gone?
Will they all dance on uplands and hillsides?
Where will they lie when darkness has come?

And then Horace stopped singing, for it was he who had led the chant, and the three filled their corncob pipes once again.

"We intend to forswear tobacco and all smoking this winter," said Horatio. "We have decided it is good to smoke no more. But we have not decided what is to take its place. Brothers," he continued, "do you think that perhaps adventure could serve as a substitute for this beguiling weed? Could we not go out with Eli and distract our deprivation with doing some notable deeds that we have never done before? Perhaps we could even go beyond the last stone walls and try our way to the passes into the Long-Eared Mountains."

Horatio then looked seriously at his brothers and, quite deliberately, reached out with his pipe and dropped it into the iron pot of fire coals.

"I have decided. I will go. And I will not smoke again."

"Are you really sure?" asked Hamlet. "Is there anything to be found beyond our final bounds that is not better found here in the hall of our father?"

"I will go with you, Eli," said Horace, "for the sake of companionship and adventure in your quest. For it seems to me you seek the favor of a worthy lady, this Marna. I will help you find whatever may have become of her parents. And then, when we return, there will be songs to sing of other places than we know of now."

And he dropped his pipe into the glowing coals where Horatio's cob was burning.

"It is hard to decide," said Hamlet. "Who will care for the goats if we leave them?"

"All the goats are dry save for Amalthea," answered Horatio. "She could come with us and give us companionship, and even help with providing our breakfasts, for we will be many days away. The others will not need to be milked until long after the ram has his way with them and they become gravid in the spring."

"I suspect it will come to trouble before the spring," murmured Hamlet. "But if there is trouble, I suppose it would be better for Eli that we three were with him than not. And we would be of help to each other as well. So if you all want such, I will go with you. Thus none of us will ever have need to smoke again." And with that, Hamlet dropped his pipe into the fire with the others, and they sat silently watching the aromatic blue smoke curl up toward the rafters for the last time.

That night Eli lay rolled in a quilt the brothers had kindly provided and thought about the goatherds and their hilltop barn. And he dreamt of youths and maidens who carried garlands of flowers in rushing, whirling, dancing chains up green and flowered hillsides. The boys and girls pursued each other in turn among grasses, buttercups, violets, and Queen Anne's lace. Beyond the sloping field where they danced and turned, Eli could discern the gray stone columns of roofless temples standing in the sunny circle of a grove of stunted trees. He walked toward the temples but hesitated, and thought of following the girls with the garlands of flowers. And then the coals in the fire pot shifted and clinked so that he awoke and watched the red glow of the dying embers reflected from the rough board ceiling.

Soon he slept again, but he dreamt no more that night.

9 BEYOND THE FINAL BOUNDS

Amalthea seemed anxious enough to accompany the four adventurers the next morning through the woods of black birch and hornbeam. She climbed over stone walls as nimbly as the stout, short-legged men and ambled quietly through the fallen leaves and the great patches of ground pine and moss. The stone walls seemed to grow farther apart as they progressed, pitiful old walls, some of them not two or three stones high, but running straight off to the left and right for as far as the eye could follow them. Several times Eli felt there would be no more walls ahead of them as they walked silently to the east, but sooner or later, they'd come to another row of stones, half buried in the leaf drifts. At last Horatio paused at the corner of one wall that turned downhill to the north.

"This is the final bound of the lands of our father, Homer," he said. "Beyond this, no one ever cleared the fields, although trees were once felled here, and there are signs of where oxcarts once brought away the biggest trunks for timbers."

Eli looked at the woods but found no sign of anything but the wilderness of the high forest about them.

"This was an orchard in those days," continued Horatio. He pointed to the rotted trunks of seven dead trees standing in a row beside the wall. They were the black hulks of apple trees, dead, broken, and covered with vines, but still, from their regular spacing, quite surely planted by some intentional hand, rather than the chance scattering of forest seedlings.

"Once," he went on, "once, in another time, they came here in the autumn to pick the fruit and load great baskets on their wagons to bear it home to their barns. But that was long ago, for even our father Homer never saw these trees in blossom or in fruit."

Amalthea rubbed her neck against the long-dead apple trunk and browsed among the shoots on the forest floor.

"But let us go on, if you will," said Horatio, "and keep the sun this afternoon between your shoulders, for that is the only thing that can guide us from this point on." They went on higher through the woodland with the sun on their backs. There was little warmth in it and Eli was grateful for the fleece-lined gloves he had received from Stanley and Staley. Horace pulled his bright red woolen hat down over his ears. "If your feet are cold," he said, "be sure to wear a hat!" This statement didn't seem to make much sense to Eli, but he pulled on the knitted hat that Staley had provided and after a while realized that he felt warmer all over.

As they progressed, the air grew misty and the shadows beneath the fallen logs grew deeper until at length Horatio called a halt. From his deep coat pocket he produced a small hatchet and set about clearing the branches from two pairs of slim, straight birch saplings. His brothers fetched lengths of dead logs and laid up a four-foot wooden wall between these uprights. They fashioned a sloping roof of long hornbeam poles and thatched it with birch switches. Hamlet ripped up streamers of ground pine with which he covered the dry leaves inside the lean-to. Horace kindled a fire with a bow drill he made from dead pine branches and a leather thong he carried in his pocket. Soon a small fire was flickering in front of the shelter, casting long moving shadows into the darkening woodland around the camp.

The night was still and there was no wind to mask the forest sounds around them. An owl spoke softly from one side and later they heard a fox barking repeatedly in a slow rhythm to the sound of its own echo. They slept somewhat fitfully, and Horatio rose several times to shove half-burnt logs farther into the fire. Amalthea calmly chewed her cud and seemed quite content with the whole situation.

In the morning Horace produced a small leather pail from the depth of his jacket pocket and proceeded to milk the goat. They breakfasted on goat's milk, cheese, hard biscuits, and raisins from Eli's rucksack. The sun soon warmed them and they set off again to the east where the bright shafts of light showed through the tangle of dark tree trunks and directed them toward distant mountains, which they still could not see. Eli reflected that it was fortunate they traveled in the autumn, for full summer foliage would have made their way much slower.

They swerved right and left from time to time, seeking the lower rises to the east, all the while allowing the sun to shine more and more on their right shoulders as they went. They could never see more than a hundred yards ahead through the trees. They traveled thus for several days, climbing all the while through a thinner woodland, until at length they came out upon a gray and yellow granite cliff where they could look out over a broad but shallow valley beyond. They stood at the edge of the rocky escarpment and stared at what was revealed before them.

The valley lay like a huge bowl stretching to the east for many miles, across to a rim of blue hills beyond. To the northeast there were notches in the hills, and through these they could discern still another range of hills beyond a still more distant valley. And beyond the farthest range they could see an enormous gray and purple shape that rose immense and featureless across the distant horizon. It was their first sight of the Long-Eared Mountains; they had traversed the passes into the high valley.

They trudged onward for many days through thin woods in the rolling valley and thicker cover of laurel in the boggier areas near streambeds. They crossed brooks on fallen trees and by jumping from stone to stone in the narrow river bottoms. Sometimes they could scarcely see the sun for the thickness of the pine woods, but on another day they camped on a little hillock of dry grass tufts in an open space between pungent juniper bushes and tall standing cedar trees.

Amalthea sampled all of the vegetation she encountered, except for the spiny juniper boughs. The lower trunks of the cedars had already been eaten bare in previous winters by the voracious deer that they saw from time to time by the brook sides and in the occasional natural meadows they crossed. She always seemed able to digest this tough vegetable matter, converting it into milk for the travelers' benefit. By now they were beginning to run low on cheese and biscuits, so it was a delight when Horatio was able to snare a fat rabbit which they roasted on a spit over the campfire. Horace had collected pocketfuls of herbs along the trail, wild thyme and rosemary, and the rabbit was seasoned with these.

As they progressed to the northeast the nights were colder, and their way brought them out onto occasional hilltops. Eventually they found signs of a trail that had been followed by earlier travelers. Once they found the cold ashes of a campfire, and Eli wondered if they had not at last come upon the tracks of Marna's parents. He wondered if his own path was taking him closer to the source of the green stones they sought.

The first snows came early that year, and each morning the small mountain streams they camped beside were fringed with small, sharp blades of cat ice. There continued to be ample forage in the tough sparse grass for Amalthea, and Eli reflected how excellent an animal is the goat who can survive happily on such fare and provide first-rate nourishment to man at the same time. Their supplies began to run low, and Horatio's snare caught no further rabbit. The days grew shorter and the nights colder as they drew closer to the towering peaks of the Long-Eared Mountains. Hunger became their constant companion.

At the easier passes of the first range they found the first trace of those they followed: a worn rucksack and an empty water bottle covered with dark brown cloth lying among the broken fragments of stone, covered with a fine powdering of new snow. On the following day they found the ashes of a pitifully small campfire and four small piles of stones that Hamlet thought might have been used to weight the corners of a tent.

As they climbed higher the way became colder, and ice and snow were all around them. Rising above were the huge rocky horns of enormous peaks, mantled in ice. By now light snows were a daily occurrence, although below the passes it usually melted before midday. The goatherds kept their red caps pulled down tight over their ears as they trudged ever upward through the mountain passes. Finally they topped a saddle between two menacing pyramids of stone and began a short decline to a narrow rocky ridge tending to the southeast. Above them hung the frozen cliff of a permanent glacier.

It was here that they came upon Marna's parents. In a small tent surrounded by lightly drifting snow, they were frozen, dead, but looking more as though they slept in their meager camp. The Sons of Homer pulled off their woolen hats and stood looking at the pitiful couple.

"We should bury them," said Horace.

"How can we dig a grave in all this rock?" asked Eli.

"We do not need to dig," said Horatio. "They could stay frozen in this bleak land forever. If we place rocks around them and cover them with stone slabs, I think they will be encased in a tomb that will last for many ages."

"What should we do with her necklace—the one with the green stone?" asked Eli. "It is still around her neck."

"If it belonged to Marna's mother," said Horatio, "it is rightfully Marna's now. Even if she may not want it, you should take it to her—at least to show her that you found her parents." And with that, he undid the clasp and took the lavaliere from the frozen neck of the woman and placed it carefully into Eli's shirt pocket.

"What if other wayfarers traverse the passes and come upon the tomb?" asked Hamlet. "They will wonder who is buried here, why they came here, and how they came to perish."

"We will put an inscription on the stones," said Horace.

So they built a large rectangular grave above the ground and placed the bodies inside. They roofed it over with flat cap stones which they selected from the flaking shale of the mountainside. Horace's deep pockets yielded up a steel cold chisel, and with the back of Horatio's hatchet as a hammer, he cut letters into the rock to identify the occupants of the tomb:

> *HERE ARE THE PARENTS OF MARNA*
> *THEIR NAMES WILL BE FORGOTTEN*
> *THEIR SEARCH FOR THE GREEN STONE UNFINISHED*
> *THEIR HEARTS' DESIRE IS UNKNOWN*
> *TO THOSE WHO BURY THEM*
> *PRAY STRANGER, THAT SUCH NOT BEFALL THEE*
> *WHO CHANCE UPON THIS WEARY PLACE*

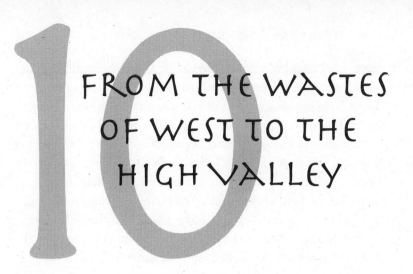

10
FROM THE WASTES
OF WEST TO THE
HIGH VALLEY

Marna's passage over the dark and forested hills and the tangled Wastes of West was surprisingly swift, although Lucindar's balloon almost seemed to hang motionless in the sky. The air was clear but chilly. She took a sweater from her rucksack and also put on her yellow waterproof jacket.

Looking out over the edge of the basket, she could see the jutting bulk of the familiar Ice and Moon Mountains receding behind her. Ahead were a pair of rounded forms that she had never seen before, although she thought one looked like a man's bald head with blunt ears and the other, slightly lower, like a close-fitting cap with a rocky outcrop on top, which was shaped rather like a gigantic stone button. Far to the north there were other mountains with steep sides and hanging valleys of snow and ice on either side, like the dangling lobes of fantastic ears.

The western wind seemed to shift somewhat to the south, and as the day wore on, Marna could see that she was being carried toward those northern places, still farther from the Valley of Spitte and the Rock Tower. But as yet she could see no cleared fields where she might set her craft down. So each time the balloon began to settle toward the threatening forest, she opened the valve a bit until the blue flame warmed the air in the great yellow and green bag. She rose swiftly above the threatening woodland. She was aware that such maneuvers could not go on forever, as soon, she would run out of the inflammable gas that heated the air to keep the balloon aloft.

And so, long before she approached the distant peaks, she began to search out a landing place, no matter how small, where she could safely bring down the balloon. She seemed to be traveling above a sizable river which originated somewhere beyond her view in the lofty valleys of the great mountains. Its water appeared almost black in contrast to the pale buff of the dry land on either side of it. Ahead, the way narrowed into a steep-sided gorge between cedar-covered hills that led farther up the high valleys to the north. Marna had not been too worried about being up in the air, but now, as she gradually descended, she felt some fear about the final landing of the fragile craft. As she moved closer to the ground, she realized that her attempt would be better made soon, while she still had fuel to control the altitude of the balloon.

Marna saw beneath her a large house with a facade of arches that faced stone-bordered terraces set with well-manicured shrubs. There was a closely mowed lawn in front of the house—a good spot for landing—so she put her hand to the ripcord that would open the top of the balloon and let the hot air out. She soon realized that she was still too high to risk such a precipitous freefall to the ground, and her descent was too slow to bring her down before the wind swept her past the house, over the rooftop, beyond the surrounding orchards, and back over the curving river beyond. Finding herself once more over the dark water of the river, she peered ahead, trying to discern another safe landing place. All she saw was a series of gorges with steep and rocky sides. This valley seemed to lead inexorably toward the snow-covered mountains to the north. Meanwhile, the balloon dropped lower and lower. Her heart was pounding in her chest now.

She saw the end of the gorge ahead of her, a closed headwall shrouded in mist that rose from a vast torrent of falling water, pouring in a mighty stream from the brink. She couldn't even see the source, but the huge mass of water fell in curtains and cascades into the mist below. Marna stood on her toes and reached up to open the gas valve. Even a few feet of altitude might lift the basket beyond the reach of the terrible force of the waterfall. She opened the valve full and watched the flame swell, but just as quickly, it fluttered and winked out.

She was out of gas at last.

Marna knew that she must lighten the basket to get the balloon to rise out of the gorge before she was swept into those falling tons of white water and foam. There were two small ballast bags of sand in the gondola. Marna dropped them over the side and the balloon steadied but did not rise. Over the side went the rucksack with her foul-weather jacket, her spare clothing, and the recorder. The balloon seemed to hesitate and hang motionless as it was swept toward the wall of the gorge. Marna sat down in the basket and pulled off her heavy hiking boots. Throwing them out of the gondola, she watched them fall into the swirling foam and rocks below.

The basket rocked from the force of her exertions and then, as she looked to both sides, it seemed to rise, imperceptibly and slowly as it continued to approach the wall of falling water. Foam and spray blew all around her, and the roar of the water almost deafened her. Huge jets of white water spurted from the face of the cascade and fell away into the mists of the abyss below. Crouching barefoot in the bottom of the basket, Marna composed herself for the end.

But the basket seemed to pause just short of the reaching jets and surges of the mighty falls. She hung motionless over the torrent and wondered what would become of her. She thought briefly of Sennet and his lonely vigil at the Rock Tower. She surprised herself by wondering what would happen to Eli, who must be somewhere in this northern land.

The basket swung from side to side in the currents of wind generated by the falling water, seemingly blown away from destruction by the air displaced from the rushing torrent. The balloon rose a bit more in the cooler air, swung forward, and skimmed slowly just a few feet above the smooth and rapid surface of the river above the falls. Hearing the boom and roar of the water receding behind her, Marna jumped up to see what had happened. She found herself moving swiftly over the surface of the broad dark water. But even now, driven helplessly by the south wind, she knew she would be in the water in a few minutes if the balloon did not cross some piece of land.

Her craft continued to blow up the middle of the stream. The only refuge from the water she could see was a small island in midstream. It was not more than thirty yards long and half as wide, studded with a dozen sycamore trees and fringed with cattails. It did not look especially accommodating, and the trees would surely make an end of the green and yellow bag of still-hot air. But for the moment, this tiny island was safer than the sinking balloon, and Marna pulled the ripcord as she crossed its southern shore.

The balloon came down surprisingly gently, for it did not have far to fall. The basket struck the gravelly shingle and tipped over, depositing a slightly bruised Marna on the sand. Once relieved of her weight, it started to blow upward until it was caught by the broad reaching branches of a tall sycamore. Marna sat up, rubbing her bruised knees, and watched the great green and yellow bag blow itself to shreds in the treetop. Shoeless, without any food, surrounded by a swiftly flowing river that led to a watery abyss, she wondered what she could do to get to either shore.

11 A RETREAT TO GO FORWARD

Turning their backs on the frozen encampment, Eli and the Sons of Homer started toward the final saddle between the mountains. Eli's mission had been accomplished, and he had now only to return the way he had come to bring the sad news to Marna. But as they climbed, the wind was rising and beginning to whistle through the high pass. The damp snow became thicker as it blew through the gaps in the rocks above them.

"If we are to return," said Horatio, "we must go quickly to get over the pass and back to lower ground, for the storm that this wind precedes will be a great one, and snow may block our way."

It was not several hundred yards up the steep mountainside to the crest, but the way over the shelving slabs of basalt and shale was difficult. The wind increased as they approached the summit of the saddle. Bent double, facing into the cold gale blowing up from the valleys they had recently crossed, they found the going hard indeed. But from moment to moment the direction of the wind changed, and as they reached the high point, a great gust of wind tore through the pass and all five stopped, unable to go farther. For a minute they stood there, leaning into the wind—the three goatherds, a boy, and a goat—as the thick snow coated their faces and their arms and the wind blew the tails of the red woolen caps out behind them like pennants. Then all five turned and hastened back the way they had come. When they reached the tomb cairn again, they stopped, and Horatio shouted over the increasing roar of the wind. "If we go back through the pass we will surely perish! If we wait here without shelter, I fear that we will be frozen to death in this place where nothing ever thaws. We must go down to the east!"

"Farther from the goats we left behind," said Hamlet.

"But perhaps nearer to other adventures or heroic deeds that we could remember for the length of our lives," added Horatio. always the optimist.

"Farther from Marna and Sennet in their Rock Tower," said Eli. "And I must bring them the tragic news of what we found today."

Horatio pulled his collar higher around his head. "We go down to the east or there will be sad news to tell of us," he said.

And then came a gust of wind greater than any before. It tore great ragged clouds of snow from the mountain and sent them swirling down toward the figures huddled by the rocky mountainside; it blew small stones from the cliff face through the air like a sheet of hail; it turned the five in their tracks and sent them sliding and scraping down a mountainside too steep to climb with the shrieking storm at their backs and the snow blowing every which way around them. Only Amalthea seemed to find the going easy, for she sprang and gamboled through the snow as though she had been born in the mountains.

They plunged down the steep side of the mountain, sliding on patches of ice and scraping their trousers on the rocks when they fell. After a half-hour of their precipitous descent they suddenly found the snow thinner and the wind less strong. By the time they had come down a thousand feet from the saddle, they found the snow less deep underfoot, and the air seemed to become warmer. Looking back up the way they had come, Eli could see the snow-shrouded ice field through gaps in the clouds. The storm was still raging above the peaks of the Long-Eared Mountains. Jagged masses of cloud streamed out from the pass they had crossed, and the highest reaches of the range were hidden in a surging, boiling, wind-whipped confusion of snow.

But the day warmed as they descended the steep southern and eastern faces of the mountains, and soon they picked their way among banks of melting snow and a few shafts of green mountain grass. Presently the sun came out and they sat down to rest on a flat rock. Amalthea foraged happily among the small white and blue flowers near the rock, and the four other travelers searched the mountains they had crossed. Gigantic towers of white cumulus clouds capped the Long-Eared Mountains, great whipped-cream clouds that billowed up into fantastic battlements enclosing the rocky peaks. From the melting meadow it seemed impossible that such a serene scene could mask the winter fury they had just survived.

"So," said Hamlet, "we are come down into the High Valley in the East. But where we are in this land, I do not know. What now, friend Eli? Do you have an idea of which way we should proceed on this quest, or other adventures that we can help you with?"

"I don't know what will be next," Eli answered, "but if my life to date is any measure of the future, I would guess that there will be a great wind from someplace that will blow us all to another adventure, or blow some adventure our way.

"Ever since my brother Reuben gave me his skiff, I have been blown to strange places and have met strange people. I mean, you are not strange, but you were not previously known to me. Everyone I've met has turned out to be a friend that will help and stand with me. So I care not what lies ahead of us here on the eastern slope of the great mountains. I have three good friends and Amalthea to share it with. My only regret is that Marna is so far on the other side of the pass, for I have no idea when, if ever, I will see her again. But let us go and see what it will be." And then he fell silent, for he was embarrassed to have made such a long speech to the three Sons of Homer, as though they were his followers and he their leader.

The three did not seem to take Eli's speech as an offense against their dignity or their years.

"I am willing to go with you," said Horace.

"And I," said Horatio.

"And if the others go, then I will go too, just for this next season of the year," said Hamlet.

And so the group continued, but with some difference from what it had been before. Eli walked with more assurance in his stride, for even if he was the least and youngest of Solomon's sons, he was, after all, a leader of a company of followers who had made a great passage and were willing to undertake still more. His followers were wise in the ways of the woodlands, while he was knowledgeable in the matter of rivers and small boats. Without asking for a pledge or giving one, they were ready to act with loyalty toward each other in their next adventure, whatever it might be.

As they sat around their fire late in the day, the rays of the pink afternoon sun lit the edges of the Ice Mountain, which was silhouetted against the brighter sky to the west. Then, looking to the south, Hamlet spied the crescent shape of a green and yellow balloon moving slowly through the sky over the high land to the right of their track. It drifted slowly to the east and toward them until it was eventually lost to their sight as it crossed the blue ridges of the neighboring hills.

The company set out again, tending to go downhill toward the stream valleys as they went. Once, crossing a cleared bluff which was studded with ancient cedar trees, Amalthea broke away from them and climbed the hill, plunging among the dark green spires of the trees. She was soon lost from their sight. The four followed, calling her to return. Eli, bringing up the rear, was last to come to the clearing where the others stood in a circle, staring in wonder at what they saw. It was a stone pedestal and next to it, lying prone in the myrtle leaves, was a stone statue of a small man or a boy.

Or at least it seemed to be a boy at first glance. Horatio and Eli rolled the figure over and then pulled it erect. Looking more closely, they could see that the boy seemed human only down to the middle of his round protruding belly. Below, he was covered with shaggy goat hair skillfully carved in the stone. His legs were as slender as Amalthea's, and he stood on small cloven hoofs. In his hand he held a willow flute, and showing through the thick curls of his sculptured hair was a pair of polished horns with broken-off tips. Oddest of all was the color of the statue: from top to bottom, it was carved out of the green stone of the Long-Eared Mountains.

"I wonder who he is?" said Eli, breaking the long silence.

"I feel as if I know him," said Horace, "but I don't remember ever seeing such a one before. He is so familiar ... I think I knew such a boy when I was very young myself. Horatio, do you know of a boy who was half goat? Do you, Hamlet?"

But neither of the other two claimed such an acquaintance. Memory stirred in Eli's mind.

"I think I was told a story once, when I was very, very young, about young animals, harts or roebucks, who shook the dew from their horns and danced to wild music on the hills. But I can remember nothing more of that story. Look at what he is made of; it is the same green stone that makes people cross mountains and wilderness to find nothing but sadness and death."

"If the stone is so rare and valuable," said Horatio, "how is it that a whole statue could be carved from it? Why, the sculptor's wasted chips from this one figure of a boy would make many hundreds of ornaments such as the necklace Marna's mother wore around her neck."

"So, perhaps it is not so rare and valuable after all," said Hamlet. "Perhaps it is only valuable to those who seek it and do not yet possess it."

"Well," said Horatio, "Amalthea values it, at least; she nuzzles at the boy's hand like a cat rolling in catnip."

"No," said Eli, "I do not think Amalthea is interested in the green stone. I think that somehow, she knows what Horatio and I cannot remember about such a boy. Whoever he was, or whoever he was intended to be, I think Amalthea knows him from some memory of her own."

The goat rubbed her back against the pedestal of the statue, looked at her four companions in a kindly sort of way, and turned to grazing on the brown and green mosses that carpeted the center of the little clearing.

WHAT THEY FOUND BY THE BLACK RIVER

The five spent that night camped in the little clearing around the base of the statue. Horatio whistled a cheerful tune and the goat boy seemed to be playing his pipe for them in the dark. Their fire outlined the dense wall of cedar branches around the shrine and the reflected light enclosed them on all sides. Overhead a cold black sky was pricked with many small white stars. The Sons of Homer regarded the familiar firmament and exchanged the names of the stars and constellations as though they were speaking of family members.

Late that night after Altair and Vega had wheeled below the trees, they caught a glimpse of Orion and the Pleiades, Taurus the Bull, and the Dog Star, Sirius, who followed them at this late season. They gazed upward and hummed fragments of old songs, but though they hummed for quite a time, no words came, and soon they rolled their coats around themselves and, turning their feet toward the fire, went to sleep. Amalthea lay down among them and regarded the statue with wise and knowledgeable eyes.

The next day's march downhill to the East brought them through more small hills and valleys, streams both straight and meandering, and many rivulets that carried the meltwater from the mountains behind them to some unknown river or sea. Far ahead they could see two huge mountain domes, pale gray-blue under the yellow morning haze. One looked like a great bald head and the other like a head in a close-fitting cap. The valley took them in the general direction of these great prominences, but there were gaps both to the north and south. To the north, between the bulk of the head-shaped mountain and the last sheer cliffs of the Long Eared Mountains, they could see a tiny patch of deep blue, as though that opposite direction led to the sea. To the south the valley seemed to turn into a broad, high land crossed by rows of pines and rolling hillocks, as though a great river furrowed the land. They passed more pine woods and cedar shrubs and odd outcroppings of rock.

And then, to their surprise, they came upon a second statue among the trees. This figure was standing securely on a circular stone. It was an image of a young and graceful girl carved from a pale orange- and cream-colored stone. She was clad in a short and flowing gown that was clasped with a brooch at one shoulder. She held a vase with two handles in her arms. From the vessel there came a stream of water that filled a pebble-lined basin at her feet. The overflow of the water formed a rill that broadened into a brook as other streams joined it and splashed down the steepening floor of the valley.

This new discovery caused them to pause and wonder even more than had the discovery of the little green goat boy. The Sons of Homer stood in the clearing beside the source of the brook and studied the land that stretched before them. There was no sign of the spring that fed the source of the water spilling from the maiden's ewer; it simply flowed unendingly from her vessel into the pebbled basin and ran on down the hill toward the valley below.

"We should follow the stream down the valley to the south," said Eli. "It may lead to the sea in the north, or it may lead between the two great mountains we can see in the distance. I have always heard that in cases of doubt, travelers should follow the course of running water, for it will lead them aright in the end."

So they went on along the green-fringed banks of the stream. As they traveled, the water seemed to flow more swiftly and darker still, until it became an ever-broadening river. Its water was cold and deep before they had gone many miles. They could hear a distant rumbling like the sound of a mighty waterfall somewhere ahead, to the south of them. Presently they could see a towering plume of mist rising from the valley. Hunger held them up at this point, across from a small, tree-fringed island in the river. They paused at the riverbank to divide the slender remains of their supplies. The last of their biscuits and cheese was separated into four portions, and they ate it slowly. They reasoned that soon they would find some human habitation, since they were now in a part of the country where statues were found in upland clearings.

"If it were not so odd to imagine it," said Hamlet, "I would say that the green and yellow foliage at the top of that great tree on the island looks more like streamers of silk than sycamore leaves."

"And the huge crow's nest among the branches—does it not look like a woven basket, a pannier of the sort that people in the olden days used to swing on either side of their mules to carry home the produce of the fields?" asked Horace.

"And below the tree," said Horatio. "If it were not so unlikely as to be my imagination, I would say that the little pile of yellow might also be cloth rather than leaves."

And while they were looking, the yellow object turned and rose unsteadily to its feet, revealing itself to be a girl in a short blue skirt and a yellow rain jacket. Her legs and feet were bare and her red-brown hair was tangled. She looked across the swiftly running water at the shore where the four travelers sat and tentatively waved her hand. With that, Eli stripped off his heavy sweater, woolen shirt, boots, and trousers, and strode into the river. The current was swift but the river was not deep for the first ten or fifteen yards offshore. The stones on the bottom were the size of watermelons, but with treacherous holes and cracks between them. Most were smooth, but when his feet slipped into a crevice he felt a sharp pain where a rock had cut his shin. He pushed off into deeper water and swam swiftly across the current.

The girl came carefully to the edge of the water, limping as she tried to cross the rocky shore in bare feet. Once in the stream she tried to swim toward Eli, but the current was too swift and she was carried along by it until she came up against a great boulder in the shallow water. She wrapped her arms around the rock and hung there in the rapidly flowing water, her legs floating out beyond the rock.

It only took Eli two dozen strokes to cross the deepest part of the river to where he could again feel the bottom with his feet. He splashed along down the course of the water, pressed along by the force of the current, until he reached her.

"Marna!" he managed to gasp. "How did you get here?"

"In a balloon, of course. You can be sure I didn't sail up that waterfall! And it certainly took you long enough to come along and rescue me. And why is it that whenever you start splashing around a river in my presence, you seem to be missing most of your clothes?"

She seemed reluctant to let go of the rock which was keeping her from being carried down the stream toward the great waterfall, but Eli gathered up her bare legs with his right arm, and, supporting the yellow-jacketed figure in his left, he carried her through the water until they had reached the shore of the island. There he set her down on the grassy bank and spoke her name.

"Marna," he said, "how did you do it? Where did you get the balloon?"

Marna spoke through chattering teeth. "Look," she giggled, "I'm delighted that you're here, but if you really are going to rescue me, you should get to it! I haven't had anything to eat in three days, and I'm terribly cold … Who are those little men with you?"

"Come," said Eli, "you will meet my friends soon enough." And picking her up, he carried her through the shallow water, moving upstream, until he reached a point across from the waiting Sons of Homer.

Marna had closed her eyes, anticipating the cold moment when she found herself in the water again. Being carried in Eli's arms was an unfamiliar experience for her, and at first, she couldn't decide what to do with her own arms, which seemed to be in the way, until she finally locked them around Eli's neck and put her face against his wet, scarred shoulder. Eli waded into water up to his chest for most of the first half of the crossing, until he had to push off into deeper water and keep them both afloat. With one arm around her and swimming with the other, he reached the shallows of the other side in less than a minute. Even so, he was winded and ready to collapse on the grass by the time he had reached his three companions and Amalthea on the bank.

Hamlet, Horace, and Horatio moved swiftly to bring the two of them over to the fire they had just finished kindling. Eli introduced Marna to his friends, and pleasant greetings were exchanged. Taking off their long coats, they dried the girl and soon had her clad in Eli's woolen shirt and his heavy sweater, which hung down nearly to her knees. Eli managed to get into another shirt from his rucksack and Horatio's coat. But Eli also discovered a long laceration along his right shin that continued to bleed until it was tied up in a handkerchief from Hamlet's pocket. Wet clothing was draped over sapling branches in the sunshine next to the fire where it slowly began to dry.

"We have sad news for you," said Horatio, after a time. He seemed to sense that Eli was reluctant to bring up the fate of Marna's parents.

"We found your father and mother too late for Eli to persuade them to return," said Hamlet, "and perhaps too soon for them to have even found

THE HOUSE OF
UMBERTO

CASA SAPIENZA

the treasure they sought in the Long-Eared Mountains."

"But though they are gone from this life," said Horace, "we made a marker in the form of a stone cairn and put an inscription over their burial place."

Eli put his arm around Marna. She did not weep, but instead, sat quietly as they told her about how they had found more of the green stone in the hills, where it seemed to be a common material for making statues.

"I am sorry for them," Marna said finally. "They never even made it to the strange and wonderful land that they sought to enter," she said. "But I *am* glad they did not live to see their jewel of great price turn out to be merely a semiprecious curiosity. Perhaps they went to sleep in the cold that night, trying to keep each other warm, keeping faith with each other, still hoping that the next day would bring them to their goal. Do you think so, Eli?"

"I cannot read the heart of a frozen person, Marna," he answered, "but if you are their daughter, the fruit of their love, they must have had some generosity and kindness in their natures, along with their desire for treasure. Maybe your mother gave her warmer clothes to your father in an attempt to save him when she knew the end was near." He paused for a moment as he reached into his pocket. "I have brought you this," said Eli, "since it belonged to your mother." He slipped into her hand the lavaliere that bore the fragment of green stone.

"I won't wear it," she said. "But I am glad that they are gone now rather than still seeking for something that made them unhappy to seek, and left them unsatisfied for so much of their lives. I won't miss *them* so much as the love and relationship I never really had with them. Perhaps they are at peace now, and I can go back to the River and the Rock Tower with this mission fulfilled. I may now be an orphan, but I still have a grandfather who waits for me to be mistress of the Rock Tower."

And they spoke no more of the quest to bring the daughter of Sennet and her husband back to the river.

Marna looked to the west and then looked at Eli and the Sons of Homer, who were looking downstream, to the south. "I never intended to come to this eastern country at all," she said. "Which way should I go to get back?"

"You cannot return the way we came—at least, not at this season of the year," said Horatio. "Ice, snow, and glaciers block the way."

"Perhaps you must wait for another balloon and a wind from the east to blow you back again," commented Horace.

The three brothers seemed to have little real advice to give her, and Marna declared herself unwilling to try to travel by air again, no matter which way the wind should blow.

"There is much we must do before nightfall," said Hamlet. "We need a camp, a shelter, food, and more wood for our fire."

Marna smiled indulgently at the four companions and told them of what she had seen. "You fellows should try looking at things from up in the air," she said. "You would find your way quicker. I have seen a great house not more than a few miles from here if we go due south. The river curves back to the west below the falls. If we go over the upland here beside us, we should find it soon enough."

The three men, the boy, and the goat listened to her explanation and her description of the landforms she had seen from the balloon, and then started up the hill that led them away from the riverbank they had been following. The day was growing late and the sun beginning to turn orange as it approached the ragged blue pattern of the western mountains. They walked swiftly through pastureland where they had to tug Amalthea along to keep her from the distraction of the lush grass. Marna, still without shoes, wore two pairs of knitted woolen socks that had been contributed by Horatio and Horace.

Their minds were on food and dry clothing as they came down toward the river again and saw beyond them the limestone and tile-roofed shape of a big building with a high gabled upper story and many arched windows. The house was of noble proportion and dominated the cliff above the stream. Beside the house there were several laundry lines where two girls in black uniform dresses with white aprons were taking in a great number of linens that flapped in the fading afternoon sunshine.

At the sight of the band of strangers, the two maids, clutching the laundry in their arms, looked wide-eyed and startled.

"Don't worry," called Eli, suddenly realizing how ragged their costumes must appear in this civilized place. "We are harmless even though we're hungry. We have come walking over the mountains on foot, except for Marna, who came in a balloon and had to drop her shoes, and Amalthea, who sort of prances along. Can you tell us where we are and where we can get something to eat, and perhaps even a pair of shoes that would fit a girl's foot?"

"You have come to Casa Sapienza, the home of Dottore Umberto and La Dottoressa Donna Elizabetta, his sister. But no one comes here from the north! How did you cross the mountains?"

"It was long, but not very hard," said Eli. "Coming from the south in a balloon was probably harder. But who are you?"

"I am Maria," said one of the girls.

"And I am her sister, Margaretta," said the other. And both Eli and Marna realized for the first time that the two girls looked very much alike except that although they both had black hair, one had brown eyes and the other hazel.

"I think you should all come to the house," said Maria, putting her bundle of laundry in her sister's arms and straightening her own ruffled white apron.

"Except for your goat," said Margaretta. "Perhaps she could stay in the rear court outside the kitchen door."

So the group divided around the back and front of the house, and the oddly clad Eli and Marna, along with the three red-capped Sons of Homer, entered the stately doorway at the west end of the house. They passed through the entrance arch and Maria opened a pair of tall walnut doors with gleaming brass hinges and bolts.

"Padrone!" she called. "Padrone! We have unexpected guests, and one of them is a girl who has no shoes!"

A tall man in a dark red velvet jacket arose from a writing table where he had been reading a book. There were a number of books on the table and many more in the shelves around the room. Only one wall lacked shelving for books, where a walnut mantelpiece surmounted a large fireplace framed in lavender marble jambs and lintel. A small fire glowed between black and irons in the shape of a pair of large sitting cats who seemed to be guarding the flame. The man wore a ruffled white shirt and had a black velvet patch over his right eye.

"Welcome," he said in a quiet voice, not much above a hoarse whisper. "Welcome to Casa Sapienza. I am called Umberto." He bowed formally to Marna and then extended his hand to Eli.

"You all look as though you could use a change of clothing before dinner. Maria, tell the Dottoressa that we have five guests this evening and that, with nine at the table, we could perhaps have a *bollito misto*. And when you show our guests to rooms in the east wing, perhaps you and Maria could also find a moment to show this young lady the guardaroba in the green bedroom, where I am sure you will be able to find something for her to wear."

He smiled at Marna and said, "I don't mean to imply that you do not look well dressed as you are now, but I think you would be more comfortable in something warmer and dryer. And what is your name?"

"Marna," she answered. "Granddaughter of Sennet who keeps the Rock

Tower in the West. And I hope someday to be mistress of the Rock Tower and keeper of the upper reaches of the River Spitte."

"And we are the Sons of Homer: Horatio, Hamlet, and Horace," said the first of the brothers.

"And I am Eli," said Eli. "I am the least of Solomon's sons, from Salem on Spitte."

"All the way from Salem on Spitte?" said Umberto with some surprise. "That is a long journey indeed. You must tell us about it at dinner." And then he bowed again and gestured to Maria, who brought the troupe of travelers through a high-ceilinged hall and up a broad stair that led to the rooms along a wide corridor above.

THE GUARDAROBA

Maria and Margaretta together brought Marna into a large south-facing room and immediately hurried her into an adjoining dressing room where they undid her muddy braids and prepared to put her into a deep tub full of hot water and bubbles, perfumed by rare herbs unknown to the girl from the West. Being a seafaring girl, she was not accustomed to such things and she tried to protest. But the two maids had four hands to her two, and they soon got her clothes away from her and were shampooing her in the pleasant depths of the hot water. Her protests did no good, and Margaretta confiscated all of her clothing and took it away to the laundry. So, while she was waiting for something else to put on, she stayed in the hot water, under the bubbles, studying the plaster modeling on the ceiling where sculptures of little fat babies seemed to be flying above her. Presently the two girls returned, wrapped Marna in a big yellow bath sheet, and opened the double doors of the guardaroba, which turned out to be a sort of huge, free-standing closet that took up most of one wall of the room.

"These things have been here for many years," explained Margaretta. "They are dresses and gowns that were made for Donna Lucrezia, who was the great-great-grandmother of one of the ancestors of the Padrone. She lived many years ago, but she had such great beauty and her clothes were so lovely that they have been saved by many generations of her descendants and we, my sister and I, keep them clean and free from moths. And on Christmas or at other great feasting times of the year, when there is a candlelight ball at Casa Sapienza, we dress ourselves in the fashion of the ladies in the paintings in the dining room and dance very late into the night."

There were many dresses on elaborate wooden hangers and drawers full of silk petticoats and underthings beneath them. Marna tried to protest again, and even to give orders to the two enthusiastic girls, each not much older than she was herself, but they shushed her with happy giggles and insisted. Soon she was clothed in a dark green velvet dress trimmed with rich gold embroidery, the scalloped neckline edged with dark gold galloon, as were the hem and the long sleeves.

"That is a very pretty *scollatura*," said Maria, adjusting the bodice. It was a much lower neckline than Marna had ever worn, and she wasn't at all sure that she liked it.

But when Maria and Margaretta led her to a tall mirror that was on the inside of the wardrobe door, she was startled at the sight of the girl in the reflection. Her skin was pale against the soft dark material, and her eyes seemed more luminous and her lashes longer than she remembered. When Margaretta and Maria brushed up her hair and wrapped it in a string of pearls, she decided that she liked her new appearance. By the time the older girls had finished with her hair and produced a pair of dull golden slippers for her feet, she was reconciled to the change, and walked carefully in the long dress that just touched the floor.

Then Maria and Margaretta said they had to go quickly to help in the kitchen and change their own dresses before dinner.

"Do you have special uniforms for dinner too?" asked Marna.

"Not uniforms, but gowns almost as gorgeous as the one you are wearing," said Margaretta.

"You see," said Maria, "we are not really servants here at Casa Sapienza. We are orphans and the wards of Umberto the Padrone. He always has several orphan girls here, where they learn to compose and perform music, and pursue philosophy and mathematics until they are old enough to look after themselves—or until a young man asks them to become his wife and live in the south, where there are cities and ships and commerce."

"But married or not," continued Margaretta, "we will go out ready to follow our own good professions as expert musicians because of the teaching of the Padrone and the Dottoressa. Several of the orphan girls who came here years ago now play in the great orchestra of Berrymor, and one of them is its concertmistress. Another is the first woman to be the principal kettle drummer of any orchestra in all the land of the East. Some dance in the theater of Lucro where the greatest commerce is said to take place. But sister, come, we have much to do and very little time to do it."

And with that they vanished down the hall and left Marna to think about the fact that she was also an orphan now, and of her own interest in marine science and mushrooms and mathematics and music.

She studied the girl in the mirror for a few minutes, uncertain of what to think of her. She thought of wearing her mother's green stone on her pale bosom, but decided that what she saw was already different enough without adding anything else to it. Lifting the hem of the dress a careful few inches from the floor, she began to traverse the hallway and the wide staircase to the library below.

THE FOLLOWERS OF THE RED PRIEST

When Marna descended the great stairway, she saw a very different company than the one she had left a few hours earlier. Eli and the Sons of Homer stood in a semicircle at the foot of the stairs. They were dressed in black velvet sleeveless jackets over white, full-sleeved linen shirts. Their boots were gleaming with polish and the hair and beards of the three older men were snowy white, neatly trimmed and brushed in place. Eli's head looked slightly less damp than when he had arrived on the island to retrieve Marna, and it was obvious that he had been subjected to something of the same sort of rehabilitation as she. All four stared at her with speechless wonder as though they were not quite sure who she might be. She decided she liked the look of amazement in Eli's face best of all, and she smiled at them as she came down the stairs.

"Good evening, Signorina," said Umberto. "Donna Elizabetta, may I present Marna of the Rock Tower who has come to us from the West."

Although she had never done it before and had no idea that she even knew how to do it, Marna surprised herself by making a deep curtsey to the tall lady who stood beside Umberto. She was even more surprised when the lady responded with a similar gesture toward Marna.

"I am greatly delighted to have you with us at Casa Sapienza. Guests are rare here and thus always prized, but you are even more welcome because your companions tell me that you are two things that we value most highly here: someone who has lost her parents, and is also a musician."

This combination seemed very odd to Marna, and her face must have shown that she was puzzled, but Umberto took her arm and followed Eli and the Dottoressa into the dining room across the hall from the library. The walls of the room were hung with paintings in ornate frames. There were paintings of bearded men in black and scarlet gowns who held black velvet caps with gold tassels in their hands. There were paintings of women and girls in dresses of every hue, embroidered with jewels and trimmed with lace.

Maria and Margaretta, now dressed in brocaded crimson dresses that came to their ankles, joined them at the table, and all folded their hands while Umberto asked a blessing. The prayer was in a language Marna did not understand, and though she had heard many languages from sailors who came to the Rock Tower, she was almost sure she had never heard this tongue before.

"I see that you do not recognize our grace," said Umberto. "The language is actually Latin, but the pronunciation is that of Venice, as it was spoken several hundred years ago. You see, we take our inspiration from a man of that time, a priest with red hair who devoted most of his life to music and to girls who had no parents. His name was Antonio Vivaldi, and here, although we study many things, we are greatly fond of music such as his."

"So, are you then all Catholics?" asked Horatio.

"No, nor all Italian either," said Umberto, "although we all learn that language. We are all students and musicians, and we all honor Signer Padre Vivaldi, the Red Priest. You will find as you grow older that the love of music is more universal than religion."

They were each served an ample amount of a simple linguine in a delicate pink and white dish with chopped fresh basil and a sprinkling of Parmesan cheese. But shortly thereafter the two girls rose and took away these dishes. A moment later Margaretta came back bearing an enormous round silver platter with a domed cover on it. She set it in front of Umberto and lifted the cover.

A steam perfumed with many spices and the aromas of savory meats came from under the silver dome. There were six separate items glistening in the steamy sauce: a beef tongue, a fresh ham, the breast of a fat capon, a ruddy brown sausage, an eye round of beef, and a stuffed pig's trotter, which Umberto explained was called a *zampone*. Using a long, silver-handled carving knife, he sliced and laid delicate servings of each of the various meats on large flowered plates which Maria held and then brought to each person at the table.

"If you have not had *bollito misto* before," said Donna Elizabetta, "you should know that there are many sauces that go with it. There are curries and chutneys and fruit mustards and other spices that add piquancy to the boiled meats."

The Padrone and his sister, as well as the Sons of Homer, all sipped from tall wineglasses of a slightly bubbly red wine which they called Lambrusco, but the younger people were provided with a pale yellow beaded cider. After the short rations of their recent adventures, the five newcomers to Casa Sapienza quietly gave thanks both to God and Signor Padre Vivaldi, and did justice to all the delicacies of the table.

Umberto quizzed his guests politely but thoroughly about their journeys through or over the mountains. He heard about the fruitless quest of Marna's parents, about the snow in the high passes, the stone cairn where the doomed pair were buried, and about the statues of the goat boy made from the green stone and the maiden whose vase was the source of a stream.

"I have heard of such statues. They are relics of a people who lived long ago and whose language no one can read today. I think the statues had some religious significance, and out of respect for the maker's beliefs, I am glad you set up the faun—for that is what goat boys are called. I study the lost language from the gravestones and boundary markers that are found in the woods and in the far hill country. I have identified a number of words, but it will take many years and the attention of many scholars before we can know much about what they thought, or if they sang songs or were only warriors," said the Padrone. "They valued the green stone, quite surely," he continued, "although much of it is found in this country, so it was not valuable because of its rarity. It seems to have been sought because of the lasting beauty of things that could be made from it, for it is hard and durable."

After they had all eaten what seemed to Eli a great deal of *bollito misto* and green salad, each was served a small, ice-cold yellow pear and a miniature slice of Gorgonzola cheese. After this, they were ready to leave the table when Donna Elizabetta arose. The company did not return to the library after dinner, but passed along the broad corridor beside it and entered an ample drawing room. Here they found another inviting fireplace, flanked by a pair of large couches which bore long plump cushions that were covered in striped yellow and blue fabric.

On the opposite side of the room there was a large polished table on which there were a number of wooden flutes and recorders of various sizes, and several stringed instruments as well. In the center of the wall stood a large musical instrument of a sort that Eli had never seen before. Shaped rather like a grand piano, it was dark red in color, and there were gilded decorations all around its edges. It had two keyboards, one above the other, and on the underside of the uptilted cover, in carefully designed capital letters, were the words:

NELLA MUSICA SI PUÒ TROVARE LA SAGGEZZA.
LE PAROLE DELL'ISTRUITO SONO SAGGEZZA.

Eli later learned from Horace that the inscription inside the harpsichord read: *In music can be found wisdom. The words of the learned are wisdom.*

Donna Elizabetta and Signor Umberto sat across from each other on the two couches and the guests selected places beside them. Eli waited until all of the others were seated before selecting a place where he could also look at Marna while he was looking at the musical instruments, for he found himself continually occupied with regarding this new version of the girl he had thought he already knew well. As for Marna, she seemed to pay no attention to him at all and directed her questions to Donna Elizabetta, Margaretta, and Maria. The three Sons of Homer sat in a row, very straight-backed and dignified in their black and white costumes.

The two older girls went to the table and the harpsichord. Maria selected a mandolin and Margaretta sat on a gilded stool in front of the double keyboard. They began to play a piece of music so merry and with such movement that Eli thought it was a dance. But then it seemed so poignant and so full of longing that he scarcely knew what to think of it. And then Maria put down the mandolin and took up a large viola which she held vertically between her knees and played with a bow. (Later on Marna told Eli that it was called a *viola da gamba* and had six strings and frets on its fingerboard like a guitar. The pieces the three girls played that night were concertos for mandolin and recorder by Antonio Vivaldi.)

Margaretta invited Marna to join them in playing some dance tunes. Marna selected a small soprano recorder from the collection on the table and stood beside Margaretta to read the music from her score. The melody of the treble pipe floated above the dark harmony of the viola da gamba and the bright and merry movement of the crashing plucked strings of the harpsichord.

The Sons of Homer seemed to accept the musicale as a normal sort of event, as did the Padrone and Donna Elizabetta, who listened with grave approval. But Eli was mesmerized; he had heard nothing like this before, and his eyes were wide with wonder and his ears were amazed with the sounds of such music and the sight of such musicians. When the evening was done he went off to bed in a sort of daze, with the figure of the pale girl in the dark green velvet dress still before his mind's eye, playing intricate melodies on the wooden flute to the rich accompaniment of the stringed instruments.

15 THE PURSUIT OF LEARNING

B ut Eli soon learned that life at Casa Sapienza was not entirely a matter of *bollito misto* and sparkling cider. He awoke in the morning and, dressing in his own clothes again, which had appeared clean and dry in his room, he set out to find some breakfast. The Sons of Homer were there before him in a sort of great hall and kitchen that smelled most deliciously of coffee and fresh-baked bread. The three girls were there too, but now Marna and the other two orphans all wore simple black dresses with white aprons and had their hair tied back with white ribbons.

"Good morning," he said quite formally to the assembled company. "If I'm not early, at least I'm glad I'm not the very last."

"Oh, but you are," said Marna. "The Padrone and la Dottoressa were up hours ago and are already at work."

Eli wondered what sort of work the two older people would be doing in the early morning, but he decided not to ask just then and went in search of coffee and a roll. Maria supplied him with these, as well as a brightly colored pot of peach marmalade and a small pitcher of hot milk for the coffee.

"We must hurry," said Margaretta. "We have to practice our musical instruments and tend the garden before the mathematics lesson in the library at ten," she explained to Eli. Although nobody seemed about to ask him to do anything in particular, Eli decided he should join the bustle of activity that seemed to be going on all around the great house. He found Horatio down on his hands and knees in the garden, rapidly pulling weeds from between the plants of an extensive row of basil, and another area devoted to rosemary and sage. Horace was watering a brilliant array of rusty red and yellow chrysanthemums, using a large copper watering can with a very long spout. Hamlet was over at the other side of the garden, tying tomato plants up with string to wooden frames that could support the heavy fruit and keep it off the ground. The three girls traveled through the garden at great speed, cutting flowers for the vases in the house and gathering vegetables for the day's meals. Onions, carrots, and a few parsnips came out of the earth. Marna was gathering a bushel basket of white beans. Eli joined her, and together they filled the basket in short order. But long before they were through, he could hear the pleasant droning of the viola da gamba in a series of intricate intervals in various combinations.

"That's Maria doing her thirds," said Margaretta.

"Does she do them every day?" asked Marna. "They don't sound like much fun."

"No, they're not," said the older girl, "but the only way to become a really good player, like the Dottoressa, is to do your intervals and scales every morning. You just have to do your thirds and your fifths especially, and things like your C sharp minor scale, so that everything in the music will be easy."

Getting to be really good on the recorder would probably be even more difficult than getting to be skillful in a canoe or a sailboat, Eli thought.

The garden and kitchen chores completed, the Sons of Homer set out on a tour of the garner and outbuildings of the farm, for Casa Sapienza really was a farmhouse which Umberto said had been built after the plans of a man named Andrea Palladio. This architect had made designs for a good number of large farms in the past. His drawings had been published in four great books, and in that form had come to this high valley in the foothills of the Long-Eared Mountains many years ago. This was evidently in the ages before the present time, even before the time of the people that the Sons of Homer knew about, perhaps even as long ago as the time of the Wall Builders, but not nearly so long ago as the time of the statue makers of the green stone.

Shortly after ten in the morning, the four younger people gathered around the large table in the library. Umberto drew on a sheet of paper a triangle with one square corner. One side of the triangle was three centimeters long, another was four, and the longest side, across from the square corner, five centimeters. He then drew three perfect squares, making the first side of each square from each of the three sides of the triangle. He then divided each square into one-centimeter squares. The smallest side bore nine, the middle sized one sixteen, and on the longest side, he drew a square of twenty-five boxes.

"Now you can see," said Umberto, "the two smaller squares added together equal the big square."

"Does it always work out that way, for any triangle?" asked Maria.

"Let us find out," he said. "Just be sure that one of the angles of each triangle is a perfectly square corner."

All four drew different triangles, and measuring the sides, began the laborious process of multiplying the sides by themselves and seeing if the two smaller sides together equaled the larger. Some came close; Marna found that sides of 94 millimeters and 74 millimeters, squared and added, came close to the square of the 120 millimeters she measured on the long side of her triangle. But only Margaretta found an answer that added up exactly. The length of her sides were 12, 13, and 5 centimeters.

"So does it work in all cases?" asked Eli. "I think we cannot measure well enough to get it precisely right. These millimeters are very small, and it is hard to figure halves and quarters in between them."

"What you have shown so far is that the theorem works for cases that are integral," said Umberto. "That is, if the sides can be measured in whole numbers. But the man who first wrote the proof of this theorem down, Pythagoras from Samos in Greece, knew that it was true of all triangles with one square corner. He proved it by taking triangles that could be drawn by cutting up the squares made from the two shorter sides of the triangle andputting them together like a jigsaw puzzle to make up a big square, whose areas together would be exactly the same as the area of a square set on the longest side of the triangle. If you know just how to cut up the large square, you can do it too."

So more triangles were drawn and more squares erected on their sides. With compasses they measured the sides of the squares and even worked out how to cut them in half. None of them was able to work it out alone, but Marna kept at it longer than the others, until at last Umberto suggested that she draw four triangles inside a square. Suddenly, when she had done this, she could see that the area of the square on the longest side was equal to the sum of the areas of the two squares on the other sides.

"You will be a fine mathematician, Marna. What do you seek to do when you are older?" asked Donna Elizabetta when she was told that Marna had worked out a geometrical proof of Pythagoras's famous theorem.

"It is hard to decide," said Marna. "But I feel I would much rather be a leader than a follower if I am able."

"That is an admirable goal," said Donna Elizabetta. "Since you feel that way, I have a riddle for you to solve: What leader needs no follower, what follower needs no leader, and who needs to neither lead nor follow?"

Marna looked thoughtful for a moment. "I don't know the answer to that yet," she said. "But I promise you, I will solve it someday."

Donna Elizabetta smiled and patted her hand. "I know you will," she said.

16 A FAREWELL TO CASA SAPIENZA

The late autumn days went by quickly at Casa Sapienza In addition to their gardening and other chores, both Eli and Marna enjoyed learning more mathematics and experiencing more music. Marna developed her skill in classifying mushrooms by poring over a number of exquisitely illustrated works on mycology in Umberto's library. Umberto said that these books of plants were called *herbals*, and they always had beautiful illustrations. He also said he was unsure what to call an herbal that classified mushrooms, since fungi are hardly plants like other herbs and have no stems, seeds, leaves, or roots. But the watercolor illustrations in the books were beautifully detailed, and Marna learned much about mycological classification from studying them. Studying the mushrooms made her think often of Sennet, who had taught her so much about them, but she found she dwelt little on the death of her parents while she was occupied with her busy life at Casa Sapienza.

Eli also enjoyed reading in the library, and in particular studied the books about the names and positions of the stars and the rudiments of celestial navigation. He had always loved the stars, and learned the names of many of them.

Horatio favored the military history books, of which there was a sizable collection. Hamlet read volumes of jurisprudence, while Horace pursued the poetry of the earlier ages. In the evenings, before the day's music was performed, they all shared the results of their research. From Horatio, Eli learned of the brave Spartan, Leonidas, who fell with all his men defending the pass at Thermopylae. Hamlet told them of Solon, Sargon, Hammurabi, and other codifiers of laws. But Horace's contributions were more often brief poems. Some were about the flowers of the fields and some about the loves of youths and maidens, but when he recited these, Marna studied the paintings on the walls or looked fixedly at the backs of the books in the shelves. She thought Eli was looking at her, and she did not want to look at him for fear of finding that he was not, for that would have been very disappointing.

But rich though this life was, all five travelers knew that sooner or later they had to start out again if they were ever to find their way back to the West. As the late autumn days slipped away, Umberto grew concerned. He felt that the route through the mountains would be impassable by winter. He advised going down the Black River to the city of Verity, whence they could cross the Black Lake and then follow the River Mohr to Round Head on the Great Northern Sea, where they would be likely to find a ship that could take them to the West again on the far side of the Moon and Ice Mountains.

"Your river trip will be with the current," said Umberto, "and will take you through several fair cities. Some of these cities are mere towns, and some are of very great size and wealth. But there are some things even I do not know about these places, so you must proceed with care. I do know it has been said that not every thing in these towns is always what it appears to be. Be shrewd and wary.

"I think you will be safe in Berrymor, which is one of the most beautiful of places in the eastern country. It is very old and has governed itself for many years in ways that have developed according to their own traditions, which make it the safest of all communities of such size in the whole world. Everyone there obeys the laws of their council.

"Perhaps your parents wished to go to the great city of Lucro," Umberto continued, "which is far to the south and separated from the sea by the long and dry stretches of the Sorrel Plain. All say that Lucro is a place of stunning beauty, and it is also the center to which people come if they seek to gain great wealth. But somehow no one has ever told me that they wanted to tarry there long. Few have ever come back to Casa Sapienza from that city, but several have written me letters saying that they were moving to some other place. I know it is a city where quick judgment and sharp wits seem to be more revered than human affinity. As a result, there is very little religion practiced by its citizens, and there are few churches there. Still, some of our students have gone there and have met other like-minded people and become friendly with them." And with that, Umberto concluded his advice.

The "Barge" of Casa Sapienza, which hung in davits on the stone dock that fronted the river below the great house, was a twenty-foot pulling boat with stations for two or four oarsmen and much space in both bow and stern for other passengers and cargo. Umberto said it was due to be hauled out at a boatyard farther downstream for repainting and repair. Eli thought the barge looked in very good repair indeed, and he suspected the Padrone was being kind in finding an excuse to send them downstream swiftly and in comfort. Umberto directed them to deliver it to the boatwright, Harold Naufragio, who would paint and repair it and bring it back to Casa Sapienza in the spring.

So in the cooling season the little company packed up supplies and spare clothing and made ready to depart. Maria and Margaretta bade farewell to Marna with much giggling about their certainty that Eli had what they called a *debole*, or "weakness" for her. Because the long gown Marna had worn for the evenings of music wasn't suitable for travel, it was returned to the guardaroba in hopes that Marna might come back someday and wear it again. But the two girls worked late to sew up a "dancing dress" for Marna after the design that they had seen in illustrations of girls in very ancient times. It was made of thin white linen, short, and pleated so finely that it could be twisted like a rope and tied into a figure-eight knot to be packed in a rucksack. Donna Elizabetta gave her a gilded silver clasp to fasten the light garment at the shoulder, as well as a pair of tiny brass finger cymbals and the rosewood recorder she had played on her first night at Casa Sapienza.

Umberto presented the Sons of Homer with small leather bound notebooks in which to record their adventures, and a half-case of Lambrusco to cheer their hearts during their journey. But to Eli he gave silver-plated hand-bearing a compass in a brown leather box With this little instrument, Eli knew he could find the true direction or bearing of distant objects such as church towers or mountain peaks. Plotting the lines of bearing on a chart of two such prominences would locate the navigator's position at their intersection. But Eli also knew that to do this, he would have to have a mathematically accurate chart; no mere map would do. Umberto provided him with such a chart of the Low Land to the east of Cap and Hat Mountains, the valley of the Yellow Brown Mohr and the Sorrel Plain beyond.

Despite all the bustle of preparation for their parting, there was time for a final evening of music in the stately music room. The Dottoressa played the harpsichord and Maria the viola da gamba, while Margaretta and Marna played treble recorders. This time the major work was not by Vivaldi, but by Johann Sebastian Bach, his Fourth Brandenburg Concerto. The Padrone himself took up a long tenor recorder and joined the ensemble. Donna Elizabetta explained that the music of this period was often composed for nearly any combination of instruments that might be available when a group of musicians came together.

Early the next morning the entire company gathered at the stone dock by the river, and Eli and the Sons of Homer lowered the barge into the Black River. There were a few shared tears at the affectionate good-byes of the girls, and a few words of careful advice from the Padrone and the Dottoressa. Then, with Marna at the tiller in the stern and Amalthea standing in the bow, the four oarsmen dipped their oars in unison and the boat moved smartly out to midstream. There the current of the river augmented their speed, and they rapidly moved beyond the view of the great house.

The color had gone from the leaves and most of the meadows bordering the river were brown or pallid buff, but even autumn weather in the lower valley of the Black River turned out to be pleasant. Each day that the rowers moved south brought them toward a more temperate climate. The sign of the waning season was above and behind them, where the far-off Ice Mountain and the distant western peak of Toe Top were mantled with deep snow. Head and Cap Mountains to the east would turn white and pink with gleaming ice in the low sun of each passing afternoon.

Their passage down the river took them past few houses or farms, but in less than a week they sighted, beyond a turn in the river, a flagstaff with cross trees and a gaff, bearing pennants of many colors. There were flags with stripes and diagonal divisions, burgees with a variety of devices, eagles, swans, hawks, and a turkey. The backgrounds of the flags were orange and apple green, dark blue, bright red, and golden yellow.

On the shore behind the flagstaff was a large, dark red building shaped like a long high barn and a small forest of timber scaffolding that surrounded the partially completed hull of a large boat. Standing on a plank fixed to the scaffolding around the boat stood a man in a blue shirt who was pounding a long strand of cotton caulking into the seams between the planks with a mallet.

Marna steered the barge up to a dock that met the river in front of the flagstaff.

"Up oars!" she commanded as they approached the shore, and the rowers lifted the blades until they stood vertically above their heads. The boat continued to make way until Marna steered it close alongside the dock. In a moment they had made fast, shipped the oars, and disembarked.

"That looks very like the Padrone's barge from here," called down the man on the scaffold.

"It is indeed," responded Eli. "He asked that we bring it to you for paint and repair."

"Looks pretty well painted to me," he observed. "But considering I built it and painted it myself, I suppose that's no more than I ought to say of it."

He climbed down from the scaffold and approached the five travelers and the goat.

The boatwright, who announced that his name was Harold Naufragio, inspected the barge and decided that it could indeed stand a coat of paint. He then welcomed the group to inspect his yard and see what was under construction there.

The large boat on the stocks was a trading vessel being prepared for the merchants of the south, who regularly came to this upriver country where the presence of good stands of timber made boatbuilding a favored occupation. The boatwright had stacks of felled trees behind his sheds and stacks of carefully piled-up boards seasoning inside them. He had ruddy and sweet-smelling fir and pale yellow spruce cut and stacked, with wooden spacers between the rough-sawn planks to allow the air to circulate while the timber was drying and seasoning. In another part of the shed, there were thick beams of white oak timbers that were destined to become the keels and stems of other boats when the wood was ready. And all around there were tools.

There were racks of different-sized chisels with gleaming and burnished edges. There were many sorts of planes: scrub planes, block planes, jack planes, and rabbeting planes, some with wooden bodies of beechwood and cherry, others with old iron frames dark with age, but none of them rusty. It the middle of it all was a great band saw with two huge wheels supporting its long blade above and below the sawing table. Each wheel was almost a meter in diameter. There was a lathe and a thickness-planing machine powered by belts that ran overhead to pulley wheels that turned on a long axle, which in turn was hung from brackets fastened to the ceiling of the long shed.

"What source of power turns the axle that drives all these machines?" asked Eli.

"There is a canal that leaves the river a half-mile upstream from this place," said the boatwright. "It brings water to a sluice above and behind the shed, from where it drops down a broad pipe to a water turbine that spins fast and powerfully in the basement. The spinning turbine is connected to the axle by rods and gears so the one turbine can transmit power to all the machines in the boat shop."

Inside the shop was also another boat, seemingly complete and gleaming with dark green paint. Twelve meters long with a stubby oak bowsprit extending its bow, the new vessel had a white deckhouse with four round port lights on each side. Her decks were laid teak planks and her cabin top was painted a rosy buff. Two gleaming spruce spars lay on her deck, waiting to be stepped when the boat was brought out of the shop. Everything about the little ship seemed ready—and greatly appealing—to Eli.

"And when will she go in the water?" he asked.

"By rights she should have been finished weeks ago," he responded, "but I built this boat for a very particular customer: Ben the Maker, of Berrymor. He wants a bright yellow cove stripe to accentuate the sheer and some fancy scrolling at the bow, and I haven't got the cadmium yellow paint to finish the job."

"What does Ben the Maker make?" asked Marna.

"Almost anything that people want made in Berrymor, except boats," answered Harold. "He makes coffered ceilings in the houses of rich people and wooden chopping blocks for the shops of butchers. He makes bedsteads and tables, chests and wardrobes, and I am told that he has even made coffins for those that want to have them constructed before they actually die. But most of all, he likes to make musical instruments, flutes and lyres, tambourines and fiddles, and some instruments that no one has ever heard before—he has produced the first of their kind," said the boatwright. "He asked me to build this little schooner for him, and I have done it all except for that last bit of paintwork."

Eli nodded and smiled. "Then perhaps it is fortunate that we have arrived when we did," he said. And with that he went back to the barge to fetch his rucksack. After rummaging about in the bottom of it for some time, he eventually produced Stanley's jar of Cadmium Yellow that he had carried across the mountain passes.

"The very color!" exclaimed the boatwright. "How could you have known, and what price do you want for it?"

"Take it with the compliments of Stanley and Staley of the Cove," said Eli. "And please take the other jar too, the bright Cerulean Blue. You are more likely to find a use for it than I."

"Well and good," said the boatwright. "I will accept the gift of the one gladly, and suggest that if you will stay with me while I paint the stripe and the ornamental scrollwork at the bow, I will engage your services to deliver the finished boat to the owner, in Berrymor near the mouth of the River Mohr. I am sure you will find sailing better than walking along the riverbank."

"We happily accept your offer," said Eli. "And I can chart the river as we go." But as soon as he had said this, he looked around at the faces of his companions to see if they agreed with his speaking for the whole company. The Sons of Homer nodded in unison, and Marna seemed to acquiesce, but there was a questioning look on her face. Eli realized for the first time that she had joined the expedition under other circumstances than the three goatherds.

"Marna, you will sail with us, won't you?" he asked.

"Of course," she said. "It seems the only way to seek my way home. And if you four are decided to go by that route, I must go too. I have no balloon to take me directly to Lucro or the Valley of Spitte instead."

Harold painted the stripe in a rounded groove carved from stern almost to the stem of the planking of the little schooner. Forward of the end of the groove, there was a series of curved and twiggy furbelows and arabesques cut into the planking. Harold carefully painted all of these with the bright yellow paint. The job took him the greater part of a day of careful work. Then, because yellow pigments seldom cover dark paint underneath in a single coat, he repeated the process on the following day. He also painted the ship's name, *Polaris*, on the transom, with her homeport to be, BER-RYMOR, in smaller letters beneath it.

In the evenings of these few days, the Sons of Homer, who had often been rather guarded during the conversations at Casa Sapienza, were voluble in discussion with the boatwright about wood. Together they mourned the elm and chestnut trees that had been taken by blights in prior years. They extolled the merits of the tropical hardwoods, true mahogany and boubinga, ironwood and angelique. White cedar was recognized as being resistant to rot as well as having the remarkable quality of having its knots held fast by a natural resin so that they would not fall out even after the wood was seasoned and dry. They agreed on the virtue of the natural lubrication of lignum vitae that made it suitable for sheaves and pulleys. They also discussed the use of natural crooks which could be made by slicing vertically through the roots and branches of the deciduous conifer, the larch tree. The boatwright recommended locust for treenails (which he pronounced "trunnels"—meaning long wooden pegs used to hold the planks to the ribs of a ship). The upland goatherds seemed to know the name and usefulness of everything that grew in the forest, and the boatbuilder seemed to delight in discussing the best way to saw, stack, and season this harvest of the hill country so that it could be turned into curved and graceful shapes of shallops, skiffs, and sailboats by the skilled hands of a boat carpenter.

But on the morning of the third day of their visit, they turned to helping Harold move *Polaris* down to the water. They raised the cradle on which the boat rested by lifting each of the four corners with a long spruce lever, shoving wedges under each corner in turn. As they worked many times around the hull in this way, the whole structure was soon high enough for a stout wheeled carriage to be rolled underneath it. Then, with a long block and tackle, they urged it out of the shed and to the water's edge.

"By rights she should be christened with champagne," commented Harold, looking at Marna. "But I wouldn't want to hit her on the nose with a bottle if I had one."

"Would a bubbling red wine do as well?" asked Horace. "We have several bottles of the Padrone's Lambrusco with us."

The substitution approved, the wine was carefully uncorked. Marna was nominated to perform the ceremony because Harold said it was traditionally done by the oldest and most honored woman present. She climbed on a stepladder and poured a good measure of the foaming wine on the bowsprit, calling out in a clear voice, "I christen thee *Polaris!*"

There was hearty applause from the five males, and the balance of the wine was served so all could drink a toast to the safety and success of the new vessel. They eased the boat down the sloping bank on wooden tracks which fitted the wheels of the undercarriage. She floated free of the cradle and was warped up to the dock with lines held by Horatio and Hamlet. Made fast near the barge of Casa Sapienza, she looked very grand, and much larger than the other boat.

Dressing the two masts with running and standing rigging and stepping the big spars was several hours' work. Harold had produced a silver coin to place under the heel of the mainmast to bring her speed and good luck. Rigging and tuning the shrouds and headstay took longer, but by nightfall, the little ship was rigged and ready to sail.

17 MASTER AND CAPTAIN

T

he night before the start of an expedition is always a time of happy anticipation and sometimes of feasting as well. Harold Naufragio's larder was not filled with elaborate things, but his garden was bountiful, even if he provided his guests with a simpler meal than the elegant fare of Casa Sapienza. A large earthenware pan of baked lasagna came bubbling from the oven, running with beef juices and crowned with mozzarella and ricotta cheeses. The hot pasta was accompanied by a salad of many greens: lettuce, arugula, romaine, and pink radicchio. These were combined with quarters of small plum tomatoes, slices of pale green zucchini spiced with a piquant vinegar, and drenched with a deep green olive oil.

Sitting long at table after dinner, Harold gave them advice about the unexpected changes of weather they might find on the Black Lake, and told them that putting into Verity could be a confusing experience since the citizens of the town did not always tell the truth to strangers, or even to each other. He said that the descent of the Lesser Mohr would be an easy passage because the west wind would be behind them, on their port quarter most of the time, so there would be no need to beat to windward. Although the way would be long, the prevailing winds should continue to favor them until they rounded Round Head and entered the Bay of Birds on their way to the Great Canal, which would lead them to Berrymor itself, where Ben the Maker would expect them.

But despite the favorable winds they could expect, the journey would not be without the possibility of peril, and the boatwright cautioned them to protect the newly launched vessel most dil gently. He told them of the steep chop that could come up in the shallow reaches of the Black Lake in a sudden thunderstorm, and how to find calmer seas where the water is deeper. He spoke of the rushing current of the Lesser Mohr where it ran through the Great Gorge, and of the stagnant reaches of the Flume that acted as an enormous filter of the polluted waters of the Yellow Brown Mohr, turning its water clear again before it joined the Lesser Mohr, became the Greater Mohr, and reached the Northern Sea.

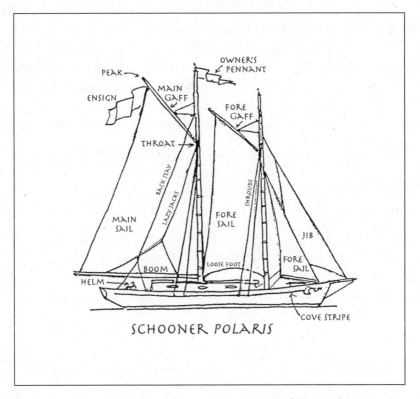

SCHOONER POLARIS

He told them of the ancient city of Berrymor, built on islands in the sea where there were houses which lined the banks of canals that served as streets. It was, according to Harold Naufragio, a city of music and painting, sculpture and noble architecture. Ben the Maker was well known in Berrymor, and they were told that they would have no difficulty in locating his studio, high up in the loggia of an ancient building that faced on the stone wharfs bordering the sea. He directed them to the mouth of the largest canal at the ocean front, and then to face left and ask the first person on the quayside to direct them to the studio of Ben the Maker.

Early the following morning they boarded *Polaris* and Eli, looking at his crew, realized that he and Marna were the only experienced sailors in the company. More daunting was the fact that he had never before sailed a boat this large, or with such a complex rig. He set Hamlet to undoing the sail stops that kept the mainsail furled to its long boom and began to wonder how he would manage to set the bow of the boat into the wind while raising the sail, for the wind was in the west and was blowing (rather gently) across the breadth of the boat. Marna noted his hesitation and suggested a course of action.

"Mister Captain, sir," she said, "I suspect that if you set the foresail while still at the dock, you will be able to get under way most easily."

Eli felt the mocking edge of a challenge in her manner of address, but he realized immediately that Marna was right. The big mainsail would have been very hard to control before the vessel was moving. The smaller foresail was much easier to handle, and would provide sufficient driving power to get the vessel under way without requiring the setting of the larger canvas.

Horatio and Horace looked at Eli with unspoken questions in their old wise eyes.

"Hamlet," he said, "belay a couple of those stops on the main and let's get the foresail up first."

The loose-footed foresail went up smoothly and trailed out to the lee side while Horace and Eli tugged the gaff up tight to an angle that seemed proper to Harold's practiced eye.

Good-byes were called hastily as the docking lines were let go and pulled aboard. Eli asked Marna to take the helm and called on Horatio to trim in the foresail sheet. As the wind filled the sail, the schooner moved slowly away from the dock and down the river. They gave a hasty wave to the boatwright and then moved to set the forestaysail and jib, which increased their way to a modest speed.

Eli eyed the big main with some apprehension. Its boom was a full twenty feet long, longer in itself than any boat Eli had ever sailed. Pressed by more than fifty square meters of sail, that heavy spar would require careful handling. He glanced at Marna.

"May I offer some assistance, Captain?" she asked.

"I wish you wouldn't emphasize the 'Captain' stuff quite so much," he answered. "How would you go about it?"

Marna smiled. "If you show the crew which ropes I am talking about, I can get it up with their muscle and a little of your brains." Then she pointed to the starboard side and began to call out a stream of clearly enunciated commands.

"Horace, ease off the leeward backstay, and Horatio, set up the one on the windward side. (The lee side of a boat is the side away from the wind. Things on that side of the vessel are said to be to "leeward," which is pronounced *loo-ard* by knowledgeable sailors like Marna.) Hamlet, cast off the rest of those sail stops. Horatio and Eli, stand by to raise throat and peak halyards. Hamlet, haul up on the topping lift and get the boom free of the gallows! Now, up she goes, boys, keep the gaff level till she's up! Horace, cast off the main sheet and tend it when it swings off. Eli, sway up that throat halyard and belay it. Now Horatio, up with the peak and sway on the halyard till she's chockablock! Eli, help put some strain on it. Now, belay the peak! Hamlet, let off that topping lift! Horace, now trim her in till she's full and bye. We're sailing!"

Responding as though it understood her orders, the big sail rose, billowed out to leeward, and then, as the angle of the sheet and the weight of the boom brought it under control, seemed to adjust itself into a perfectly curved wing that lifted the boat forward with a great burst of power.

Through the day, *Polaris* surged down the Black River, and Eli and the Sons of Homer took soundings of its depth and noted the location of sandbars and snags along the shore. Because the good west wind only slackened slightly at sunset, they continued on in the gathering darkness, keeping carefully to the deep water in the center of the channel. Horatio lit the oil lamps inside red and green running lights that were mounted on boards lashed to the shrouds of the foremast. Eli set a white light in the stern to be proper, although it seemed unlikely that any vessel would overtake them from that direction. Then he relieved Marna at the wheel and steered down the center of the river.

The black water turned a deep blue as it reflected the starry sky, and the riverbanks on either side darkened to a velvet black. The southern stars of the winter sky rose before him and wheeled slowly toward the west: Aldeberan, the ruddy eye of Taurus the Bull; the sparkling Pleiades; Castor and Pollux; and Sirius, the dog, brightest of all fixed stars.

But the warm glow of the oil lamps in the cabin called him to the cheerful place below, and the long day's sail required rest for the whole crew. Coming at last to a westward curve of the river, Eli brought the schooner up into the wind, and the Sons of Homer dropped the sails under Marna's direction. With the little steerage way still provided by the boat's momentum, they brought the bow around into the current and let go the principal anchor in what seemed to be about twelve feet of water.

"Give it plenty of scope," said Marna. "With the current of the river pulling at us, besides the twenty feet of chain that's on that anchor, I want about seventy-five feet of anchor rode to keep the hook flat on the bottom and well dug in. The longer the rode, the better I sleep."

Hamlet washed down the foredeck where Amalthea had been tethered and had unintentionally fouled it with her droppings. Horace set out their simple supper of bread, cheese, and some of Harold's basil and tomato soup. Horatio, who seemed to have a natural affinity for nautical things, set an anchor light burning brightly in the bow. Very shortly thereafter, all the members of the crew were rolled up comfortably in their bunks and soon sound asleep.

FROM RIVER TO LAKE

With a favorable wind on their beam and the steady current of the stream to help them, the passage of the lower reaches of the Black River required but a few more days' sailing. The weather became significantly warmer as they moved to the south. The distant peaks of the Long-Eared Mountains sank slowly from sight beyond the northern horizon. But before they wholly disappeared, Eli had the opportunity to take sights on several of the tallest mountaintops and compare their lines of bearing with cross bearings he was able to sight on the rounded Dome of the Broad Hump to the west. The distances to these prominences was so great that Eli was not totally convinced of the accuracy of his fixes, but he delighted in practicing a new skill and becoming more familiar with the elegant little instrument that Umberto had given him. He recorded his observations in a notebook to bring them back to his father Solomon someday.

Marna sometimes practiced her intervals, major and minor, on the recorder when someone else took an extended turn at the helm. Once, when Eli was awakened early by an unfamiliar sound on deck, he came up through the after-cabin hatch to look around.

Nothing unusual was visible aft, but looking forward, he discovered her. Dancing on the foredeck with the finger cymbals tinkling in her hands, she was wearing the short, pale cream-colored dress the girls of Casa Sapienza had made for her. Her motions were slow and deliberate, punctuated by the high bell tones of the cymbals. Her unbraided hair was caught back with a ribbon and hung to the middle of her back. Because she too was facing forward as her body swayed to some musical theme played by imagined instruments in her mind, she did not notice Eli until she spun in a barefoot pirouette and found herself facing the boy who was staring at her in amazement and delight.

"Good morning," she said, "I was just doing my exercises."

"They are beautiful," said Eli. "Please don't stop."

But Marna was gone in an instant, disappearing down the forward hatch to the head and dressing room that occupied the forward part of the cabin. She emerged minutes later in her more customary costume of blue trousers, gray sweater, and sneakers, and finishing the final braiding of her red-brown hair.

Later that day they realized that the river was widening and following a more direct southerly course. The current seemed to be slackening and the distance ahead was no longer bounded by the continuous tree-fringed riverbank. There were broad reaches of pale green eelgrass and meadows bordered by cattails to their right while the dark blue water stretched to their left farther than the eye could see. They had entered the Black Lake. The water was actually not at all black, but an almost wine-dark purple, flecked with traces of white where small waves tossed off whitecaps farther away from the western shore. *Polaris*, heeled well over to port, made rapid way in the fair breeze from the starboard side out of the west. But the sky in that direction was growing less distinct, and already the familiar bulge of the Broad Hump had faded into the jumble of cloud forms that darkened the sky to starboard. Far ahead, silhouetted against a pale orange sky, they could see the towers of the little city of Verity.

"It looks as though we might have some rain," said Horatio.

"And perhaps some more wind," added Marna, who was busy lashing Amalthea by a system of halters and lines to the grab rails that ran along the top of the cabin trunk.

"But look," Eli pointed ahead. "There's Verity. I think we will be in the harbor before that weather gets here."

Horace looked to windward and began to sing the words of an odd little song that Eli did not know:

IF THE RAIN BEFORE THE WIND, TOPSAILS, SHEETS AND HALYARDS MIND!
IF THE WIND BEFORE THE RAIN, THEN YOU MAY MAKE SAIL AGAIN.

Marna searched the sky in both directions, gauging the positions of the advancing weather front and the distant port.

"Sooner or later," she said, "we're going to have to shorten sail."

"But if we did it now we would lose speed then, and the chance of getting into Verity before the front passes will be lost."

"My grandfather had an expression about this sort of situation: 'Always shorten sail before you have to,'" said Marna, continuing to look to the west.

"But how do we know that we have to before we have to?" asked Eli, as a few drops of rain began to scatter on the water.

"Because of that big black cloud that is starting to cover the sun," she said quickly. "And look at the color of the water!"

For the lake was beginning to live up to its name. As the squall approached and the western sky darkened, the water became truly black, and even the whitecaps cresting beside *Polaris* seemed to turn a greenish gray. The schooner was driving hard on her course and Eli looked longingly ahead toward the still-distant town of Verity. But, loathe though he was to submit to Marna's advice again, he realized it was getting close to a time when reefing the sail would become harder and more dangerous to accomplish. He put the wheel hard down to the lee and brought the bow up into the wind.

Horatio went forward and had the big jib down in an instant, Hamlet helping him smother it on the foredeck and haul it in from the bowsprit. Marna and Horace uncleated the main halyards and let them off just as the big boom swung over the gallows frame and dropped into the center notch with a heavy thump. The gaff followed it down, thrashing from side to side in the quickly freshening wind, but effectively confined by the lazy jacks, lines from the boom to fittings high on the main mast.

And then with a savage gust, the storm was on them.

Still under foresail and staysail, the schooner veered off the wind to port, rolling her lee rail under and heeling steeply over until she gathered way again and began to plunge slowly ahead into the sudden spray and gathering waves.

"Get that foresail down!" cried Marna. "We can keep steerage way with the staysail!"

The three Sons of Homer moved swiftly over the sloping deck and cast off the foresail sheet which took the pressure off the sail but sent it billowing out to leeward. They cast off the halyards at the base of the foremast, but the pull of the wind was too great to let the sail drop of its own weight. Horatio reached up to grasp the lowest mast hoop and pulled with all his might. The sail came down a foot or two and then another foot. In stages they dragged the sail down onto the deck, but there were no lazy jacks on the loose-footed foresail and the gaff swung away from their grasp.

"Put her into the wind, Eli," called Marna in a remarkably calm voice.

Obedient to the sound of experience in her command, Eli put the helm down again and the stout little schooner struggled and then lifted her bow into the waves piling up from the west. In an instant Hamlet and Horatio had secured the foresail gaff, and Marna and Horace completed tying stops around the mainsail. Letting the boat off the wind before she lost steerage way this time, Eli was able to put the vessel back on course without coming as near to a knockdown as he had before.

"Now, ease her off the wind a bit more," said Marna as she regained the cockpit. "She can't take bashing into this chop and get anywhere, and besides, we're not in a race to get to Verity anymore—the squall has already caught us."

"All right, *Capitanessa mia*," said Eli. "Thank you for speaking up when we needed you. I am glad for your good advice."

His thanks and acquiescence to her authority were unexpected, and so sudden that Marna was left without an immediate response. She smiled and then blushed when she saw the look of obvious appreciation in his eyes.

"Then let's keep her on a broad reach until this thing blows out," she said. She had somehow gotten into her yellow foul-weather jacket and her wet face, looking up at him, seemed to Eli to be surrounded by a bright golden halo.

TROUBLE TRYING TO TELL THE TRUTHERS

The violent squall ended almost as quickly as it had begun, and left *Polaris* and her crew in an almost placid sea with a much-diminished wind that had backed around into the northwest. The change in the wind direction flattened the steep and choppy seas, and they were able to make sail again and resume their course under full canvas for Verity, which was still plainly visible before them.

The channel leading up to the stone wharf that seemed to occupy the center of town was well marked by red and green buoys. Marna and Eli stared at these markers as they approached the first set and then looked at each other.

"If we go between them, we will be leaving the red buoy on our port hand and the green one to starboard!" said Eli, "That's backwards!"

"Of course it is," agreed Marna. "The markers should always be 'red right returning,' and we are 'returning' to Verity in the sense that we are coming in from sea to land, even though we've never been here before. Could they be marking a rock or shoal in the middle of the channel?"

"Maybe so," said Eli, "Let's luff up into the wind and get some sail off her so that we can do this a little slower before we are right on top of those markers." The crew was by now well practiced, and the mainsail, jib, and forestaysail were downed quickly by the Sons of Homer. The schooner was able and easily maneuvered under foresail alone.

It was Horatio, standing on the bowsprit, who discovered the next surprises in the harbor.

"Eli!" he called. "Look ahead. There is another pair of buoys, arranged just the same way. And there is another beyond that. It appears to be a regular thoroughfare of markers leading us up to the big stone pier, and all of them have the red on the left and the green on the right."

Eli found this arrangement hard to believe, and he fetched up a lead line from the cabin and set Hamlet to taking soundings as they moved slowly up the "thoroughfare" under foresail alone. There seemed to be better than fifteen feet of water beneath them even when *Polaris* slipped between the first set of markers, but Marna was unsettled by the experience of sailing where everything she knew told her that her ship would come to grief.

"There must be some reason for it," said Horace. "It is consistent all the way up the channel, so it is not just a mistake."

"The buoys are telling us something," said Eli. "That is what buoys are for. I do not know what it is that they are telling us, but I think it may be important."

There were spires and cupolas that rose from the buildings of Verity and gave its skyline a jagged and unexpected shape. It was a larger town than Eli had ever seen before, much larger than Salem on Spitte. Perhaps, he thought, it was really a small city.

"I know very little of towns or cities," said Horace.

"I am told they are sometimes the seats of universities and thus places to seek learning," said Hamlet.

"I think they are places to go to when business must be done, but perhaps not as pleasant a place to live as our hilltop farm over beyond the Long-Eared Mountains," concluded Horatio.

In a matter of minutes they had brought *Polaris* up to the spiles that lined the outboard side of the pier and made her fast to the smooth old mooring cleats set in the pavement of the quay. People walked past on the cobble-stoned street, and there was a quiet bustle to the town, but although the passersby smiled at each other and at the little troop of sailors tying up their boat, no one seemed inclined to say anything to them. Even odder, it seemed to Eli and Marna, was the fact that although they smiled and nodded when they passed, few were heard to say a word to another. There were courteous hat doffings, bows, and an occasional curtsey, but the citizens of Verity seemed disinclined to enter into conversation with their acquaintances. Finally Hamlet could stand the eerie reception no longer and placed himself squarely in front of a tall man wearing a large yellow hat who emerged from one of the largest buildings along the dockside.

"Pray tell me, sir," said Hamlet, "does no one speak on the streets of this town? Are all the people of Verity mute and merely nod and smile when they meet?"

The man stopped and looked down at the little goatherd. He carefully removed his yellow hat and held it in front of his body as though he was shielding himself from Hamlet's questions.

"Why surely," he responded in a deep voice, "you must know that all of us in Verity always speak the truth when we do not speak falsely. But, to be sure which is which, we are slow to speak at all. Take me, for instance: I am a member of the Guild of Truthers who are pledged from birth to utter no untrue statement, no matter what provocation we may receive from our fellows of this town who are members of the Guild of Liars, who never make a completely true statement when speaking to a Truther or a stranger or even to the members of their own guild."

"What a remarkable place," said Hamlet. "But how fortunate it is that we have met you, a Truther—first of all, so that you may tell us about the town and direct us to the wisest men who live here. We only wish to traverse the Black Lake and continue our journey, but we need supplies for ourselves and for our goat."

"Fortunate indeed!" said the tall man, clapping Hamlet on the back, "for if you had chanced to meet a Liar first of all, he would have confused you greatly about the customs of our town."

"But wait, brother," said Horace. "How can we be sure that this new friend who is so helpful to strangers among all these silent people is truly what he claims to be? If he were a Liar, would he not have responded in just the same way that he has just now when he assured you that he was a Truther?"

"He would indeed," said Horatio, regarding the tall inhabitant of Verity. "Tell us, sir, how can we tell that you are a Truther as you say you are, and not a complete and total Liar, as you say the others of this town are?"

"Ah, to be sure!" said the tall man. "There is no way of telling unless you are a member of one of the two guilds yourself. As for me, I am one and can tell you surely that I speak the truth. In fact, I am Bugiardo da Palo, and I am the first undersecretary of the Ancient and Most Honorable Guild of Truthers of the City of Verity."

"Well," said Hamlet, "if what you say is true, and you are therefore a Truther, we will never be able to find out if you are speaking true or telling the most dreadful lies."

"That doesn't give us much help," said Eli.

Marna, who had been coiling down lines on the deck of *Polaris* and generally tidying up the boat, stood amidships with Amalthea and regarded the little gathering on the quay with some curiosity, although she did not join in their disputation.

"It is no help at all," said Horace. "We don't even know if Bugiardo da Palo is your real name."

"Of course it's my real name," answered Bugiardo (or whatever his name was, or was not). "I would like very much to help you find answers to the somewhat confusing questions you are asking yourselves."

"By which you mean," commented Horatio, "that either you will help us learn the difference between the Truthers and the Liars, or you won't, and instead will mislead us at every turn."

"Perhaps," suggested Bugiardo, "you should avoid asking questions that admit of a true or false answer and just say things like 'good morning' instead of 'How do you do?', which requires that the person you ask commit him- or herself to an answer that is either true or false."

"I am beginning to think that I am sorry we ever came into this port," said Eli.

"Any port in a storm, eh friend?" commented Bugiardo.

"Now a platitude like that might be true, or it might be false," said Horace. "Just let it pass."

"Look," said da Palo. "You might find help at the meeting of the Joint Committee of the Guilds of Verity, where the leaders of the Truthers and Liars sit around a table to discuss the rule of the city. I never like to go myself, but you could go to one of the two guild halls and visit the meeting of the Joint Committee."

"Which means, I guess," said Hamlet, "that either we will find help at the meeting of the Joint Committee or we will not, depending on whether you are telling the truth or lying."

"That, I cannot help you with," said the tall man, replacing his hat.

"You cannot or you will not," remarked Eli.

But with a smile and a nod, Bugiardo turned on his heel and left them, quite puzzled, standing on the stone dock.

ELI LINGERS WITH LIARS

After a brief discussion on the afterdeck of *Polaris*, it was decided that Eli and Horace should go into the city and seek to determine who was telling the truth and who was prevaricating. They all agreed that it was worth finding out which guild was which in order to arrange for supplying the vessel and getting properly started on their way again. After all, what would happen if they were sold water for lamp oil, or even if the opposite substitution was foisted on them? Since Horace seemed to have much experience with poetry and other uses of words, he was deemed the best companion for Eli. Marna's participation in the expedition was ruled out by the three men and the boy as being too dangerous for her in case some terrible calamity took place while they were in the guild hall.

"Stuff and nonsense!" she commented, but she stayed on board and set to making a large vegetable soup from the turnips, potatoes, parsnips, and beans they had on board. Hamlet peeled and sliced vegetables, and Horatio set out with Amalthea to locate a lawn or park where the goat could forage.

Eli and Horace walked toward the center of the little city where they could see the towers of two stuccoed buildings with pointed, blue slate roofs. One was painted a gleaming yellow with white trim and bore a sign over the large front door that read:

HALL OF THE GUILD OF UNITED TRUTHERS OF VERITY

The other building, quite as imposing as the first, was painted white with yellow window casings and doors. It too bore a sign over the front door on which an inscription was boldly lettered:

THE WORSHIPFUL GUILD OF TRUTHERS OF VERITY
THE LIARS GUILD WILL BE FOUND ACROSS THE STREET

"Which one will you choose?" asked Eli.

"Since it could be either," said Horace, "I think we should try the one with the shorter inscription, since the blunt truth is usually communicated very simply."

Eli agreed, and the pair entered the yellow building and found themselves in a large rotunda surrounded by a spiral stairway that seemed to lead to an upper room. The walls of the rotunda and stairs were covered with frescoed flowers and leaves, and above them was an elaborately lettered inscription in old-fashioned characters:

DEDICATED TO THE DISSEMINATION OF THE TRUTH
THE WHOLE TRUTH
AND NOTHING BUT THE TRUTH

Eli and Horace climbed the stairway and found themselves in a large chamber with a round table in its center. More than twenty chairs were set around it. The table was covered with a generous layer of dust, and some unknown finger had traced the words "Down with all liars!" at one side. There was no one in the room, so they descended again to the street.

"No wiser yet," said Eli. "Let's try the other hall."

The white building seemed better kept than the one they had entered first, and, as they started up the steps to the entrance, they were joined by a number of smiling and nodding citizens of Verity who were chatting with each other. Those taking part in these quiet conversations seemed in agreement about whatever it was they were discussing, but whether it was true or false Eli and Horace could not determine, so they entered the building and joined the considerable group climbing the broad spiral stair to the upper room. There was no dust here on the table, which was large enough to accommodate two dozen. A smiling member of the company brought chairs for Eli and Horace and invited them to sit with the members of the council.

"Welcome to Verity!" said the man on Eli's right. "Welcome and good wishes to you who come before the United Joint Committee of our city. What do you seek from us?"

"Well," said Eli, thinking to himself for a moment that the hearty exclamation could be a wish for either good or ill, depending on which guild the speaker represented, "we are in need of a number of things for our vessel; lamp oil, for example. But first we need to know how to tell if the merchant who sells it to us is measuring truthfully and is selling good oil that will burn all night long in our anchor light, or whether he is deceiving us and telling untruths about the contents of his cans and the quality of his oil. So how can we tell who is telling the truth here in Verity?"

The man looked very solemn when he heard what Eli had to say. "What you ask is surely a most impertinent question," he answered. "If strangers who come to Verity were to learn what you seek to know, our secrets, the previous inheritance of our guilds, would be made public and the mystery of our mastery of truth and falsity made clear to all the world. Where then would we be, deprived of our identity and our tradition? You may seek your answer in any way you choose, but I tell you truthfully, for I am a Birthright Truther and cannot tell a lie, that you will be imprisoned if you are inconsistent and speak to us in falsehoods some of the time and tell the truth at other times. We value consistency above all else, and when I tell you that, I speak the truth!"

"No he doesn't!" exclaimed the next man to the right. "He is seldom consistent and is indeed a most foul liar. And down with all liars, say I!"

"Now see here," said the next man, glaring at Eli, "I am here sitting between two liars, listening to the false drivel they have been speaking to you. You must realize that I am a Truther."

"But I am a Truther!"

"And I!"

"And I!"

The voices came from all around the room. And at that point every man pointed to the man seated beside him and said "But not him! He is a Liar! He tells the most monstrous untruths in all of Verity!"

And each pointed to the one beside him and made a similar statement. Oddly, there seemed no rancor in these accusations, merely a good-humored statement of fact.

"What?" cried Eli. "You all accuse your neighbor of prevarication and claim truth for yourselves. How can this be?"

"I think," said Horace, who had been thinking deeply with his eyes closed, "I think I can see how it works out. If every other man around this table tells the truth and the ones in between always tell lies, then each will say that his neighbor is a liar. The truth tellers would be telling truth and the liars would be running true to form in their own way by accusing their neighbors of falsehoods."

"So," said Eli, "if my neighbor here is a Truther, then the man on the other side of him must be a Liar."

"Quite so," said Horace. "But if the first had chanced to be a liar, then the positions must be reversed all the way around the table."

"If only they all weren't so consistent!" said Eli.

"But, friend and captain," said Horace, "that may be the least of our troubles. Look, by the door!"

And, as he spoke, four tall men in scarlet coverall suits entered the room and approached Eli and Horace.

"Seize them and confine them to the Library!" came a voice from the far side of the table.

"Away with them! Chain them! Enbibliate them! Lock them up with the books!"

There was a chorus of other voices in such confusion that it was impossible to tell who was saying what.

The scarlet-clothed men laid their hands upon Eli and Horace and hustled them off down the grand stairway to the rear wing of the guild hall and marched them in through a set of tall doors into a room carpeted in emerald green and set all around with bookshelves and glass-topped exhibition cases.

"You will be kept here on bread and water until you repent of your wretched ways and learn to accept the authority of the guild masters!" said one of the tall men in scarlet.

And with that, the double doors were shut with a loud bang and the brass rim locks were heard to click over several times as the bolts were shot home.

21 WHAT THE LAMPLIGHTER SAID

Hamlet and Marna had worked busily at making a sort of freshwater bouillabaisse during the afternoon. Using sign language, they had obtained Black Lake crawfish from an itinerant fishmonger on the dock, as well as a pair of bass and several trout. Marna knew that any firm-fleshed fish would make a splendid stew when combined with crustaceans and shellfish. A great variety of vegetables and spices went into the pot, along with garlic and onions, and by the time the sun began to set beyond the distant Broad Hump, they had created a savory soup of noble proportions.

But neither of the two shore parties had returned to *Polaris* by evening. The big kettle in the galley bubbled gently on the gimbaled stove, and delicious aromas of vegetables and shellfish filled the cabin of the schooner. Hamlet began to worry.

"What do you suppose could have happened to them?" he murmured. "And if we ask what could have happened to them, we won't know if the answer we get is true or not. It is terrible to be in a town where you don't know whether or not to trust anyone at all."

But at that moment Marna, who was standing on the second step of the companion ladder that led up to the cockpit from the cabin, gave a happy cry of recognition.

"But I've got him!" she said.

"Got who?" said Hamlet.

"The lamplighter!" said Marna. "Look, here he comes in his skiff. He must have been out in the harbor lighting the lamps on the navigational markers. He is our solution."

And she stepped to the stern and looked down at an elderly seafaring man with a lantern and a large can of lamp oil who was sculling his skiff up to the quay.

"Ahoy, lamplighter!" she called. "Is that good-quality lamp oil in your can?"

"Not really," said the lamplighter. "It has so many impurities and so much water in it that it will almost surely foul the lamps I've put it in."

"Good," said Marna, "then it's just what I need for my stove. I will buy all you have left in your can."

The can held more than a gallon, and the man heaved it up over the gunwale onto the deck of *Polaris* with a broad smile. He accepted the coins Marna offered him without any comment.

"I take it you are a Truther," she commented with a knowing smile.

"Of course," he answered. "My family members have all been Truthers for many generations."

By this time Marna was on the dock and helping the lamplighter to tie his skiff to one of the old iron cleats.

"Would you care for a bowl of soup?" she asked.

"Oh no," said the lamplighter. "I'm not hungry at all."

"I thought so," said Marna, and taking the old man by the elbow, she steered him down the companionway to the cabin and settled him at the table.

"Quick, Hamlet, a serving of soup in our biggest bowl, and a plate of pilot biscuit for our truthful guest."

The grizzled mariner made no comment, but he seized the spoon Hamlet provided and began to devour the soup. He bit through the crawfish shells and sucked the meat out of the carapaces. He consumed the floating potatoes and the chunks of tomato in the spicy stew and began to munch on a large round pilot biscuit.

"Pretty good soup, isn't it?" said Marna.

"Heavens, no. Worst I've ever tasted!" said their guest heartily, wiping his mouth on the back of his sleeve. "Disgusting—simply dreadful!"

"Eat all you want," said Marna, "but when you have finished, you will come with us while we find our friends."

"Oh, I could never do that," muttered the man while continuing to spoon up the soup. "I couldn't possibly."

"Splendid," said Marna, and in a few moments, she was walking up the broad street toward the center of the town with the elderly lamplighter in tow.

22

THE BARBER
OF BERRYMOR

The room in which Eli and Horace found themselves had no
resemblance to a prison, nor did there seem to be any sign of
either bread or water about. But whether that was evidence that
the guards had told a lie or the truth seemed hard to determine. Perhaps
the dinner hour would give them a clue.

"What was it they said they were going to do to us? I've never heard of
being *enbibliated*. It doesn't sound like something you would do to someone
you liked. Do you think it will hurt?"

"The word is new to me too," said Horace, "but I think it comes from
Latin roots, as so many words do, and means something like being put with
the books or being booked for a crime, or maybe being put away among
the books. And whoever said it must have been a Truther."

They surveyed the room, which was long and had an arched ceiling
decorated with painted birds and flowers. There were shelves of books
along both sides, some open and others covered with elaborate doors
of bronze screening and locked with brass locks. There were tables and
glass-topped cases down the center of the room, and on top of one case there
was a very thick volume that turned out to be an unabridged dictionary.

Horace started to look up *enbibliate*, but as he turned the pages
and surveyed the key words, his eye was caught by the fact that not
only was the word missing from the large dictionary, but also, there
didn't seem to be any words in the English language that began with
the letters "enb." The closest entries in the dictionary were a pair of

French phrases that didn't seem particularly useful to their situation. Horace, who was almost as fond of surfing through dictionaries as he was of making up verses, decided to continue with the E's while he thought about making up some useful words that could be used in his poems.

Eli missed some of the results of this research since he was exploring the farther end of the room in search of a way out. At the farthest corner of the library he discovered that they were not alone. A large, robust man with an immense black beard was seated on the top of a short stepladder. He was reading a small, leather-bound book.

"Good day," said Eli, "Are you the librarian?"

"No," the man responded with a snort. "I am a barber. In fact, at one time I was *the* barber."

"Aha! Then you must be one of the liars," said Eli, "for I have never seen a bearded barber before."

"No, not so!" answered the barber. "I am a member of neither of the guilds of Verity. I am the Barber of Berrymor and have been enbibliated here because of a foolish consistency that relates to my commission to trim or shave other men while here in Verity."

Eli, seeing that there was no exit from the place of their enbibliation in the far corner of the room, settled down on the carpeted floor.

"Horace!" he called, "come hear what our companion in incarceration has experienced. Maybe he will be able to help us figure out a way to get back to *Polaris*."

Horace had just gotten on to words like *elegiac* and *eisteddfod* and seemed reluctant to leave the dictionary, but he came to look at the black-bearded man on the stepladder, and bowed politely to him.

"We are Horace and Eli," he said, "two troubled travelers who have transited the tops of mountains and sailed the length of the Black River to come to this place of capture. And you, sir?"

"I am Occam, the Barber of Berrymor. I came because I was bored with my steady but dull employment in Berrymor and decided to travel across the moors to the Lower River Mohr, and then up the Lesser Mohr until I came to this town where I heard there was a great need for an industrious man who was skilled in the use of a razor."

"And did you find employment here?" asked Eli.

"Not only employment," replied Occam. "I was given an exclusive commission to shave all the men in Verity who did not shave themselves. Indeed, I was required to shave them at the expense of the Commune of

Verity. Since almost every man in Verity shaved himself, I had very little to do at first."

"That must have given you a good income," said Eli.

"But I never shave," said Horace, "nor do either of my brothers. Does that mean that you are to shave me?"

"Those were the terms of my commission," said Occam. "But, worse yet, worse than removing the whiskers of unwilling graybeards like you, and I suppose, your brothers, whoever they may be, think of what I was expected to do to myself. If I did not shave every day, I would be derelict in duty to shave a man quite under my direction who did not shave himself. But if I took the razor to my own face, I would be shaving a man who also shaved himself, something forbidden me under the terms of my commission."

"But what happened to you? Why were you enbibliated?" asked Eli.

"Well, while I was trying to think of some simple way of solving the problem," said the barber, "a few days went by and my beard began to grow. Soon the men in the scarlet uniforms were outside, surrounding my shop. Two were ready to arrest me if I did not get on to shaving myself as I was required to do, and the other two were ready to lay hands upon me the instant I began to lather up my own face, since I was forbidden to shave anyone who did the job for himself. Before I had done the left cheek to the satisfaction of the first pair, the other two had me in handcuffs and brought me here to throw me in among the books where the municipal archives are kept."

"But why here?" asked Eli. "Why in a library?"

"Because," grumbled Occam, "because here all the worthies of the town worship the consistency of logical thinking, and they say that in these books are found the laws of the town and the rules of logic that govern the commune. They said that I should stay here until I had learned the difference between right and wrong, between truth and falsity, between what often is and what is always meant to be. And so I look through the books hoping to find a solution to my plight and subsist on the bread and water they bring me twice a day. But I am yet to find any answer to my problem in any of the books I have found so far."

"And how long have they kept you in this place?" asked Horace. "Aside from the bread and water, it seems a rather nice place in which to be enbibliated."

"Well," he answered, "I had only a stubble on my chin when I was first locked in," said Occam, "and now you see ..." And he stroked the luxurious length of his bushy black beard with a sorrowful gesture.

"Of course, I hardly ever have to shave at all yet," said Eli, "so you are safe in my company, in any case."

"And I don't intend to let you shave me, unless it could help us gain our freedom," said Horace. "We may be here for a long time. I think I'll go back to the dictionary."

"There has to be some simple, direct, and uncomplicated way to get out of here," muttered the barber.

And at that moment they heard the locks on the tall doors click back. A voice intoned solemnly: "Criminals pay heed, your food is delivered to you!" And there came a clink and a crash of the doors closing again.

The three prisoners turned and went quickly to the door. There they found a small wooden tray holding three brown crusted kaiser rolls, a tall silver pitcher, and three large blue-glass goblets.

"It's the same thing every night," said Occam, "but sometimes the goblets are green or yellow. That is all that changes here, the color of the goblets I drink my water from. But the books on the shelves and the manuscripts in the cases are all different and I continue to read them in hopes of finding a means of escape. Something tells me that there is a simple way to escape, one that does not involve force or the manufacture of great machines or siege engines to break down the walls. Perhaps it only requires asking the right questions."

23 TRUSTING THE TRUTHLESS TURNS THE TRICK

The light was beginning to fail as Marna and the lamplighter came to the center of the town and approached the twin guild halls. Bright lights showed in all the windows. As she watched, a pair of tall men in scarlet suits emerged from a bakery that faced on the square. One carried a small basket that contained something wrapped up in a large white napkin. The other held a silver tray with a tall pitcher and three blue goblets.

"Quick!" said Marna. "Lamplighter! Is that a preparation for a ceremonial toast for an honored guest, or is it fare for a prisoner?"

"Food for a triumphant victor, to be sure," he answered. "Can't you tell by the way it looks and the elegance of the waiters?"

"I feared as much," said Marna. "Come quickly—we must follow them!"

"But it is forbidden to follow the men in scarlet suits. Their task is secret and their orders severe."

"Really? I had hardly hoped for that good luck," said Marna. "But tell me, lamplighter, are the men in scarlet tellers of truth or lies?"

"Both, or neither," he responded. "The day shift is as truthful as can be, but after dark they all become prevaricators of a most ingenious sort, and it is impossible to understand anything that they say."

"How wonderfully fortunate to have your consistent guidance in this confusing matter, lamplighter."

"Well, you don't deserve it!" he said with a smile, "not after having made me eat all of that wretched soup!"

They threaded their way through the streets of the town, sometimes following painted signs on the corners of the buildings, sometimes ignoring them depending on which way the lamplighter urged Marna to go. She carefully did the opposite of all the things he suggested to her and shortly came out in the central square, where they found Horatio seated on a bench watching Amalthea. The goat was happily cropping the grass of a little lawn that grew around the pedestal of a statue of an almost naked man standing beside an empty barrel and holding a lantern aloft.

"Some will tell you this is Diogenes of Apollonia," said the lamplighter. "I am not really sure, but now that it is getting dark, I must light his lantern." And with that he withdrew a slender taper from his coat pocket and lighted it with a match. He then reached up to light the bronze lantern in the hand of the sculptured figure.

"A very good idea," said Horatio. "It does seem to be getting dark."

"But Horatio, don't you see?" said Marna. "Diogenes must have been a man who did something unusual with his lantern, because our lamplighter is a proven liar, and he is now in the very act of lighting his lantern as the light fades in the west."

"How do you know he does not tell the truth?" asked Horatio. "He looks like an honest man to me."

"Because," she answered triumphantly, "he lit the red and green Fresnel lamps on the navigational markers in the harbor. Hamlet and I saw him do it. And you know that they are exactly backwards from the way they should be. If the buoys tell lies, the buoy tender cannot be a Truther."

The lamplighter merely smiled and seemed to be waiting for someone to tell him what to do.

"And now we must find Eli and your brother Horace," Marna said. "They have disappeared into the city, and I fear they may have come to harm."

"Oh, I'm sure they're likely to be in great danger by now, probably from overeating in some tavern, and will be back to your ship shortly," said the lamplighter.

"Not so bad as I had feared," said Marna. "Safe, but locked up somewhere with nothing to eat!"

"I think I begin to follow your method," said Horatio. "Now tell me, lamplighter, what is the very least likely place in the whole city to find them?"

The lamplighter looked very solemn and then leaned over to Marna and said in a loud whisper in her ear, "The men in scarlet suits would surely never allow them to get into the library which is in the guild hall on the right-hand side of the square."

A few moments later the three had reached the door of the Library in the left-hand building, where they found the doors locked but with a large brass key projecting from the handsome rim lock on the outside of the door. Horatio turned it and looked into the darkened room inside.

"Horace!" he called. "Eli! Are you in there?"

Horace, Eli, and Occam were out of the Library in an instant.

"However did you do it?" asked the barber as soon as he had been introduced to Marna and Horatio.

"Oh, it turned out to be very simple," she said. "Once we were sure that our friend here was a congenital liar and incapable of speaking the truth, it became as simple as just asking him the right questions."

She patted the elderly lamplighter on the shoulder, and the ancient mariner smiled with modest pride at having his accomplishments so well appreciated.

"But we must get back to the ship before our absence is discovered," said Eli. "I don't think they will be back again before morning, but I'm not really sure what they might do when they find we've escaped."

By the time it was really dark, they had retraced their path to the dock and found Hamlet had the running lights burning brightly in the fore shrouds and the cabin glowing in the warmth of the copper lanterns that hung from the overhead. The fish soup had been set bubbling again on the galley stove.

"Would you join us for another meal, lamplighter?" asked Marna.

"Oh, that would be impossible," he answered. "And besides, I detested that revolting soup."

And so all seven crowded around the cabin table together and finished every scrap of crawfish and every drop of the fish stew. And after supper Occam told them in great detail who both Diogenes of Apollonia and Diogenes the Cynic of Sinope were, and how the latter carried a lighted lantern in the daytime to search for an honest man in Athens. Occam had spent so much time enbibliated in Verity that he had read a great deal about the Greek philosophers while his beard was growing in the guild hall of the Truthers. He said he was sure that the Library belonged to the Guild of Truthers because it would have required a needless multiplication of books to make sure that a Liars' library had no truth in it at all.

FROM THE LOWER TO THE LESSER MOHR

A fair north wind had sprung up in the predawn light as the Sons of Homer cast off the docking lines and helped haul *Polaris* around to face the wind. The foresail was set and the forestaysail boom held out to windward by Horatio to push the bow off to the east. Then the final line was let slip and hauled aboard, and under easy canvas the little schooner sailed slowly down the thoroughfare of the harbor of Verity and passed between the red and green lighted buoys which appeared predictably on the wrong sides of the channel.

By midmorning *Polaris* was dancing along through the waters of the Black Lake and her crew was enjoying big mugs of *caffelatte* while seated along the windward rail. This breakfast drink, composed of one part very strong, very black coffee and three parts very hot milk, was another of the delights of the kitchen that Eli and Marna had learned from Margaretta and Maria. But the brew on board *Polaris* was even richer than that at Casa Sapienza because Amalthea had been feeding on an unusual diet of oats and table scraps since she had become a seafaring goat, and her milk was heavy with cream.

Occam served as an experienced pilot as they left the lake behind and entered the swiftly flowing narrows of the Upper Mohr. Here the water was deep and there was little danger of going aground, but the current neared five knots as they approached the towering bulk of Hat Mountain. The north wind seemed to funnel between the steep hillsides that confined the river. With the wind free astern, *Polaris* was making nearly her best speed, more than seven knots. This combination of wind and current was propelling them through the valley at nearly twenty kilometers per hour, a speed that appeared breathtaking from the deck as they passed close by the high banks of the Mohr.

(Marna knew from the nautical lore she had learned from Sennet that the speed of a hull through still water was governed by its length, because the waves formed by its passage through the water began to mount farther and farther aft as speed increases, until finally the stern of the boat begins to settle into the low point behind the wave forming off the after part of the hull. When this happens the boat must be pushed uphill by the wind, and it requires a huge force to further increase its speed. But since the waves are about the same distance apart, the longer a boat is, the faster it can go before its speed is limited. A simple way to figure out the "hull speed" of a boat in knots— nautical miles per hour—is to multiply the square root of the waterline length of the boat—measured in feet—by 1.34. Thus, Marna's canoe, which was about 14 feet long on the water, would glide through the water at about five knots: the square root of 14 being about 3.75, which, multiplied by 1.34, gives a product of a bit more than five.)

Now they progressed swiftly down the river and, since they had a large-enough crew to stand watches of two crew members each, there was no need to stop for sleep. Even when the wind slackened, the current carried them onward to the northeast. A winter gibbous moon lit their way when all the lights were out, and the tiny orange lantern of the binnacle compass was the only light on deck between dark and dawn.

Occam's presence provided an extra member of the third watch and allowed for some members of the crew to exchange places without rear-ranging the basic schedule. By the second day Eli had managed to work things out so that he and Marna stood the first morning watch together from four in the morning until eight.

"I love the dawn watch," she said. "Do you know the hymn about it?" She sang the words softly:

A THOUSAND AGES IN THY SIGHT
ARE LIKE AN EVENING GONE,
SHORT AS THE WATCH THAT ENDS THE NIGHT
BEFORE THE RISING SUN.

TIME, LIKE AN EVER-ROLLING STREAM,
BEARS ALL ITS SONS AWAY;
THEY FLY FORGOTTEN AS A DREAM
DIES AT THE OPENING DAY.

O God, Our Help in Ages Past

1. O God, our help in ages past, Our hope for years to come,
2. Un - der the shad - ow of Thy throne Thy saints have dwelt se - cure;
3. Be - fore the hills in or - der stood, Or earth re - ceived her frame,
4. A thou - sand ag - es in Thy sight Are like an eve - ning gone,
5. O God, our help in ages past, Our hope for years to come,

Our shel - ter from the storm - y blast, And our e - ter - nal home.
Suf - fi - cient is Thine arm a - lone, And our de - fense is sure.
From ev - er - last - ing Thou art God, To end - less years the same.
Short as the watch that ends the night Be - fore the ris - ing sun.
Be Thou our guard while trou - bles last, And our e - ter - nal home.

"Eli," she added thoughtfully, "do you think we will disappear like a dream someday and just not be anymore?"

"I'm not really sure," said Eli, "but I hope that if all the sons are carried down the river of time, at least one of the daughters of time comes along too."

"Because you need someone to rescue you if they put you in jail again?"

"No ... more because I would like being with you. And besides, I wasn't in jail," said Eli. "I was enbibliated, and above and beyond that, sometimes you need someone to rescue you, too, when you land on islands in rivers."

"I don't want to be rescued," she said, "and I would rather lead than follow." This reminded Marna of Donna Elizabetta's riddle, which she had yet to solve. *What leader needs no follower, what follower needs no leader, and who needs to neither lead nor follow?* When would she find the answer to this puzzle? Eli's reply interrupted her musings.

"All right," said Eli. "I'll just follow around after you, but I won't rescue you anymore, unless you ask me to and really mean it.

"Look east, Eli," she said. "The dawn ... the day is opening."

"I'm glad our watch is short tonight," said Eli. "But I also wish it could be a long night. I think I would rather spend time with you than do anything else."

But then Amalthea, having seen the coming of the dawn, bleated repeatedly from the foredeck, and shortly thereafter Horace emerged from the forward hatch and began to do Chinese exercises in the lee of the forestaysail, and to recite poetry about goats and pan pipes to himself. Eli and Marna turned to talking about the course of the river and the set of the sails, still sitting close together on the windward side of the cockpit. Their legs touched when the boat heeled in a puff of wind, but they pretended not to notice.

Polaris entered the Gorge of the Mohr and the still swifter current bore them toward a V-shaped opening of dim yellow light between the black bulk of the mountains on either side. The opening seemed to grow wider and brighter during the next hour, until they passed the last shoulders of the mountains and came out into the full sunshine of a winter morning on the Mohr.

But though it was now December, it was not cold in these eastern lands, far away from the snows of the Long-Eared Mountains. There was still greenery along the banks, rhododendron and mountain laurel, as well as cedar and juniper on the higher terraces above the river. They had descended many kilometers from the High Valley and the headwaters of the Black River, and they were now in a more temperate land. The speed of the current became less, and far ahead they could see headlands and a clear high sky that promised their eventual arrival at the sea.

"Look," said Occam, a few days later, pointing ahead. "There, off the starboard bow; that blue knob on the horizon is Round Head, where the Great Canal that leads to Berrymor joins the sea at the Bay of Birds."

The winds grew fluky now, and sometimes *Polaris* barely had steerage way through the dark water. But the current was steady and they continued to progress at a rate of three or four knots, even when their speed through the water was half that rate.

"I would guess we are passing that tree at about six or seven kilometers per hour," said Occam. "Why, Eli, do you worry about knots, rather than using the logical kilometers? It seems you are needlessly complicating things."

"Are kilometers really logical?" said Eli. "I always have to try to multiply miles by one-point-six to find distances in kilometers. And then I have to multiply nautical miles by about one and a seventh, or one-point-fourteen, to make land miles out of nautical miles."

"That is why kilometers are better," Occam replied. "A kilometer is one ten-thousandth of the distance from the North Pole to the Equator."

"But is it now?" asked Horatio. "Who measured the distance from the pole to the equator before you divided it by ten thousand? What kind of tape measure did they use?"

"They estimated it from astronomical observation," said Occam, "and then they divided it by ten million (which made any error in their estimate very small), and finally, they made a metal bar just that long and put it in a special museum in a city very far away. Now they say a kilometer is a thousand times longer than that bar of metal.

"And if they were wrong in their measurement of the distance around the whole earth by as much as a hundred miles, their kilometer might be wrong by no more than seven or eight feet," Occam concluded.

"Not much," Eli agreed, "but a lot on a journey as long as ours. Remember that your mistake gets bigger and bigger the longer you travel. No, I prefer to use nautical miles because although they are a distance, they don't come from measuring a distance on the earth to begin with, but from an angle that you can always go back to and you don't need a metal bar in a museum to refer to." Eli continued his explanation: "If you divide the circle of the meridians that pass through the north and south poles into three hundred and sixty degrees and divide each degree into sixty minutes of arc, then we call the minute of arc on the surface of the earth one nautical mile."

"But why is it better to use angles and degrees instead of lengths and distances?" asked Occam. "Isn't that just making things more complicated than they need be?"

"Because navigators figure things out in degrees by the angles at which they observe the stars," said Eli.

And that answer seemed to satisfy even Occam.

During the days that followed, Eli sought every possible chance to talk with Marna without the presence of Occam and the Sons of Homer. He seldom found much opportunity. One or another of the Sons of Homer seemed always to be about. Horace spent much of his day surveying the pleasant landscape that bordered the river as they moved slowly to the northeast. All the while he sat on the cabin trunk while working out bits of alliterative verses about the farmland they were passing on either side. Alliterative verses, he explained, are a bit like the opposite of rhymes, in that the beginnings of words match up instead of the endings.

So no new snow melts along this Lesser Mohr
Old meltwater slides silently in the silver light.
Sparkling waters spring fresh from the fair fields,
Spilling noisily near the leafless shore.
Listen. The reedy margin of mud-caked river meadows
Sound with winter whistles of bobwhite quail.
Quick struts and jiggles on the wind-pressed shore
Pecks and turns to show his pushed-up plumes,
Pauses, preens, and pensive, he whistles once again.

Marna told Horace she liked his verses, but Eli began to feel that the older goatherd was with them too much of the time.

Hamlet continued to produce stews and soups in turn in the galley, but he was always popping up the after hatch to ask Marna a question about herbs or spices, or how long the pasta or the black-eyed peas should be boiled. He never seemed to make up his mind about anything if he didn't talk about it first with someone else.

Even Horatio, who was usually very sure about what he was doing on the schooner, seemed to want to talk with the two young people whenever he was at the wheel or on watch near them.

"Someday I will sail to Sicily," Horatio said. "I have been told that there are wonderful ruined temples there, and ancient fountains of wonderful water that has the best taste in the world. And there are beautiful ladies that can heal old wounds in palaces there. Would you like to go there too, Eli?"

"No," answered Eli. "I would like to get to Berrymor. Then, after I have all the soundings of this river and the harbor of Berrymor, I would like to go back again to the Valley of Spitte and go sailing with Marna whenever I wanted to."

"There are ships that pass from the Bay of Birds to the north and west," said Occam. "They come to shore just before the entrance to the Great Canal and take on what cargoes they can find before going around Round Head and the peninsula of the Northeast Moors to Berrymor."

Eli was interested in the shipping and the cargoes of the Northern Sea, but he was even more interested in Marna, and he shortly extracted the two of them from the discussion and went below to seek the seclusion of the cabin to "do some trigonometry and work out the sights of the hand-bearing compass" that would fix their current position for the cartographical notes he was keeping for his father. But he soon discovered that, besides the charts and nautical navigational instruments, the cabin also contained Occam, who was wielding a soapy brush and a murderous-looking straight razor with a red handle. Since they had the two riverbanks to guide them to its mouth, the coastal piloting wasn't exactly necessary, but there was Occam in the cabin, and he had to be spoken to.

"Hullo, Occam," said Eli. "What's new?"

Occam looked up from the sink where he was lathering his lower jaw. In fact, his entire face was covered with a rich and creamy lather, and he soon began busily scraping away the remains of his beard with the large, red, ivory-handled straight razor.

"It's so simple," he said. "Now I have no complicated and self-contradictory laws to get around. When I want to shave, I shave, and when I don't, I don't."

"But I liked your beard," said Marna.

"I did too," said Occam. "But having the freedom to choose and regulate one's life according to conscience or one's own taste is a great delight when you have been oppressed by somebody else's values and decisions," he said, holding up the end of his nose between his thumb and forefinger and shaving away the last trace of his mustache.

"Perhaps," he added, "the freedom to follow one's own conscience is the only freedom that matters in the long run."

As *Polaris* reached the waters of the Lower Mohr and approached the sea, Marna and Eli did find time to be close in each other's company. Even if they got no closer than they did during that dawn when their knees touched in the cockpit, they now sometimes held each other's hands when they walked to the foredeck at night, away from the glow of the binnacle lamp when one of the other members of the crew was at the wheel. When they discussed the loss of Occam's beard, Marna reached to Eli's face and touched his smooth cheek with her fingertips.

"Will you grow a beard too?" she asked.

"I will if you want me to," he said.

"I don't know yet," said Marna. "It might be very nice, and I think it would make you look older."

"Do you want us to be older, Marna?" he said softly.

"I do.... I think I do," she answered.

Then Eli took her cheeks between his hands, tilted her face up to his, and kissed her very softly on the lips. Afterwards, neither spoke for quite a long time, but stood looking into each other's eyes. They had just begun to kiss again when the sudden rising of the fore hatch behind them announced the arrival of Horatio on deck, ready to milk Amalthea before breakfast.

At length *Polaris* arrived at the Bay of Birds, under the shoulder of Round Head, where the Mouth of the Mohr joined the bay and the Great Canal that ran on east to Berrymor. In an uneasy anchorage they came to the wind and set their largest anchor just at sunset. All around them there were lights of other ships and small boats, some red and green and others white, yellow, and orange, strung in pyramids around the masts of the fishing and trading boats in the roadstead. Several of the masts supported lighted, multi-pointed Moravian stars. It was late autumn and the flotilla was already dressed in Christmas colors.

FAREWELL,
FAITHFUL FRIENDS

I t was on the first morning in the anchorage at the mouth of the Bay of Birds that they saw a cloud of wheeling terns and gannets, and a solitary willet. They noticed an old black ketch anchored near at hand. Ill-painted, square-sided, and with stubby masts, she presented a marked contrast to the elegant lines and shiny new paintwork of *Polaris*. Her name board was almost illegible, but Eli knew the boat instantly.

"Gormley! Reuben!" he hailed. "*Mercy* ahoy! Who have you aboard?"

A shaggy white head appeared from the cabin hatch.

"'Tis only I and my paid hand," said the old sailor, settling a black visored cap on his plentiful shock of hair. "Who are you that you know my name?"

"I am Eli, Reuben's brother," he answered. At that point Reuben himself emerged from the cabin.

"Eli!" he called. "Where did you come by that fine vessel? It is a trifle larger than the one I left you with in Salem."

Shortly, the crews of both boats were aboard *Polaris*. Introductions had been made, explanations offered, and invitations to breakfast extended. They gathered around the gimbaled cabin table while Hamlet cooked innumerable pancakes which he set before them with a great crock of sweet butter and a gleaming amber flask of maple syrup that Gormley fetched from the galley of the old ketch.

"We will sail to the west in a short while when we find the right weather and a favorable falling tide tomorrow morning," said Gormley. "I cannot go to Berrymor again. Years ago I was there and loved the beauty of the place, but I did some commerce there that roused the ire of the Council of Seventeen, and now I cannot go back. We will soon sail back to the Northwest Cape. From there you will be able to find your own way back to the cleared fields beyond the upper reaches of the Spitte."

"Will you come with us, Eli?" asked Reuben. "It might be a stormy passage at the Northwest Cape at this time of year, and we will most probably spend Christmas at sea, but it would bring us all home to Salem together. I have many notebooks of soundings and positions of capes and headlands to bring to our father in Salem; it is time for me to deliver them for the preparation of the next volume of charts."

"I cannot," said Eli. "I have promised to bring this vessel to Berrymor and deliver it to its owner, Ben the Maker. I cannot abandon it here."

"That was a serious bargain we made with Harold Naufragio, the boatwright, and I expect you will do your duty," said Horatio.

"But I am ready to go back now," said Hamlet, "with you, my brothers, and our goat, if you are ready to return now."

"I too begin to long for the farm," said Horace.

"I am going on to Berrymor, in any case," said Occam, "but I cannot sail this boat by myself, even if it were towed through the Great Canal."

Marna was silent and looked down at her folded hands in her lap.

"No," said Eli, "I must go on to Berrymor. There will be other ships later on this winter, or perhaps in the spring. I must finish what I promised to do, and also complete the survey of the river route that I have under-taken to explore and chart for our father Solomon's charts. But Reuben, Gormley, you can bring Marna back to the River Spitte and to the Rock Tower, where her grandfather, Sennet, awaits her return. He may believe her dead after such a long absence."

"No," said Marna. "I will go where you go, Eli, and your course will be my course, and your adventure will be my adventure. In any case, we will find our way back to the river valley in the spring."

"And we three are sufficient crew to bring *Polaris* to her owner," said Occam. "It is the simplest plan."

"But be careful where you search for adventure," said Gormley.

Farewells on the deck of *Polaris* were restrained, but there were many promises of an early renewal of the friendship between the lad from Salem and the three goatherds from the little farm with the great gray barn above the last cleared field. Marna kissed them all good-bye in turn, and the three little men each brushed away tears from their bright eyes, beneath their shaggy white eyebrows.

"Good-bye," they repeated. "Farewell, and God be with you. Come up the river to the Cove past the dock of Stanley and Stalcy as soon as you are back in the West, and we will be waiting for you on our hill."

And with that, Reuben waved to his brother, levered up the anchor with the windlass, and the ketch gathered way under her mizzensail and inner jib. Gormley looked thoughtful as he swung the wheel to head the ketch toward the mouth of the Bay of Birds that led to the open sea. A cloud of gulls and terns wheeled about them as they moved slowly to the west.

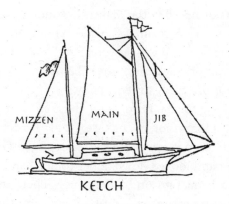

KETCH

IN THE GREAT CANAL

A t the entrance to the Great Canal, *Polaris* joined a string of three larger boats which were being taken in tow by a small black steam tug. The tug was squat and wide with bulky paddlewheel guards on either side that made her appear to be broader than she was long. Her tall pilothouse was like a miniature tower that projected well above the arched tops of the guards, and the deckhouse aft was surmounted by a slender black stack that rose more than ten meters above the deck. Supported by a complicated web of rigging and guy wires, the stack was topped by a ring of projecting points that looked like a blackened crown.

They entered the first lock at the top of the high tide, being worked inside by the tug's crew with considerable help from Eli and Occam, while Marna took the helm. With four boats and the tug inside, the great lock gates were swung closed behind and the lockkeeper opened the valves that let the ships settle the few feet to the level of the water in the canal itself.

"The locks are needed at both ends of the canal," explained Occam, "because the time of the tide at Berrymor is three hours later than it is at the Bay of Birds. Without the locks there would be fearsome currents running through the canal, changing directions several times a day and eroding the banks so swiftly as to block the canal itself in a few months. The mechanical equipment of the lock gates and valves may indeed be very complicated, but sometimes I must admit that complex things are necessary. It is only when there are two ways of doing something or understanding something that I am quite sure the simplest answer is always the correct one."

They traveled through the cleft in the winter countryside all day, sometimes in broad lakes and sometimes in narrow, dug channels that had been cut through the low moorlands to reach the next long lake ahead. Ahead of them the tug sent up a column of gray-black smoke that drifted off to the south and brought a faint smell of sulphur to the air. By nightfall the stack emitted occasional sparks, and the smoke plume glowed pink against the clear black sky.

That night, moored to dolphins (huge wooden pilings set out from the banks alongside of the channel), the diminished crew was less talkative than it had been on the previous night when the three goatherds had been aboard.

"I wonder how they are doing," said Eli. "This north wind is fairly gentle, but they have to point into it as they go to the northwest, past the Cliffs of Care."

"I would like to see the cliffs from the ocean someday," said Occam. "I fear that place and its memory thrills me. Many years ago I went up the coast on foot and visited there to see it from the top, on land. We walked across a friendly farmstead on a pleasant afternoon and asked the farmers how we could find the Cliffs of Care. We were told to walk until there was no more land in front of us and we would then see the cliffs.

"Eventually, we realized we were coming to the end of the land in a green pasture that faced a clear sky, but we still could not see the sea. Then we came to the top of a little rise and suddenly, there was the Northern Ocean at our feet, a hundred and fifty meters below us. That is a terrible height to look down, almost a tenth of an English mile, close to five hundred feet straight down beneath our feet. When you see an escarpment like that, you can feel the height in the pit of your stomach. The cliffs drop almost directly to the sea, and at their base is a white surge of bursting waves always forming and breaking in the black-green water of the Northern Sea.

"The tumult of that sea is dreadful to behold," Occam continued, "but it was so far down from where we were standing that we could not hear any sound but the gentle sighing of the breeze and the chatter of birdsong in the meadow behind us. That silence was more frightening than a warning roar of breakers would have been. If a ship came in to that coast and could not sail to windward, away from it, there could be no hope for it. There is no beach or harbor of refuge, only sheer blocks of pink and gray stone that are smashed again and again by the returning green waves of the sea." Occam's eyes had a faraway look as he finished his tale.

"I hope the Sons of Homer and their friends never come close with that shore under their lee," said Marna, pausing to think for a moment. "But if their weather gets worse, at least the wind will go around toward the east and they will have a fair course out and around the northern headlands."

"Many times," said Occam, "things have to get worse before they get better. And sometimes, it's things getting worse that causes things to get better. But at other times, things just get worse until they are really terrible."

"That sounds rather like the riddle Donna Elizabetta told me that I cannot solve," said Marna. "I'm still working it out," she said. "Nevertheless, I think things are always on the way to getting better and better. Is it time to set the anchor light, Eli?"

"Better than that," he answered. "The night's almost half gone, and it is time to go to bed."

Eli and Marna slept in high pilot berths on either side of the main cabin, while Occam occupied a transom berth below and between them. He was soon snoring resonantly while the two young people found themselves wakeful, their minds still full of the events of the past days and imaginings of what tomorrow would bring.

"Do you think we could rent him to a church as an organ pipe?" murmured Eli.

But at the sound of Eli's voice, Occam rumbled and rolled over in his bunk.

"Ssshhh!" whispered Marna. "You'll wake him. Go to sleep, you silly idiot. We can talk in the morning."

Eli slept, and in his dream he kept finding Marna in one terrible plight after another. Usually she was in a storm or in the raging surf of a terrible, windswept shore, always wet, often muddy, and he would plunge through the dream night to wrest her from fen or ocean, and then ask permission to rescue her. When she nodded, he would carry her slight body in his arms, looking for some place of refuge that he could never quite locate. Always searching for some dry, warm haven where he could lay down the sweet burden he carried ... He would wake to realize that she was there on the other side of the cabin where Occam snored between them.

But Marna's dream brought her to places she had not even imagined before. In a hot desert land she entered a long Bedouin tent and sat cross-legged on a rich red and blue carpet that had been spread over the sand. The master of the tent, a great sheik with a delicate black beard and mustache, nodded and smiled at her, and she knew it was her command to dance. Barefoot on the carpet with little silver bracelets on her ankles, she began a slow, sinuous movement, holding her hands high above her head. She was not wearing the dancing dress she had brought from Casa

Sapienza, but sheer crimson silk pajamas and a golden silk cloak that came almost to her heels. She had a pair of silver hawk's bells on the backs of each of her wrists, and they jingled in the slow rhythm of her undulating bare arms and the motion of her hips. She saw the sheik smile when she looked in his direction, but most of the time, she kept her eyes on the tent overhead or on the gorgeous patterns of the carpet beneath her feet. She danced until the sheik rose up to his full height of nearly two meters. As he stood, his foot touched a brass pitcher and basin by his side, and they fell over with a sound like tumbled pots and pans.

She awoke to find Occam rattling about the galley, making breakfast coffee and porridge.

BERRYMOR

The helpful tug was under way again shortly after dawn, raising its column of smoke in the still December morning as the little fleet was herded into the eastern lock, where they returned to the sea level of the local tide. Within an hour they had cast off the tow and were under sail again on a light northerly breeze, heading directly into the rising sun which provided a golden background for the towers and domes of Berrymor. It was a view unlike anything Eli or Marna had ever seen before. Tall bell towers rose up in several places and a trio of huge globular domes stood atop great churches on the waterfront of its southern side. The winter sun reflected from the water made a shifting golden path that seemed to lead directly to the entrance of a canal that beckoned them toward the interior of the city. Fantastic buildings pierced with arched and mullioned windows stood on both shores of the canal. The facades of the buildings were pink and rose colored, fringed with balconies and decorated with multicolored mooring posts on either side of dignified doorways that faced the water. The wooden posts were painted in stripes and topped by gilded knobs. Each building seemed to have its own landing stage. Many boats were moored to the gaudy mooring posts. There were boats everywhere. Steam tugs and tall ships moved about the great anchorage. There were rowboats, barges, wherries, shallops, and even thin and delicate single-sculled shells that moved on the surface of the water like tiny insects whose buoyant feet hold them up on bog waters and in woodland ponds.

"We cannot go through the main canal," said Occam. "Our masts are too high for the bridges that connect the halves of the city. We must go around

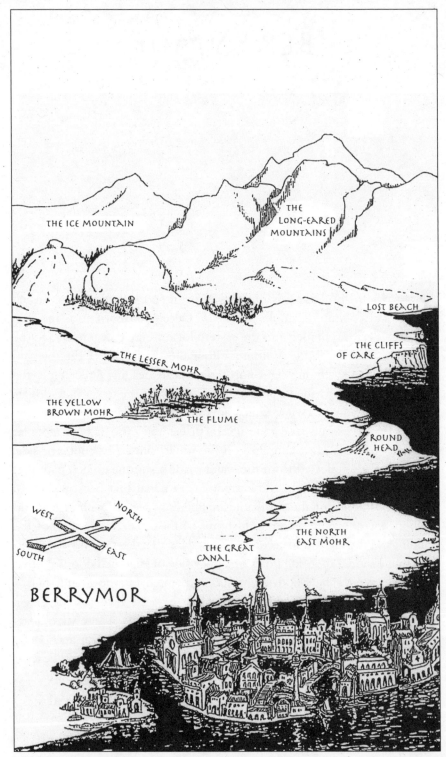

THE ICE MOUNTAIN

THE
LONG-EARED
MOUNTAINS

LOST BEACH

THE CLIFFS
OF CARE

THE LESSER MOHR

THE YELLOW
BROWN MOHR

THE FLUME

ROUND
HEAD

NORTH

WEST

EAST

SOUTH

THE NORTH
EAST MOHR

THE GREAT
CANAL

BERRYMOR

the south end to reach the embarcadero of the east side. Where were you told that you could find the studio of Ben the Maker?" he asked Eli.

"To the east of the south entrance of the biggest canal," said Eli.

"Not far from my old shop," said Occam. "I wonder if Alberto and Tomaso, my old partners, will take me back again. I long for the simple life of an honest barber who does not have to tangle with the complex notions of truth and untruth that I found in Verity."

They sailed slowly under foresail and inner jib, to the south, leaving the city on their port side, finding their way among a forest of channel markers and colored buoys, but this time the green cans were properly on their starboard hand as they moved gently in the direction of the open sea.

It required most of the day to work *Polaris* around the island city in fitful winds, and it was late afternoon when they came in sight of an unoccupied floating dock beside a long stone quay that seemed to invite their landing. The wind held light but became remarkably steadier in the north, and Marna was able to make several passes back and forth with the little schooner before attempting to bring her in to shore by turning directly into the wind just as they approached the landing. *Polaris* bore slowly up alongside the dock where a few passersby stopped to watch as Eli jumped ashore. Occam tossed him a stout line to snub around an ancient bollard. The momentum of the boat was not great, but it was enough to require Eli to take three turns around the old iron fitting and let them slip off slowly with a great creaking sound until *Polaris* finally came to rest. He then ran forward to catch a bowline and make it fast while Marna let go the helm and went forward to drop the slatting sails.

With the ship secured, the three turned to thoughts of food. There seemed no dearth of places to eat, but Occam led them inland, over a stone arched bridge and along the side of a deep green canal. They walked through a very dark alley where they passed a little niche that contained a small statue of a woman with a child in her arms. It was illuminated by a flickering candle in a red glass globe.

"The *Madonnina*," said Occam. "She looks after everyone that comes through these alleys."

After a few more turnings they came to a lighted doorway with a crudely lettered menu of two or three items posted in a picture frame. Neatly carved into the top of the frame were the names CARLO and MARIA, and above them was a sculptured basket of long loaves of bread and bottles of wine.

"Let us go in," said Occam. "They will remember me here and they will feed us well."

"Occam!" called out a high tenor voice as they entered the restaurant. "Where have you been? Come in, come in! Maria come, bring a liter of the best Frascati. Occam is home and brings beautiful young people with him!"

Carlo and his wife were composed of circles: Their faces were round, their smiles semicircular, their girth generous, and their extended arms embracing. The three sailors were installed at a table bearing a red candle that dripped its wax into the saucer of a blue and yellow pottery candlestick. It cast a warm light on the red-and-white-checked tablecloth.

Their supper began with bowls of thin spaghetti gleaming with oil and butter, perfumed with garlic, and dusted with grated cheese and a sprinkling of parsley and basil. Then a grilled sole appeared alongside of a small, crusty wedge of polenta, produced as if by magic along with a salad of plum tomatoes and infant zucchini slices arranged on brightly figured ceramic plates. There seemed to be no prejudice at Carlo's table against the younger people drinking wine, for Maria poured it herself from a blue and yellow ceramic pitcher. The host and his wife then sat down with their guests and all five raised their simple wineglasses in a toast to Occam's return, as well as Marna and Eli's arrival.

"It is so good to have you back to celebrate our fast before the feast," said Carlo.

"This is no fast," said Occam. "What feast, my friend, could be better than this?"

"But no meat tonight; this is Christmas Eve," said Maria. "Have you been away so long that you don't know the season of the year?"

"And I fear that you will not find room at any inn in Berrymor tonight, as there are many visitors in the town," said Maria. "So you must stay with us, and after you are settled in, you will come with us to midnight mass at our little church beside the next canal," and she reached across the table and patted the back of Marna's hand with a smiling gesture of possession.

So after the supper and a very small cup of very strong black, steam-brewed coffee to keep the tired sailors awake for midnight churchgoing, the three went back to *Polaris* and brought their sea bags ashore to the apartment above the restaurant. When she passed the statuette in the alley for the fourth time that night, Marna thought that perhaps the little Madonnina really was looking after her.

They joined a file of others as they walked along the stone fundament and crossed several small bridges with wrought-iron railings on their way to the church, located beside a canal full of tied-up boats. In the dark it seemed a small building, but it was tall and encrusted with carved stonework. There were fluted columns with leafy capitals that supported a great triangular pediment trimmed with dental moldings and bands of egg and dart decoration. They pushed their way through a dark opening and came to an interior lit by a thousand candle flames.

Eli and Marna found themselves standing in the midst of a crowd of worshippers, for there were only a half-dozen pews in the front of the nave, and these seemed to be occupied by the very oldest people. Christmas carols echoed through the high interior and the rising sound seemed to return from the dome above, and from the dozens of gilded cherubs that disported themselves about the architectural details of the ceiling.

God rest ye merry, gentlemen,
Let nothing you dismay! Remember ...

Marna remembered Christmas at the Rock Tower and how Sennet's beard always let her know who Santa Claus really was, despite the stories she had been told. Eli wondered if there was another verse that wished a merry rest to the ladies as well as the gentlemen. They stood close together in the dimly lit rear of the church, facing the glowing burst of candles that surrounded the altar. Marna's hand sought Eli's, and he looked down to smile at her when their fingers met and twined together.

At the end of the carol, there was a jingling of bells and a priest in a white and gold vestment appeared, accompanied by a man carrying a large red leather book. They entered from the shadows of the rear of the church and were preceded by a half-dozen white-robed boys and girls, most of whom were only slightly younger than Marna and Eli. They carried tall brass candlesticks as they came from the sacristy door. The priest was a slight black man with a neatly trimmed gray beard. The dignity of his bearing made him seem taller than he was, but actually, he was shorter than most of his altar servers, and his creamy, brocaded, gold-trimmed chasuble came down almost to his heels. A wisp of pungent blue smoke came from the censer carried by one of the altar girls. A grown boy of about Eli's age carried a long pole surmounted by a silver cross as he led the procession.

In later years Eli tried to remember the words of the service, but he could only recall a few: ... *before the day star I have begotten thee ... The grace of God has dawned on all men alike ... We are ransomed from our guilt ... For unto us a child is given.*

The priest gave a short sermon, not more than a few minutes of slowly spoken, clearly announced words: "... because He first loved us, we are a holy people and our sins have been forgiven. And if we are not always perfect and do not always live up to His example, we will be forgiven as we have forgiven others. Let us give thanks."

Later, after the priest gave thanks and raised a golden cup and a small white wafer of bread, he spoke of peace, and then said to all those gathered, "Peace be with you."

And all turned to their neighbors to clasp their hands or to embrace. Since Eli and Marna were already holding hands, it seemed the only thing left to do was to kiss each other in the presence of so many smiling people before they returned the offered handshakes of Occam, Maria, Carlo, and the others around them.

At the end of the service, the voices of choir and congregation rose up to the cherubim above and cascaded back from the shadowy ceiling:

> THE ANGELS SANG, THE SHEPHERDS SANG,
> THE GRATEFUL EARTH REJOICED,
> AND AT HIS BLESSED BIRTH
> THE STARS THEIR EXULTATION VOICED:
> VENITE ADOREMUS ...

THE STUDIOLO OF BEN THE MAKER

A bright yellow sky in the east made the forms of the towers and loggias of the ancient buildings stand out in clear relief. Eli rose and went to the window. It was Boxing Day, the Feast of St. Stephen, but also the day when he and Marna would deliver *Polaris* to her owner. They applied themselves to a thorough cleaning of the little schooner as one always should when about to return a borrowed or chartered boat to its owner. After they had dusted and swept the cabins, cleaned the sink, and washed the head with soap and sponges, they put a drop or two of liquid soap in the bilge and then pumped it dry. They washed the decks, re-rolled the sails in a proper "harbor furl" with no lumps or bumps in them, hung the coiled halyards on their cleats, and flemished down the docking lines, winding them into the shape of flat disks on the deck beside their cleats. By the time they were finished, the boat looked quite as new as when they had first boarded her. Finally they ran Harold the boatwright's vermilion burgee up to the truck of the main mast where it would soon be replaced by its new owner's personal signal. Last of all they went to a ship's chandlery and secured a large flag of the City of Berrymor, a gorgeous banner of broadly striped crimson and gold, and set it on the ensign staff at the stern, the proper place for it when the sails are furled.

Ben the Maker proved to be a close neighbor of Carlo and Maria's; they knew him by his reputation as a famous craftsman. His *studiolo*, they explained, was on the second floor (which he called the first floor, because the lower level was called the "ground" floor) of an ancient palazzo, fifty meters farther up the stone bulkhead and floating dock from the landing stage where *Polaris* was moored. They climbed a curving stairway to a hall that led to many dark wooden doors set in an expanse of peeling plaster and neglected paintwork. Each door had a carefully lettered plaque with a name in small Roman capitals: BALDASARRE, PICO, NICCOLO, PIETRO, ALDO, and, finally, BEN.

Eli knocked. There was a long pause and then a rattling of a chain being undone on the inside. The tall door swung open to reveal a tall, smiling man who was holding a long ivory pipe in his left hand.

"Come in," he said, and then, putting the end of the instrument to his lips, began to play a plaintive melody in a deep bass tone on the open pipe. It was an odd melancholy sort of music that Marna had never heard before. He turned away and Marna and Eli followed him down a lengthy hall to enter a large room with high arched windows that looked over the docks and water below.

In the center of the room stood a Christmas tree with sparkling ornaments buried in the recesses of its branches, and bearing a scattering of tiny but richly robed angels carrying censers, trumpets, and lutes. The little angels seemed to be flying about the upper branches of the tree.

"We have come to deliver *Polaris* to you, sir," began Eli.

"I know," said Ben. "I saw you arrive yesterday from these windows. She is a pretty boat and your pretty helmsman sailed her prettily. Will you take coffee or tea?"

Marna and Eli soon learned that all business in Ben's studio was conducted over tiny cups of something hot, either bitter black coffee or bitter green tea. Perhaps because of the lack of sweetness, the slightly acid distillations of bean and herb seemed to sharpen the mind and make the bargaining process of business go on longer and in a more ceremonial manner.

They had just gotten around to arranging for the price of the boat being deposited to Harold's account at one of the banking houses of Berrymor when there came a loud knock at the door. A visitor entered without waiting to be admitted, since Ben had left the chains off.

"The Academy has announced a new exhibition and a public symposium for a month from now!" said the newcomer.

"Pico, my friend, don't be so enthusiastic. As always, the Academicians want to show the best work but give the least time to prepare it. Perhaps this year I will stay home or go sailing on my new boat."

"Bosh, Ben," said Pico. "You might snub the exhibition, but you could never give up the chance at the symposium. You love to hear yourself talk—or think—out loud."

Ben chuckled and went back to blowing on his pipe. But at that moment the door flew open again and an enormous man with fiery red hair came stalking down the hall.

"Ascanio!" said Ben. "Will you show your sculpture in this sudden exhibition?"

"I have no choice," said Ascanio. "We are not all as successful as you, Ben, exhibited in the great museums, patronized by the rich and famous of many cities, and paid what you ask for the things you make. Why, I could live for a year on what you receive for a simple wooden flute. And now I hear you have bought a yacht, a cruising boat. What did that cost you?"

"Two bassoons, a viola da gamba, and a full set of kettle drums," answered Ben. "I also supplied a lovely, balanced baton for the conductor, made of boxwood, but I didn't charge for it."

"And I," countered Ascanio, "if I want to show anything new, I must begin today and complete my work in less than a month. And I have not even begun to plan or draw what I will carve."

But at that point his eye fell upon Marna and he straightened up to inspect the girl more closely.

"Have you ever modeled?" he asked her.

"No," said Marna. "I have danced, but only for fun and exercise, and I have played the recorder, but only for pleasure."

"But why deprive the world of your beauty?" asked Ascanio. "If I carve a statue of you as a dancing girl, you will gladden the hearts of men for all time thereafter."

Marna blushed, glanced at Eli, and then said defiantly, "If I do anything to help or delight other people in the future, it will be done by my learning, my taste, my judgment, or my skill—not just for the way I look."

"But you can do both, my dear," said Ascanio. "Beauty and truth can live together in the same person, in the same work of art. And a work of art you will be when you are shown in the new exhibition at the Academy. Your brains should not be allowed to obscure your beauty any more than the other way around."

"I remember a poem by a fellow named William," said Pico. "He addressed a beautiful girl with yellow hair who wanted to be loved for herself alone and not just for her yellow hair."

"And what was her history?"

"A blank, my friend. She became consumed with green and yellow melancholy because, as he pointed out, only God could love her for herself alone and not her yellow hair."

All this talk of loving people and their beauty was beginning to embarrassMarna and Eli. They interrupted with a request that they settle the business of the boat. Ben served more green tea and they went back to their discussion while Pico and Ascanio argued about the role of art in unifying sacred and profane desire.

Another knock at the door was followed by the footsteps of another guest.

"Ha! Antonio, now we will know what the musicians think of the Academy's new project," said Ben.

"Very little," said Antonio. "They will give no prize for opera or concerto or ballet. I will die a poor man."

"You old rascal," Ascanio snorted. "You are paid every time a person comes to one of your concerts! No one pays me if they look at one of my sculptures. I must make my entire living from a single sale of my talent while you can collect again and again, seven nights a week."

"But I work seven nights a week," countered Antonio, "while you lie about in bed waiting for inspiration and do nothing until someone gives you a commission for a tombstone or a garden fountain! No, my friend, you have chosen the easier life."

"Easy!" exploded Ascanio. "Easy to pound marble into dust, to dig hard chips of wood out of the folds of imaginary drapery, or to make granite as smooth as the skin of a child? You are the one who has it easy, with nothing to do but make little black marks on fine lined paper while thinking of sweet tunes in your head, or waving your little stick in front of others who really make the music you are paid for."

"And not well enough paid at that!" roared Antonio. "And now I hear that there is a boy musician coming to Berrymor who plays so well and writes music so swiftly that he seems to be merely copying it down from a score he carries in his head. Soon there will be no work for an honest composer at all."

Ben stopped playing and looked up from his pipe. "The best of all music is that which is made up and played without ever being written down. It is played only once and then forgotten while something else, new and spontaneous, takes its place."

"But if you want to make money from your music, Antonio," said Pico, "you must combine art and commerce. Go to the south—go to the city of Lucro and you will be able to find buyers for your compositions and people that will contract for your performances, too."

"But I must finish my business with my young guests before we go on with this symposium," said Ben. He rummaged about in a credenza that stood between the windows and produced a pen and a sheet of heavy cream-colored paper. Then, sitting on the floor with a wooden lap board, he wrote the following letter:

TO THE BANKERS OF BERRYMOR

GOOD SIRS,

BE PLEASED TO·PAY AT THE DEMAND OF ELI, SON OF SOLOMON OF THE SPITTE, WHO IS THE BEARER OF THIS ASSIGNMENT, THE SUM OF 2,200 SCUDI TO THE ORDER AND ACCOUNT OF HAROLD NAUFRAGIO, THE BOATWRIGHT OF THE VALLEY OF THE BLACK RIVER, THE SAME BEING FULL VALUE RECEIVED BY HIM FOR THE CONSTRUCTION AND DELIVERY OF THE SCHOONER YACHT POLARIS HERE IN BERRYMOR ON BOXING DAY THIS YEAR. YOU WILL BE PLEASED TO PAY ALSO A DELIVERY COMMISSION OF ONE PER CENTUM, OR 22 SCUDI, TO ELI, THE BEARER OF THIS ASSIGN-MENT.

PAY ALSO A COMMISSION OF 14 SCUDI TO THIS SAME ELI FOR HIS RECOMPENSE IN THIS MATTER.

SIGNED BY MY OWN HAND,

BEN THE MAKER

He signed the document with a flourishing squiggle at the end of his name, blotted it on the rug, and handed it to Eli.

"Take it to any of the company of Bankers of Berrymor and they will complete your transaction by placing the money at Harold's disposal."

"Thank you, sir," said Eli. "You have used us generously. We will be on our way to complete the business as soon as we have allowed you the time to inspect the yacht."

"I already have," said Ben. "I looked it over shortly after dawn today and noted only that it needed to be swept and tidied. Then I saw you working on it for several hours when I looked out my window, so I assume that it is now immaculate."

"Then we will go to the bankers now," said Eli, and stood to leave.

"But do not take my model from me so soon," said Ascanio. "Will you not consider posing for me as temple dancer?"

"No, thank you," said Marna. "You are kind to flatter me so, but I will decline."

And the two young people set off down the hall, descended the broad stairs, and came out onto the cobbled streets to look for the Bankers of Berrymor.

OF DANCERS' DRESSES AND DECORATIONS

Marna exercised and danced for a half-hour every morning. She usually wore the dress from Casa Sapienza while she stretched and whirled through a graceful series of demanding movements. In her room above Carlo and Maria's restaurant there was a large oval mirror on a mahogany stand that could be tilted so that she could see herself from head to toe while doing her workout. Ascanio's insistence that she model for his sculpture had bothered her at the time, but as she looked in the mirror, she was surprised by what she saw. She stopped to examine the girl in the glass. It confused her that she should be made so that Ascanio should admire her even though she did not want to be admired. Did Eli see the same person that Ascanio had seen, and that she saw now in the mirror?

She looked at the simple open neckline of the dancing dress and wondered if her mother's necklace would improve her appearance. Without really deciding or thinking about it very much, she rummaged among her things and took out the amulet. When she slipped the chain over her head, the stone came just to the top of the shallow valley between her breasts. It looked appropriate, and she thought that either Ascanio or Eli, or even Lucindar, would approve of it.

By the time the routine of her exercise was complete, she felt her mind was clearer on the subject of being admired. The mirror told her that her face and body were certainly attractive. Perhaps Pico's poet had been right: Only God should be expected to appreciate her mind and accomplishment without regard for her good looks. She carefully undid her braids, brushed back her hair, and tied it with a ribbon so that the loose auburn curls cascaded down her back. Then she dressed in her usual sailor's clothes. But when she moved she could still feel the presence of the green stone under the heavy sweater.

Eli was already at breakfast in Carlo and Maria's still-empty restaurant. He looked up and then stood when Marna entered the room.

"*Caffelatte* and hot rolls," said Maria, coming out of the kitchen and wiping her flour-dusted hands on her apron. "What will you have with them, Marna? Blueberry jam or honey?"

"Both, thank you, Maria," said Marna, sitting down to join Eli who was tearing a large orange into sections with his fingers. The smell of fresh coffee, the perfume of the orange, and the aroma of baking bread filled the room.

"Your hair's different. What did you do to it?" said Eli.

Marna shrugged, smiling slightly.

"Now that we are here, before we find a boat to go back to the West, I want to see the sights of Berrymor today," Eli said. "Let's go right away, after breakfast. And I hear that there will be New Year's parties in the streets and in the big square every night for the next four days."

After breakfast, Marna and Eli headed out to explore the city. They crossed many canals and explored the length of a number of alleys and arched tunnels before they found themselves at the edge of a larger canal where there was no bridge. But people in small boats were crossing the water all the time, and they soon were able to make the passage for the expenditure of a few small coins. On the other side they threaded through more narrow streets and over more bridges until they emerged suddenly in a great square, bordered with the arcaded facades of large buildings on three sides, and faced by an ornate cathedral at its east end. They crossed the sunny square past flocks of pigeons, through a grove of flagpoles, and beside imposing columns where, they were told, the people of the town had once hanged a wicked ruler who had desired too much power for himself and his family. People in the square told them this and other stories, and Eli and Marna surmised that this town was very unlike Verity. Here you generally knew that people meant what they said, with very little possibility for doubt or confusion.

They visited the house of the Council of Seventeen, which, they were told, was a group so powerful and so secret that no one in Berrymor dared to commit a crime because the Council could imprison or even execute any criminal who was accused before them. Such accusations were a serious matter, especially because the accusers often made their complaints in secret to keep from becoming victims of revenge by relatives of the accused. These secret accusations were made by writing out the complaint and placing the message in the mouth of a stone leopard who stood as though he was guarding the door of the Council chamber. The mouth of the leopard communicated with an iron-bound box from which the youngest member of the Council, the seventeenth, would withdraw the complaints, bringing them before the other members for judgment.

Even though the decrees of the Council were severe and their judgments often secret, the citizens of Berrymor were nonetheless proud of the fact that there was so little crime in their town. People told Marna and Eli that even a vegetable merchant would be careful that his scales weighed honestly if a false measure might cause him to be taken away in the middle of the night to disappear into an unknown prison.

When they entered the great church, they found the light dim at first, and Marna took Eli's hand as they walked toward the domed center of the building. All above them were millions of golden stones that formed the background for the colored mosaic figures of saints and angels that surrounded an immense, solemn figure of God, sitting in judgment high in the dome. But not all of the surrounding figures wore the gilded haloes of holiness. Some seemed to be representations of ordinary people— soldiers, students with books, and even farmers and fishermen. In one area there was a figure of a young woman in a fur-trimmed bright red dress who seemed to be dancing with her graceful arms raised. She held something above her head. But when they came closer Marna could see that the object was a jeweled platter that bore the severed head of a bearded man.

"She must be Salomé," said Eli. "She was supposed to be a wonderful dancer, but her mother told her to do something terribly wrong. Her name is in a book by a man named Flavius Josephus."

"I think she is in a book by Matthew, too," said Marna. "I wonder what her dance was like that made her stepfather, the king, promise her anything she wanted?"

On New Year's Eve there were masked partygoers in the streets of Berrymor, from early in the day until late at night. Marna and Eli sought out a shop that sold the papier-mâché masks that both young and old were wearing. Carlo explained that the masks allowed both the simplest and the loftiest of people to go to the same parties and dance to the same music because no one knew precisely who was who. Of course, friends could recognize each other because they knew what masks their friends were wearing, but at a party, a kitchen maid might dance with a member of the Council of Seventeen without either of them knowing who the other was.

Eli selected the mask of a bearded faun with small horns and a grinning mouth because it reminded him of Amalthea the goat and her three cheerful masters, Horace, Hamlet, and Horatio. Marna looked over the collection of fantastic faces for a very long time before she selected an almond-shaped face with bright blue makeup above its eyes, arched black eyebrows, and a pouting mouth painted a deep red. She thought the mask looked more like Salomé than any other in the shop. Although they spent some of their money on the masks, Eli still had about fourteen scudi left in his wallet. They returned to Maria and Carlo's for supper before changing into their party costumes for the evening.

Marna had no proper party dress at hand, but she borrowed a long black cloak from Maria and put it on over her Grecian dancing dress. At the last minute, she added her mother's amulet to complete her costume. Eli, in a black wool watch cap and sweater, looked both playful and slightly wicked in his satyr mask.

They joined a throng of other people both young and old who strolled the banks of the canals and swarmed over the arched bridges. A number of the great houses were open to all costumed visitors, and they soon found themselves in a glittering ballroom on the upper level of a grand palazzo where there was an orchestra of white-wigged violinists, pretty young girls playing flutes and oboes, and a number of kettle drummers and trumpeters A beautiful dark-haired woman played the harp. The music was merry and dancers whirled and coupled in an intricate series of patterns that everyone seemed to know by heart.

"Come on, Eli, let's dance!" said Marna.

"I can't. I don't know how," he answered.

"Do I have to teach you everything?" she said. "Look!" And dropping her cloak on a chair, she whirled away toward the center of the room with her arms held high above her head and her bare legs flashing in the glittering light of the chandeliers. Other dancers made way for her, and soon she was performing in the center of an admiring circle of masked revelers, the green ornament swinging free from her dress. Eli watched but felt helpless to join her. He gathered up the cloak from the chair and stood waiting for the music to end.

Marna returned, slightly breathless. "Come on," she said, "let's try another party. This one is fun, but I've done my thing here, and there is more music across the canal!"

And so it went throughout the night. At one gathering Marna danced with a huge man dressed as Harlequin with a pattern of large black-and-white squares on his costume. At another she found a clown with a round red nose and a huge white ruff standing out around his neck. When midnight came, everybody embraced, but Eli did not know where Marna was at that moment and he stood alone, holding the black velvet cloak Marna had borrowed from Maria.

Then Marna came toward him, holding by the hand a young man who wore lavender knee breeches, a yellow silk shirt, and a silver mask with a pointed mustache.

"Eli, this is Pedrolino. I think he's the best dancer in Berrymor tonight."

"No—not to compare with this little Columbina."

Eli acknowledged Pedrolino with a nod, and then, draping the black cloak around Marna's shoulders, he took her by the hand and started for the door.

"Come on," he said, "it's past midnight now. It's time to go home."

"Now don't be jealous just because I danced with another boy."

"I'm not jealous," said Eli, "but I think he looks silly in those purple pants."

"You certainly are jealous!" said Marna. "And remember, you don't own me. I'm a person in my own right. You think you should own everything just because you're a man—like the money we got for delivering the boat. I earned it as much as you did, but you took it all and you have been making the decisions about what to do with it. I know you bought me a mask, but you made all the decisions as though I were a child who didn't know enough to make her own choices!"

Eli walked along in silence, but he took the leather wallet from his pocket and thrust it into Marna's hand.

"Here, take it," he said. "Take it all if that's what you want. You don't even have a pocket in that dress that you can put it in."

"Now you're really sounding jealous," said Marna. "My talk with Pedrolino was strictly professional. He is a member of a troupe of actors, and he said that I was good enough to be a part of the company, to dance and take part in their plays!"

"If that's what you want, that's what you ought to do," answered Eli. But by that time they had passed through the alley where the vigil light over the Madonnina was flickering low in its little red glass cup. Soon, they had arrived at the door of Carlo and Maria's restaurant.

"Good night," he said. "I'll see you tomorrow."

Marna turned and went up the stairs without looking back.

30 COMING APART

Marna did not find Eli at breakfast the next morning. Maria said that he had gone out very early and had not told her where he was going. Not about to miss the chance to explore the sights of Berrymor just because of a silly argument, Marna set out by herself to learn more about the town. She wandered the banks of canals and went into galleries of ancient and wonderful paintings. In one vast church she paused to study the representation of a lovely woman in a scarlet gown rising through a golden sky past dozens of childish cherubim.

Marna lunched at an outdoor table in the winter sunshine where a bearded man sold grilled sausage wrapped in crusty slices of bread, liberally daubed with spicy mustard. She sat for a long time in a small piazza near a wooden bridge where she drank tea and read an illustrated magazine that had articles about painters and poets, singers and actors, all of whom were currently being admired by the people of the city on the water. While she was sitting under an umbrella to shade her from the bright sunlight, a young man stopped and stared at her.

"Hello," he said, "I am Pedrolino. Aren't you my little Columbina of last night?"

"I guess I am," she answered, "but I'm not sure who you are. I've never seen your face until now."

"I recognized you by your pretty arms—and my face doesn't matter," he said. "I change it all the time. Sometimes I think I have a thousand faces. Sometimes I am a lover; sometimes a bragging old soldier. I can be a clown and a tumbler or a zany, depending on what the show requires for that night's performance."

"Are you doing a show tonight?" asked Marna.

"Certainly. We will be showing on the south side of the Art Academy, right up against the middle of the blank wall where there is a little stone plinth that we use as a stage. Come at eight o'clock."

"I will," said Marna, and she smiled at Pedrolino. "I surely will."

Marna continued to explore the city throughout the afternoon, but she saw no sign of Eli. By evening she was beginning to worry about his absence, but she kept up a good pretense of not being overly dependent on him when she talked with Maria at the restaurant.

"When Eli comes in," she said to Maria, "tell him I went to see the players on the south side of the Art Academy." And, wrapping herself in the black cloak, she set out alone for an evening of entertainment.

Later, Eli was not able to remember exactly everything that happened on the morning after the masked ball. Marna had said he was jealous, but he only knew that he had been angry. He was angry with Marna for her outburst at him. After all, hadn't he done everything he should have done to care for her, to keep her safe, to provide for everything she needed? He was angry with Ascanio the sculptor for even *wanting* to look at Marna, let alone make a statue of her. He was angry with Pedrolino, whoever he might be, for putting ideas in her head that she should join a company of actors and dancers who traveled about putting on shows for people who paid them very little when they were in a theater, and next to nothing when they were out of doors. He was also angry with himself for being angry, and that was the most difficult thing to forgive.

He started out that morning just as the darkness was beginning to pale into the pink and gray of the early dawn. It was chilly, and he thrust his hands deep into his pockets, which were as empty as his stomach. He crossed a great wooden bridge over the largest canal, where he came upon a painter with an easel set up at the very crest of the arched bridge. His paints were laid out in the half-light and an empty canvas was set up before him.

"What are you doing?" said Eli. "How can you see what you are painting in this light?" he asked rather bluntly.

"I don't always paint what I see," said the artist calmly. "Sometimes I paint what I feel. And your manner makes me feel like punching you in the nose."

"Well, go ahead—I'll knock you into the canal!" responded Eli.

The artist responded by mixing a great brushful of red paint from his palette and jabbing it in Eli's direction.

"Get out of here!" he said. "I have to make a painting to sell to the tourists by midmorning, and I come here when dawn breaks and there is no one here to bother me, and what do I find? A simpleton seaman who barges in where he has no business and tells me I don't know what I am doing!" The artist sputtered angrily. "How would you know, you stupid sailor? Besides, you are a foreigner; I can tell from your accent. You don't belong here at all. Go away!"

The artist began to hold his paintbrush like a fencer's sword, making thrusts like a fencer in Eli's direction.

Just then two young men came up from the opposite side of the bridge and watched the argument develop.

"Go to it!" said the first one.

"No, get them apart! They might do some damage," said the other.

"Foreigner?" said Eli. "I'll show you who knows how to speak properly!" He reached out to grasp the wrist of the artist who was now trembling with rage.

The two newcomers seized Eli and pulled him away, across the bridge toward the farther side.

"Don't be such a fool!" said the first stranger. "He has every right to be on the bridge; he paints there almost every morning. He could call the guard to have you arrested for molesting him."

"And he is known to have a hot temper. They say he almost killed an art dealer whom he accused of cheating him."

"Go along, young sailor," said the first of the peacemakers. "Go along and stay out of trouble."

Eli stumbled away from the bridge and went in the direction the strangers had pushed him. He was still fuming; in fact, he was nearly shaking with rage, but he knew that they were right, and that it was his remark that had started the whole incident. He was ashamed of having lost his temper rather than having patched up the misunderstanding, but he remained angry nevertheless.

An hour later he was sitting by the waterside feeling sorry for himself. He was hungry, he didn't have any money to buy a roll or a slice of cheese, and he was still annoyed with Marna. He was too proud to go back and ask her for his wallet, which contained the fourteen scudi they had left from the payment they had received from Ben the Maker. He paced the waterfront for another hour before retracing his steps toward the wooden bridge. As he approached it he noticed a group of fifty or more people had assembled in the little square nearby. He also saw the tall, shiny gold and crimson helmets of the Berrymor Watchmen in the middle of the crowd.

"There he is! That's him!" someone shouted, pointing at Eli. "He's the sailor who was fighting with the artist!"

One of the burly members of the Watch came toward Eli. "Were you here this morning?" he asked.

"Certainly," said Eli. "I came across this bridge a couple of hours ago. Why? What's the matter?"

"The matter is," said the Watchman in a solemn tone, "that an artist has jumped—or was pushed—into the canal and has drowned, leaving his half-begun painting and easel at the crest of the bridge."

"He must be the one," said a member of the crowd. "We heard them shouting at each other just after dawn!"

"Let me see your identification papers," said the other Watchman.

"But I don't have any," said Eli. "Nor any money either. I gave my wallet to my girl last night, and I haven't been able to get it back yet," and he held out his arms to both sides with his empty hands spread to show that he had nothing to hide.

But the Watchman grasped his left wrist and examined Eli's sleeve.

"Alizarin Crimson!" he said. "The very color that was on the artist's brush that we found floating beside him in the canal. You, sir, are under arrest for suspicion of murder."

Eli tried to protest, but he was hustled along the quay to a waiting steam launch where he was handcuffed and thrust into the cabin, on his way to the judgment chamber of the Council of Seventeen.

THE ARTISANS OF THE COMEDY

There was a crowd of nearly a hundred at the south side of the Art Academy when Marna arrived there. They were clustered around a stone platform that extended from the wall of the building, which was itself draped with a crimson cloth backdrop. The little stage was ringed with flickering lanterns standing around its edges. The crowd was noisy with happy anticipation of the show and buzzing with the news of the day in Berrymor. A new art exhibition had been decreed by the members of the Academy; a stranger had been arrested for the foul murder of an artist; and the newest company of players was going to present the latest spectacle of the evening.

Pedrolino, dressed as a shepherd boy, was one of the first on stage. He complained that his shepherdess did not return his love and that he should drown himself in a secret woodland spring because his unrequited desire subjected him to such pain that the only release could be in love or death. A leering old man with a round belly, a bald head, and a projecting white beard joined him on the stage. His name was Myles Gloriosus, and he gave worldly advice to Pedrolino on the subject of women and girls. He boasted of being a former soldier who had traveled all over the world gaining a reputation for great bravery and skill in war. He told stories of conquests of men in battle and of women in their homes. Some of the things he said were wise, some funny, and some indecent. Marna alternately laughed with the crowd and blushed with the other young women in the audience at the things he said. Pedrolino sighed and nodded in agreement, his eyes wide with wonder, as he played the part of the innocent shepherd boy who believed all the tall tales the boasting old man told him.

The actors succeeded each other in a number of scenes, but the tale of the youth and the maiden got rather lost among the other performers who came and went on the stage. Besides a jolly and a sad clown (one with red nose, one with blue), there was a team of three dancing tumblers who wound their bodies into contortions that made them looked like a six-legged animal while they danced to the music of a single musician. This remarkable virtuoso had a small bass drum strapped to his back, one cymbal on his elbow, and another fastened to his hip. A cord to one ankle operated a lever that beat the drum and one to the other knee activated a second pair of cymbals on top of the drum. He also played a large mandolin which he held in his hands as though he had no other care in the world. Sometimes he also played a harmonica which was supported by little braces that stood up from his collar. Whenever he stopped blowing on this instrument for even an instant he would sing in what Marna thought was a remarkably melodious and pleasant tenor voice.

The musician's songs were also about love and war, and the audience seemed to know the tunes and words to most of them. Sometimes they would sing along with him, but when he sang an aria in which he pleaded for the love of a lady, they were quiet until the end of the last high cadence, and then they shouted their approval.

The shepherdess made several appearances in the play and held off the advances of the bragging old warrior. She sang a spirited aria in which she told the audience that she really loved her shepherd but feared to admit it because she didn't know what to do with a man in love. The audience shouted encouragement to her, and when Pedrolino came back on stage they danced a series of shy approaches and increasingly passionate exchanges until at last she seemed to leap through the air in ecstasy, rising from her toes in a continuous motion as Pedrolino lifted her, and her graceful legs formed a smooth arch from one side of the little stage to the other. At the end they collapsed smiling in each other's arms, the musician produced a final chord, and the audience broke out in cheers.

Marna could not leave without telling Pedrolino how much she had enjoyed the show, so she went to the little tent beside the stage that the performers used as a dressing room. Pedrolino stood with his back to the opening of the tent. From inside came the voice of the shepherdess in a strident and unfamiliar tone.

"And if you ever dig your fingers into my ribs like that again, I'll kill you when I come down on the stage. You are a beast! That would make a wonderful tragic end to the drama! Blood all over the stage and I could smile at the audience while you played your final scene on the floor! You contemptible thug! You seem to think you can do anything you want with me just because you can pick me up in those big hands of yours! Well I'm not going to take it any longer. I am going to have Myles get a new lead dancer for the company, one that won't abuse his partner, or I won't dance for him any longer!"

"You will not!" said Pedrolino. "You signed a contract with this company, and if you walk out on it you'll never get another job as a dancer or an actress here or in Lucro! Come to your senses, Clorinda. This is a job, and it's probably the best one you will ever have!"

With that he turned to walk away and came upon Marna standing in the darkness.

Even years later Marna could never quite recall what she and Pedrolino said to each other that night, either in the coffee shop they went to or while he walked with her to Carlo and Maria's home above the restaurant. He told her how he suffered from Clorinda's terrible temper and how she always demanded more and more money from Myles whenever there was an opportunity to renew her contract. Myles usually gave in because Clorinda was popular with the audiences.

Marna told Pedrolino about many of her adventures in coming across the Wastes of West in the balloon and the storm on the Black Lake. She told him about the musicians of Casa Sapienza and how she herself loved to dance for the sheer joy of it. She felt very sorry for him because he had to dance with a partner who didn't like him. By the time they went past the little Madonnina in the alleyway, its candle had burnt out because it was very late.

THE PROTECTION
OF THE LAW

The actions of the Council were swift and effective. Eli had no money to hire a lawyer and none was provided for him. He asked to have word sent to Ben the Maker to come and vouch for his character, but the Watchman of whom he made the request obviously put great faith in the accusation of the other members of the Watch, so Eli was not greatly surprised when he returned and said that the Maker was away, gone sailing on his new boat. Eli asked about the whereabouts of Occam the Barber, only to be told that he had gone west over a year ago and no one had seen him in a long time.

"But he's back in Berrymor; I know, because I brought him on the Maker's boat. Carlo and Maria at the restaurant know where he is."

"There are hundreds of Carlos in Berrymor," said the guard, "and thousands of Marias. And besides, the accused have no rights here. Our Watchmen make just accusations and the Council would only overrule their indictment in very unusual circumstances. You will just have to wait here until your case is decided. And it won't matter much anyway, since when you are judged to be guilty of murder, there is very little else to be done. We carry out our sentences within a week of the finding, and there is only one appeal allowed to the condemned. It only takes a day or two."

"What court hears the appeals?"

"Not a court," the guard went on, "a person. You may appeal to the Bishop of Berrymor for mercy. But he is a great believer in law and order and he seldom changes a sentence."

"Then what?" asked Eli.

"Then," said the guard with a smile, "you will be removed from the society that has found you to be unworthy."

"Unworthy of what?" asked Eli. "Removed to where?"

"To the bottom of the sea when wrapped in a hundred pounds of anchor chain," said the guard. "That way there is no mess to clean up, no whiners looking for some supposed martyr's blood-stained clothing, and no expense to the city to provide a coffin or a burial place. These islands on which our city is built are small and we cannot waste the taxpayers' money buying cemetery space for criminals. Why, one grave plot for an honest citizen can cost three or four scudi!"

The trial lasted only a few minutes. The men of the Watch stated that Eli had been in a loud argument with the artist and had said something about knocking him into the canal. Others had found the painter's body floating there shortly afterwards. The smear of crimson paint on Eli's sleeve seemed to clinch the matter.

The thirteen conferred among themselves for only a few moments and then announced that Eli was judged to be guilty as charged.

"But I appeal!" Eli cried out. "I wasn't there! I am innocent! I am much too young to die now. My life has hardly begun!"

"Perhaps it were better had you thought of that before you pushed the artist from the bridge," said the Speaker of the Council as he put a large black cloth mask over his head before pronouncing the sentence. His eyes glinted through the two eye slits as he read from a scroll that was spread out on the table before him.

"Eli, Son of Solomon of Salem on Spitte, I sentence you to be taken to the place from which you were brought this morning and there to remain incarcerated until your appeal has been heard or denied, and then within a span of no more than two days further, to be brought by boat to the sea and there cast away so that the law-abiding citizens of this city of Berrymor shall be rid of your wretched presence forevermore."

Eli was taken through several stone corridors downward through the palace of the Council. At one point he passed a series of little windows through which he could see the glint of the water in a canal. Eventually he was brought to a cell where he waited in cold and despair until the Bishop of Berrymor would find time to see him.

It was three days later when he was finally brought out of the cell and across several bridges to an elaborate palace, through a doorway orna-mented with flying angels holding golden trumpets to a long stairway, up which he was hurried by the two members of the Watch who had brought him from the cell.

The Bishop was a small man who wore a long red gown over a black cassock. He had white shoes, small gold-rimmed glasses, and a kindly, somewhat distracted expression. He sat behind a desk with ornate legs carved of thin curving mahogany. There were golden handles on the drawer pulls and a dark green leather insert it its top. The desk was set with a golden tray for pens and paper clips. There were statues with sorrowful expressions standing in the corners of the room. A secretary stood behind his right shoulder and stared at Eli with watery, pale blue eyes. The secretary was dressed all in black and there seemed to be no expression on his face; he observed, listened, and assented without showing any sign of judgment, condemnation, or sympathy. Eli stood directly in front of the desk on a carpet of abstract red, buff, and dark blue designs. The Bishop motioned for the guards to let go of Eli's shoulders and withdraw from the room.

"My son," he said, "now you may tell me the evil you have done and give me reasons, if any there be, for my considering any appeal from the judgment of the Council of Seventeen."

"I am innocent and too young to die," said Eli.

"I cannot dispute your youth," said the Bishop. "But your guilt has been demonstrated before the Council, the highest legislative, executive, and judicial body in this city."

"But I could not call any witnesses in my defense and I had no lawyer to advise or speak for me," said Eli.

"Lawyers are for those who can afford them. We decided long ago that giving every common criminal a lawyer merely confused the Council and made the swift administration of justice difficult. And you know that justice delayed is justice denied."

"But there was no witness who saw me push him!"

"Yes, I admit that your case would have been neater if someone had actually been there at the moment it happened. But the Watch tell us that you had harsh words with the artist a few moments before he fell into the canal. And then there is that matter of the crimson paint on his brush and your sleeve. It all seems very convincing to me.

"But, my dear boy," the Bishop went on, "there is something even more important at stake here. If I reverse any finding of the Council of Seventeen, I will also cause a diminishment of the respect with which the people regard their decrees. If I deny the validity of the accusation of the Watch, I will cause the officers to look foolish or careless in carrying out their duty. And if I long defer your execution, it will send a message to all the evildoers of this city that their crimes may likely go unpunished and thus be encouraged to commit further acts of depredation. No, Eli, if I even let it be thought that you might be innocent, I would do great damage to the very fabric of our society here in Berrymor."

The Bishop paused for a moment. "Remember that sometimes an innocent must be sacrificed so as not to encourage the rest of the guilty. Even if we punish twenty of the innocent, that would be a small price to pay for our city to be sure that no one could ever say that we let a single guilty one go free. There used to be another Bishop of Berrymor who granted mercy to some of the guilty, but he was thought to be encouraging criminals and, in spite of his great scholarship and distinguished family lineage, he was sent away.

"You see, a society is held together by its laws and its legends. Here it is legendary that all the guilty are punished. Your death will increase the strength and validity of that legend and help to make Berrymor a better place for all its citizens."

"But do you really believe that I am a murderer?" asked Eli.

"I wonder a bit at how you could be," said the Bishop. "More because of your manner and your youth than for any other reasons. The members of the Watch were convincing. But all of that matters very little now, since your execution is by this time a matter of the support of public morality by the Council and by me, the Bishop."

"But cannot I appeal for clemency—for mercy?" said Eli.

"That is what the old Bishop would have done, but it merely made the whole system look irresolute and passive, unsure in its execution of the law. So he was sent away to pray for the miserable and the condemned in another country. No, Eli, I must at the very least make sure that all the people believe that the sentence has been carried out."

At this the Bishop paused and crooking his knuckle under his lower lip, he looked thoughtfully at Eli.

"Of course, it is always possible that there is a somewhat better solution from your point of view. You are a sailor, are you not?"

"I am, sir," answered Eli.

"And a swimmer, too?" asked the Bishop.

"A strong swimmer, sir, but not if wrapped in a hundred kilograms of anchor chain!"

"Well, perhaps you will be able to think of something that will help you out of it. I am unable to prevent the swift execution of your sentence. And if by any remote chance you survive being drowned in the depth of the Northern Sea, you will be wise to never set foot in Berrymor again, in this or another life, or you will be executed—or re-executed—very swiftly."

And with that he turned and pulled upon a brocaded cord that hung from the ceiling behind him. There was a distant tolling of a bell and the clerical secretary with the watery blue eyes returned.

"Monsignor," said the Bishop. "Have the guards of the Watch take him away now, but see to it that he is allowed the comfort of a confessor before the sentence is carried out. Eli, fare well and may God grant mercy to you."

And then the tall doors of the study opened. The Watchmen entered, took Eli by each shoulder, and marched him swiftly back to his cell to await the boat of the executioners.

BAD NEWS

Eli's disappearance annoyed Marna more than it worried her at first. She was still angry over his jealousy of Pedrolino. Only later did she grow anxious when he did not appear at the restaurant for breakfast for the second day in a row. Carlo was not able to offer much help. No one reported having seen the young sailor from the West. Maria plied her with buns and blueberry jam and said that she felt nothing could have happened to Eli. Berrymor was a decent and law-abiding town; there was almost no crime in the streets, since any robber or even pickpocket was dealt with very quickly by the honest and effective officers of the Watch.

Marna remembered the recent adventures in Verity when Eli and Occam had been enbibliated and wondered if something similar might have happened here. On the third day she set out to find Occam to see if he could help her find Eli. She walked swiftly along the stone-lined waterfront in the direction of the barbershop, and noticed that *Polaris* was gone from her dock. Ben the Maker was obviously off for a cruise on his new vessel.

She crossed several canals while she searched the facades of the houses for the red-and-blue spirals of a barber pole. Marna knew that the red-and-blue bands were symbols of veins and arteries, because barbers were the forerunners of surgeons, who disect and repair wounded human bodies. The symbol lingered on in the decorated poles, some standing in front of shops, some turning slowly beside the grand doorways of great houses. There was even one at the entry of the hospital, for this town kept to its traditions for a very long time.

At the first two sets of multicolored poles Marna found herself facing a woman at a desk who made appointments for those seeking a meeting with a brain surgeon and a doctor who altered the features of his clients to make them appear younger. Neither knew anything of Occam.

But after several more inquiries she came upon a barbershop presided over by a merry-faced, rotund, and bright-eyed man who was whipping up a huge pile of creamy white lather on the face of one of his clients. While creating the lather, he alternately hummed and sang short snatches from operatic arias and serenades from long.ago. There were three high swivel chairs in the shop and in one of them reclined a man whose face was entirely covered with a steaming damp towel.

"Sir," said Marna, slightly self-conscious at having entered such an obviously male arena, "I am looking for a barber named Occam. Is he associated with this establishment?"

"Associated?" said the tuneful proprietor. "He is in every sense a part of it. Occam is my new partner! He is a very fine fellow, a barber of *qualità*, and now in the very act of shaving one of our most distinguished clients, Pico the Philosophical Combiner."

There was a murmur from beneath the towels, but at that moment Occam himself emerged from the curtained door behind the chairs, bearing a bowl of lather and a brush in his hands.

"Marna!" he exclaimed. "What a pleasure to see you. All goes well with you and Eli?"

"Oh, Occam," she said, "I am so worried about him! He has disappeared after a stupid argument we had about a boy I met at a party. He went off the next morning and I haven't seen him for more than three days. Do you think he could be staying away because he was angry with me for having talked to another boy?"

Occam put down the bowl of lather and looked very grave.

"The simplest answer is usually the right one," he said. "I think he is being prevented from coming back to Carlo and Maria's by someone who has him locked up. Now who, Marna, would want to lock him up? Do you suppose he is being kept in a library again?"

"Eh, Occam!" said the first barber. "Is he the young sailor who is being executed for murder this afternoon? The one who pushed the artist off the bridge?"

"I never thought of that," said Occam. "I heard that the Council had condemned a young sailor, but I never thought it could be Eli. This is terrible! They carry out sentences so very quickly in this country. When did they say he was to be executed?"

"Executed!" gasped Marna.

"This afternoon," said the other barber.

"But why?" she asked.

"It keeps the town safe," replied the other barber in a matter-of-fact tone of voice.

"But we must save him!" said Marna. "Occam! You have to help me!"

"I will go with you," said Occam, putting down the brush. "But I don't know if anyone can save a condemned criminal in this town unless the Bishop grants him clemency on appeal. The last bishop used to grant a lot of pardons, but the men of business who wanted sure protection for their affairs had him sent away to a monastery. The say the new bishop has only granted two appeals in the last seven years, and both were for young women, virgins who killed men while trying to defend their own honor."

At this point the man in Occam's barber chair sat up and unwound the hot towel from his face.

"Don't worry too much, Marna," said Pico. "Remember that there are always plenty of good fish in the sea. If you lose Eli, you can always belong to some other man, as a good girl should. I think Ascanio would offer you protection."

"You beast!" she said, and turned to go.

"That was uncalled for, Pico," said Occam, wiping the lather from his hands and preparing to follow Marna.

"Just trying to reconcile a pair of difficult alternatives," said Pico. "I'm certain the young lady has a great number of other possibilities if she loses her sailor."

Later, despite their questioning of many people, Marna and Occam were unable to get within speaking distance of Eli. Almost the only ones interested in talking to Marna were a pair of writers who said they were preparing a story for the afternoon edition of a handbill and gazette that they sold in the marketplace. They wanted to know "how it makes you feel to know that your boyfriend is to be drowned by the Watchmen" later in the day. Marna could not answer at all, and she and Occam became part of a crowd that came to the waterfront to witness the Watch taking the criminal out to sea in a steam-powered launch that was equipped with a black hood over the forward part of the cockpit.

From the edge of the crowd they saw Eli hustled from the prison across the stone quay and thrust on board. Around his neck he wore a number of turns of black chain that surrounded his body, held in place by large iron shackles. The crowd made hoots and catcalls and derided the condemned man with expressions of satisfaction that he would now know that crime did not pay. In a matter of minutes the launch was under way, heading north from the city toward the open sea.

34 OF LIFE AND THE AFTERLIFE

A s the Watch boat left the dock and traveled under its silent steam power to the north, the members of the Watch discussed their day's work.

"The secretary of the Bishop said he should be allowed a confession," said the boatswain to the coxswain in the forward cockpit of the launch. He produced a thin purple stole from his pocket which he hung on a hook on the bulkhead next to the chained prisoner.

"He may want to be shriven before he meets his maker," he said to the other, "but he hasn't asked to see a priest."

But a few moments later as the launch was passing the mainland of the Northeast Moors, they overtook a smaller boat, a Whitehall pulling boat that contained two oarsmen and a passenger in the stern sheets. The passenger, who seemed to be an elderly man, was wrapped in a brown seaman's cloak, but below its lower edge was observable a black cassock with purple buttons and rosy piping around its hem. On his face he wore a mask like the ones the partygoers had worn for New Year's Eve. The face of the mask was that of Puncinello, with the protruding chin and the long hooked nose.

"Watch boat ahoy!" called the cloaked figure. "Do you carry a prisoner to his execution?"

"That we do, Father, and we intend to accomplish it with merciful swiftness so that he may not be in dread of death for long."

"Heave to and take me aboard!" called the priest. "I would hear his last confession of his sins."

The clerical passenger in the Whitehall spoke with authority, although with the high-pitched voice of a very old man. The crew of the Watch launch obeyed his instructions, and after taking the priest aboard, took the smaller boat in tow and resumed their course, although at a slower pace.

"Would you tell me of your sins, lad?" the priest muttered to Eli, "for this may be the last day of your life. Tell me what you can, and I may have something important to tell you about salvation."

"I don't want to tell you anything about me," said Eli. "My sins are none of your business, and the only salvation I am interested in is from the laws of this terrible country!"

"Your sins may not be my business, only God's," said the priest, putting one hand on Eli's forehead and the other on his shoulder, "but salvation is in many things. For example, the cotter pin from the clevis that shackles those chains about your body. If you twist and pull, it will come out. I don't know how much good that counsel of salvation will do for one so stubborn as you, but the Bishop thought you should be given the opportunity."

And with that he made the sign of the cross in the air and muttered a number of words that Eli did not understand, although Eli thought he heard something like *buona fortuna* toward the end of the formula. The priest then stood erect and the Watch crew could see the colored piping on the lower hem of the cassock. He pointed to the port side of the boat.

"Take him some way to the west," he called to the helmsman. "Be far away from the city before you send him to his reward, so that no memory of him ever comes back to Berrymor."

The coxswain said something inaudible, as though he recognized the clergyman. Then dropping to one knee, he took the masked man's hand and kissed the large purple stone in the ring on his finger.

"Grant me your blessing, my lord!" said the coxswain.

The elderly cleric said something as he put his hand on the coxswain's bowed head and then slipped swiftly over the side and down the short boarding ladder to his crew in the Whitehall. In a moment they were cast off and rowing swiftly toward the Bay of Birds.

The launch was swift, and it was not long before the headlands of the Northeast Moors and the spires of Berrymor had sunk almost to the horizon and only a featureless blue coast stretched to their south. Far ahead the rugged silhouette of the Cliffs of Care rose above the distant land.

"This will do. It's time to terminate him," said the First Officer of the Watch. "Bring 'er about and head to the east. When he goes over the stern, there will be no danger of running him down, and his end will be in the hands of God and not counted on our heads."

The boat swung about and the other two Watchmen were instantly upon Eli, seizing him from either side and dragging him to the stern.

"Good-bye and good riddance," said the boatswain. But the coxswain muttered, "Farewell, and may God be with you!"

And with a heave and a thrust he was pushed over the stern and into the gray green sea.

35 DESPAIR AND RESOLUTION

When the black boat of the Watch had borne its prisoner away from the quay, Marna's breath went out of her. She turned instinctively to Occam and buried her face in his shoulder. The sight of Eli's pale face, accented by the yards of chain wound round his black sweater, seemed too ghastly for her to look at. But almost instantly she knew that there was no comfort to be found in the shelter of this good man's shoulder, nor in the strength of any other person excepting only herself.

"I am so terribly sorry," said Occam. "I don't know what we could have done. These people are not like the quibbling philosophers of Verity. They are true believers in what their leaders tell them about the cause and cure of all troubles. Then they act quickly on principle according to what they think is right. And they never look back."

"Sorry?" said Marna, wiping her eyes with the back of her wrist. "For Eli, surely, but spare me any man's sorrow. My father left me, my grandfather is old and far away. I found a boy of strength and honesty, but he has been taken quickly away. I will not put my trust in any man forever. But I must leave this dreadful place and find some other country where I can be free of such laws and customs as I have found in Berrymor or Verity. Here skill and honesty are not enough. Chance plays too great a part."

And at that moment, she felt she had satisfied the first two parts of Donna Elizabetta's riddle—*What leader needs no follower,* and *what follower needs no leader*—and had taken hold of her own destiny. She would lead her own life no matter who might or might not follow, and she would follow no one. She turned to shake Occam solemnly by the hand, saying good-bye, and letting him know that she was planning to depart.

Occam looked at her with sympathetic eyes.

"You think you are taking the simplest route, Marna. But life is always complex, and things sometimes get tangled in knots. Someday you may have to cut through the confusion and tangle of experience and ideas to find the simplest and truest route for you. Remember me then, and take this as a memento to help you cut through the tangles and find the truth."

And he took from his pocket and held out to her his second-best barber's straight razor with a dark red handle into which the blade was folded. Although she already had a perfectly good knife that she had carried since she was a little girl on the bank of the Spitte, the gift was obviously heartfelt, and she accepted it with grace before bidding Occam a final good-bye.

While walking dejectedly back to her lodging and crossing the second bridge, she noticed that someone was beside her. It was Pedrolino.

"I heard what you said to that barber," he began. "And you may well not wish to put your trust in any man now. But if you can trust to a bond, a secure contract, perhaps there is a way in which you can get away from this city and still take care of yourself."

Marna was silent, but looked up at Pedrolino with raised eyebrows, questioning him to go on.

"Myles and Clorinda have had their last argument," he continued. "She says that she is going to marry a poet, or an artist, I cannot remember which. But she will dance no more for our company, and we need a replacement. Myles could offer you a contract, a legally sealed agreement, providing you with a salary as a member of the troupe. We leave for Lucro in the South tomorrow."

Since Marna still made no comment, the young dancer continued talking without looking directly at her as they walked along the waterside.

"Look," he said, "it's a good job. The hours are short, and Lucro is an exciting and wonderful place. The city shines with steel and polished stone. There are huge buildings with walls of glass and towers of colored tile. The theaters are indoors and have hundreds of cushioned seats. People buy places for performances many weeks in advance and sometimes, if the show is a popular one, they resell their places for many times more than they had paid for them. And dancers and actresses become so famous that they are cheered in the streets when they drive about the city in private carriages that roll along by the force of electricity.

"These vehicles are fitted out inside with soft couches and little tables of inlaid wood with recesses in them for crystal goblets and chilled bottles of the finest wines. They are long and sleek and finished in amazing colors, dark greens, deep purples, and black." Pedrolino smiled at her. "The carriages even have names like 'Lion,' 'Cheetah,' and 'Leopard.' So even when the actors draw the curtains of the long windows, the people of Lucro who are knowledgeable can tell which performers are inside each carriage, and they stand by the side of the street and cheer as their heroes and heroines ride past."

Marna listened quietly.

"In fact," Pedrolino said, "finding famous people and looking at them is what the ordinary people do whenever they can in Lucro. If they are not well known themselves, they reason that at least they can know someone else who is. And so they need famous people and must find more of them all the time. There are people in Lucro who have a business of making people famous so that other people can look at them and know that they are becoming more worthwhile because they have looked on the famous ones. And they pay dancers well while they are becoming famous.

"Look, Marna," he concluded, "I'm sorry about Eli. But you have to make a life now without him."

"Sorry for Eli, yes," she said. "He was beautiful and so young. But do not be sorry for me. I will care for myself. I will be going away."

"And so are we," said the dancer. "We leave for Lucro in the morning. Will you come with us?"

"Could Myles write me a contract that guarantees my pay, my roles, and my living conditions?" she asked. "Would he bind himself legally so that I cannot be left without help again?"

"I am almost sure he will, now that Clorinda has left the company. She met a red-bearded sculptor who wanted her to be his model and she took the opportunity to get away from me and Myles and the others. I think she felt that Myles would beg her to come back, but he wants us to move on to Lucro, and I know he would give you an audition for her place."

Marna nodded her agreement, and the two walked to the courtyard of an inn behind one of the less-frequented canals. Marna danced a solo to the music of the mandolin player while Myles scowled and muttered. Then he told Pedrolino to lift her as she leapt in to the air.

"You must make her float to the ground. Like a spirit, not a real person at all! Marna, go up on the fourth beat; he will be behind you."

Marna took three dancing steps across the courtyard and flung herself upward. Amazingly she continued to rise and float forward as Pedrolino's strong hands closed around her ribs and she found herself moving without having to control her own position. She soon came to earth again and instinctively continued dancing to the rhythm of the mandolin.

"Brava!" cried Myles. "You can do it, and you will!"

OUT OF THE DEPTHS

The pin in the shackle came out and set Eli free as he rolled over and over in the water. The chain unwound and slipped away beneath him. But his lungs were bursting with the need to take that first fatal gulp. Disoriented, he twisted and turned in his attempts to find the way up, kicking and flailing with his hands in a desperate attempt to reach the light But even as his head came to the surface of the water, he had enough restraint to allow only his face to break the surface and inhale a huge sweet draft of life-giving air.

He kept treading water, trying to keep his head low between the small choppy waves for several minutes before he shook the water from his eyes and raised his head to look around. The launch was already far off to the east, putting up a steady column of coal smoke as it returned to Berrymor. To the south and west he could barely discern the ragged blue silhouette of the shore that stretched from the mouths of the Mohr to the Cliffs of Care. Both seemed far away, but surprisingly, the water did not feel as cold as he expected the winter sea to be. Knowing where he was, Eli realized that the cause of the warm current he felt must be Lower Mohr, the combination of the three rivers that bore to the ocean the water of all the lands of the south. He tasted the water and found that it was hardly salt at all, even here, several miles out at sea.

Eli was a strong swimmer as he had told the Bishop, but he knew he could never swim so far without being overcome by exhaustion. He unbuckled his belt and struggled out of his trousers. His feet were already bare because he had kicked off his boots while he was underwater.

Dragging the wet black trousers to the surface, he tied an overhand knot in the end of each leg. Then, kicking mightily to raise himself in the water, he swung them over his head for an instant and trapped a leg full of air in each. By holding the pants upside down in the water, he produced a pair of inflated fabric balloons which he soon managed to position under his arms so that they stayed just under the surface behind his back. The buoyancy of the water wings was not great, but it was enough to keep Eli's chin just above water without his actually swimming.

His progress toward the distant shore was discouragingly slow as he kicked and paddled along, and his course seemed to keep drifting to the west, away from the Northeast Moors. The distance to land was greater in this direction, and Eli soon began to tire as he attempted to fight the current.

Then he remembered what Sennet had told him at a time that now seemed very long ago. It was the advice that brought him through the whirlpool at the Branching of Spitte. "Go with the grain when things are confused ..." Things seemed perfectly clear to Eli now: He must reach the shore soon if he was to survive, but he decided to swim more to the southwest even so. Soon the water became colder, but the cliffs began to rise higher above his head and he knew that he was approaching land.

As he neared the shore he realized that the towering bulk of the Cliffs of Care met the sea in an area of crashing waves which burst with explosions of white foam all along their base for as far as he could see in either direction. Even as the current that had brought him toward land continued to carry him shoreward, he could discern no scrap of beach or low point of land where he could safely leave the sea. Already the rise and fall of the deep sea swell was moving him toward the furious juncture of wave and rock at the base of the huge escarpment. The western sun disappeared behind the crest of the cliffs, hundreds of meters above his head. Wildly his foam-clouded eyes searched everywhere for something to grasp, some way out of the terrible surge of the waves before he was lifted and flung against the rocky wall in front of him.

And then he saw a strange thing. Just at the point where the breakers crested, tossed from side to side by the great waves, was a large wicker basket suspended by a slender rope that disappeared far above, beyond his sight. The water surged through the basket, carrying it toward the shore, but the tether drew it back as the wave receded and the water drained away, leaving the basket more or less afloat on the surface after each wave had gone.

Eli let go of his makeshift flotation device and took a dozen quick strokes toward the cliff face. A great green wave mounted up behind him and began to lift him toward the rocks. The basket, filling with the inpouring water, seemed to be making a wake and surging toward him. It looked scarcely strong enough to withstand the weight of the water, much less of Eli's body, but he reached out and grasped its rim as the waves pressed him past it. He held on until the backwash of the wave took the strain from his tiring muscles and then, with a desperate heave, he dragged himself over the braided rim into the basket.

Almost immediately he felt the basket lurch and rise. The water poured out of the basket like an emptying sieve and Eli found himself above the tumult of the sea at the base of the cliffs. He rose higher with each passing moment until, as the basket rotated slowly on its hoist, he could soon see the entire coastline stretching out in front of him: the Bay of Birds where he had come on *Polaris*, the faint line of the canal leading to Berrymor itself, and the green dome of Round Head standing to the south of the Northeast Moors. From his study of charts and plotting of positions, he knew exactly where he was, but as he rose beside the ruddy stone face of the cliff, he had no idea of where he was going.

THE WAY TO LUCRO

Marna's contract proved to have many clauses which covered everything from the number of performances in which Marna would be expected to dance (not more often than twice in a day, separated by at least an hour's rest); how much she would be paid (two and a half scudi for each performance); where she would sleep (in the caravan with two other women of the company if they were on the road, in the same inn as the others if they were in a city); to the duration of her obligation to dance for Myles (one year, with a right to cancel the agreement upon ninety days' notice on the part of either party); and, finally, that Myles should provide her with costumes for each part she was to play, all of which were to remain the property of the company.

There were other details, but these seemed to be the main ones, although there were more escape clauses for the company (in the case of there being no audience to pay them) than there were for the actors and dancers. Myles also insisted that "Marna" was not a proper name for an actress or a dancer, and insisted on the right to list her name as "Columbina" or "Clorinda" on posters or handbills that announced the performances. Marna didn't much like the idea of using a secondhand name like Clorinda, so she insisted on Columbina. But she had to accept the secondhand costumes, which were pretty if somewhat worn, and were, after all, the only things available. A few of them had huge billowing skirts with many petticoats, but most were thin filmy things cut to show off a dancer's legs. Myles's wife Antoinette set about altering them to fit Marna's small figure as soon as the ink was dry on the contract.

The next day, the group set off toward the South in three mule-drawn caravans. Marna bid a fond but unsentimental good-bye to Occam, Carlo, and Maria. She ignored the older woman's occasionally tearful advice on how to keep safe in the South, especially in the city of Lucro. She packed her few things in a sturdy canvas bag, including her recorder, her multi-bladed clasp knife with the red handle, and her razor from Occam. Since she was now an actress rather than a sailor, she wore a fashionable short dress that she had purchased with most of the money Myles had given her as an advance on signing the contract. She still had the fou teen scudi left in Eli's wallet, held in reserve. The dress was a rich brown with black lace trimming around the open neckline and the short sleeves. Underneath she wore off-white tights and dancing slippers, since she would ride in the first caravan with Antoinette instead of walking with Pedrolino, Myles, and the other men. And as had become her custom, she wore the green stone around her neck.

The pace of the mules was leisurely, but the weather of the newly turned year was pleasant, neither hot nor cold, and the sunshine was warm on their faces as they progressed to the South.

It was several days before they crossed the Blue Green Mohr, the river that drained the Blue Swamp to the east and carried its waters to join the Yellow Brown Mohr before the stream became the confused net of waterways known as the Flume. This was an almost-jungle wetland that cleaned all the water that flowed into it and emerged to join the Lesser Mohr, down which Marna (now Columbina) had come not many months before to enter the strange land of Berrymor. With her back turned to that water-laced city, she felt no desire to look back again. She reflected that there was kindness and beauty to be found there, but much more it seemed the abode of the heartless sacrifice of the individual to satisfy the desires of the many. Although the city's thinkers were a playful and inquiring lot, its government seemed to care nothing for the wrongs that are done in the name of having an orderly and prosperous city. It could have been the most beautiful community imaginable but for this deep and essential flaw in an attitude of mind that made most of its citizens think of the plight of others as being detached from their own destiny.

Eventually they came to a bridge over the Blue Green Mohr which was supported by three semicircular arches of carefully fitted stone. The keystones of the arches were decorated with sculpture in relief, but the stones were so worn with time that it was impossible to discern what the sculptures had originally represented. Myles said that the bridge had been built by a people who traveled here long ago but came this way no longer. There were ruins of this long-gone civilization wherever they went throughout the steppe land of the Sorrell Plain. It was a gently rolling country of grasses and dusty roads. To the west they could see the distant hills of the high White Land where, Myles told Marna, it was even drier. Once they camped in a little village near a very large and imposing ruin of stone arches and columns that formed the greater part of a huge oval. Inside was a jumble of ruined walls that partitioned off underground chambers. Partially intact ranks of steps all around showed where people had once gathered on graded seats to watch some sort of exhibition.

"It was built," said Myles, "by a powerful and clever people who had a market town here, where three of their great roads came together from the desert, the sea, and the mountains. They traded and created great wealth, and people came by the thousands to see their dances and their combats, their races and the games they played from the backs of animals with balls that they knocked about with long mallets. Their young men strove mightily to excel at these games and their young women gave their favors and their love to those who were the most frequent winners in their contests."

"But what became of them?" asked Marna, looking up at the delicate carving of the elaborate capitals of the columns and arches still standing along one side of the arena.

"I do not know, exactly," answered Myles. "Although they were a strong and orderly people, it seems they did not always love the order in which their affairs were regulated. Some say that the people from the sea felt that those of the desert were not honest.

"The desert people felt that the people from the mountains were too lenient toward the criminals they apprehended, and thus encouraged crime. The mountain folk felt that those by the sea were a degenerate lot who lived only for pleasure and had no real character or morals. Others have said that some of those people had a different-colored skin than others, and this made for disagreements between them. But I do not know which group had what color of skin, or even what colors their skins were," said Myles.

"All we know now is that they quarrelled with one another," he continued, "and soon the games in the great arena became blood sports in which factions from various parts of the country came to settle their differences. Occasionally someone would be killed and the crowds in the arena were horrified. But later they came to see if the show of one week would be as great a spectacle of blood and killing as the last. Soon, a set of games in which there was no death was considered a dull affair, and the managers of the arena began to contract for criminals who were condemned to die anyway and set them upon each other in the final performance of the day's exhibitions. Once all the men and boys of an entire village were killed when their argument with a neighboring village brought them here to have it out between them."

"And what was the cause of that argument?" asked Marna in amazement.

"It was a long time ago," said Myles, "and I do not really know. But I have heard it said that it was about the way they worshipped God. Some used one language in their translations of the old texts, the others a different language. They also had some disagreement about the nature of God's love and whence it came. They could not bridge these differences, so they separated themselves in different villages. In time the villagers knew only that they were not like the people who lived in the next town. They referred to each other as animals or vermin and taught their children to avoid and even to hate the occupants of the other town. Then there was a fight between some of the young men and several were killed. This led to a challenge, and the managers of the arena persuaded them to settle the affair before an audience of thousands who paid millions of scudi to see the battle. It was fairly even at first, but after a while, one side seemed to have an advantage and soon outnumbered the others. After that it went quickly, and soon all of the weaker side were dead. It is said that the victors were so exultant that they demanded a large portion of the money paid to the managers of the arena. This resulted in more fighting, and soon many feared to come back to the arena for fear of the danger of brigands and robbers who frequented the place."

Marna looked horrified at Myles's tale.

"Eventually, for some reason that is not clear, the trade routes fell into disuse and people no longer came along the three great roads. Later this place became a stronghold of desert robbers who used the arena as a fort. Then there was more war, I cannot remember whose, and the people of Lucro came and tore down half of the arena so it could not be used as a fort anymore. Now only a few passing nomads come here, and travelers such as we, and the wild animals of the dry land, the lion, the lizard, and the horned toad." Myles concluded his story as they stopped to make camp.

That night, trying to sleep in the cramped upper bunk of the caravan, Marna could see stars through the little hatch in the roof over her head. The stars made her think of Eli. He had taught her a few—the Corona Borealis with Alphecca as its jewel, and Arcturus at the termination of the arch from the great summer triangle. Although she knew that he was as far away as the ancient people who built the arena, she could not feel that he was as absent in the void of time as the wretched people who had perished there. Suddenly she knew that she wanted to see Eli again even more than she had ever wanted to find her mother and father, before Eli had brought her mother's little green amulet.

The stars were very bright in the clear dark sky of the arid country. She decided that stars would always make her think of Eli, who knew so many of them by name. *Was he truly gone?* Would she see him again, somewhere beyond the stars?

THE COMMUNITY OF THEODORIC YORB

S winging back and forth on the end of a tether several hundred meters long, Eli rose slowly in the basket, drawn upward by unseen hands or some hidden engine near the top of the Cliffs of Care. Looking down at the fury of crashing water below, he was made dizzy by the sight. Crouching in the basket, naked except for his sweater, he shivered as he hugged his knees and waited for the ascent to be complete.

After what seemed a very long time, Eli noticed that he was rising past what appeared to be large caves in the face of the cliff. There were iron railings across some of these openings, and from one, he saw a pair of hooded figures reaching out with a long hooked pole, attempting to catch the rope that was fastened to his basket. As his upward progress slowed, they caught the edge of the basket itself and pulled it toward them.

"Come," said one of the men as he fastened the basket to the railing, "take my hand. Step over quickly and you will be safe."

Eli did as he was told and a breathtaking instant later, found himself in a long gallery that ran inside the face of the cliff. For as far as Eli could see, the high-ceilinged space curved away around the edge of the cliff, where it had been carved out of the rock itself. The corridor was lit by tall openings which were protected by the railings from the two-hundred-meter drop to the sea. In places the ceilings were reinforced with ribbed vaults made of carved stone. In between the ribs the stone was painted blue and green and decorated with gilded stars and cornices of red-and-black-checkered designs.

"Thank you," said Eli, suddenly aware that he was nearly naked and that the smooth stone floor was cold under his feet.

"Brother Henry," said the first robed man, "get the lad a postulant's robe. He is cold."

Brother Henry bowed to the first man and disappeared through a stout oak door into the interior of the rock.

"What is your name, lad?" asked the man. "Have you come to renounce sin and live a life of contemplation?"

"I am Eli, the least of the sons of Solomon of Salem on Spitte," he said. "I have not come here for any purpose except to be saved from drowning, to which I was condemned most unjustly. Who are you? Do you frequently save people from the sea?"

"All who come here have chosen to leave all goods and human affections behind and dedicate themselves to the worship of God, to contemplation, to rejection of sin, to obedience, silence, and prayer. I am Father Theodoric, named for the founder of this monastery. I am also the Master of Novices here. When one casts himself into the sea in a total rejection of the things of the flesh, I try to save a few who are willing to join the company of religious men who live here above the cares of the material world."

At this point Brother Henry reappeared with a long white cotton shirt folded over his arm. Quickly Eli was stripped the rest of the way and the white garment slipped over his head. Then a rough black wool habit was produced and was pulled over his head and shoulders. Brother Henry also provided him with a pair of thick rubber and leather sandals which fit his feet quite well. A white woolen cincture was wound around his waist and the hood of the habit pulled up to cover the back of his head. Eli was surprised to discover how warm and comfortable the unfamiliar garments were. He tugged the woolen cord tight around his waist. It felt secure in the place where the anchor chain had recently unwound itself.

"Well," said Eli, "I am very grateful for your pulling me up and pulling me in, but I haven't yet quite decided what I intend to do with the rest of my life ... and, without any disrespect to you or your founder, I don't know anything at all about you."

"Ah, quite so," said Father Theodoric. "You say you didn't throw yourself into the sea, but that you were condemned? I guess that makes a difference. We will keep you here, since you have no right to the outside world. I think you should see the Prior, or perhaps the Abbot?"

"I recently was taken to see a Bishop," said Eli. "And although at first he didn't seem very helpful, he did secretly provide me with the opportunity to find my way out of the depth of the sea and into your most helpful basket."

"Prelates are often helpful in secret, even while they are being most intransigent in public," said Father Theodoric. "People who write tracts, books, and broadsides try to make much out of what they say in public, so they are almost always careful. The real meaning of their pronouncements is often found in small subordinate clauses or adjectival modifiers. I think it is because they do not want to upset the expectations of true believers who have lived by the old laws for a very long time. Come, we will seek out the Abbot. But say nothing against bishops here, for our founder went away from here to become a bishop and he was a good and holy man."

Motioning Eli to follow him, the monk set off down the long gallery. They passed many openings looking over the sea on their right and several large rooms on their left where stone stairways led upward through the rock. The third of these they entered, and climbing a flight of many steep steps, they eventually came into a high room lit by tall, pointed windows. At desks all around were men clad in black robes who were studying very large books that were open on tilted book rests in front of them. Some were writing. A few were reading two books at the same time while simultaneously writing in a third. These wore black caps with golden tassels hanging from their crests.

At a high desk in the farthest corner of the room sat a white-haired man who wore a large golden cross suspended from a green silk rope that encircled his collar. Father Theodoric bowed before speaking to him.

"Father Abbot," he said, "may I present Eli. We brought him up from the sea, although he says he was not trying to end his life, but merely hoping to escape a sentence of death by drowning. He is not sure what he should do with the rest of his life. He does not know if he is here to become one of us and renounce all sin, or if he is among us just momentarily while he escapes from his sentence."

"Ah!" said the Abbot. "If only we all could escape from the sentence we merit due to our sinfulness, we could all be happy indeed. But Eli, were you sentenced to die or merely to be cast into the sea?"

"I think the latter," said Eli. "And I have had so many wonderful adventures since I was first blown up the River Spitte that I feel there must be some purpose guiding my path. Perhaps I was meant to come here to what surely seems to be a holy place. But how am I to know that I should join your order?"

"The sense of being guided or of being preserved for some future purpose is a good sign," said the Abbot. "I would say that you have been chosen to be a member of this community. God most obviously has called you to be here. It is a vocation hard to reject, a calling from God, a powerful voice telling you that you should renounce the world and devote yourself to penitence and prayer. But, before we get on to that, what were these adventures that you have had?"

"Well," said Eli, "to begin now and work back toward the start, I have been accused of murdering an artist to whom I did no harm at all. I have been locked up in a library with a barber who was a prisoner of a logical conundrum, which is an idea and not a jailer. I have been given the use of a most splendid schooner to travel on just because I came upon its builder by chance at a time when he needed a captain to deliver the ship to its owner. I have undertaken a search for the parents of a friend, and in searching for them I have made true and loyal friends of three most wonderful men and a goat named Amalthea. I have been a guest at the house of a great scholar and musician, and learned much there about the stars and how they show one's position on earth. I have discovered in the woods a statue bearing a large jug from which there poured a perpetual stream of water that became a brook and led us to a great river."

"A statue bearing a ewer?" questioned the Abbot. "What sort of a statue?"

"It was carved all of a piece from a pale orange stone, smooth and almost the color of human flesh."

"Yes, yes, the material, I understand, but what was represented by the statue?"

"A person wearing the least fragment of clothing pouring water from a ewer," said Eli.

"A most pagan statue," commented the Abbot. "And one that was unlikely to have been intended for you by God. I suspect that you have had an encounter with the evil spirit."

"It didn't mean much to me, but the goat seemed familiar with the statue," said Eli. "And shortly after that time, I met again with a friend, a most dear friend, helpless and barefoot beside the remnant of a crashed balloon on an island in the Black River. It was thence I rescued her."

"Her?" said the Abbot, aghast. "Were you not told that the name of woman, even that pronoun, is forbidden in these holy halls? When a novice renounces sin here, the first vow taken is that we shall neither speak nor even think of women again. For such thoughts are disturbing to monks and we have come here to contemplate God without disturbance."

"I am not sure that Marna is really a woman yet," said Eli. "She is rather more like a grown-up girl. But I do think about her quite a lot."

The Abbot's face contorted into an expression of something between anger and nausea. "This will never do," he said. "Thinking about such a person will almost surely lead you into sin. This monastery was built here inside the top of these cliffs so that we could lead lives of peace and contemplation, where no woman would ever penetrate to unsettle our dedicated lives."

"Perhaps that is the message that I am being sent since my rescue from the sea. For shortly before I was falsely accused, she briefly left me and went for a time in the company of a man with wildly waving blond hair who had powerful muscles and danced with her.

"When we kissed each other while we were on the boat, I felt I knew as pure a joy as I could ever imagine, and I wanted nothing but for her to love me and be as happy as I could make her. But I don't think she wanted that anymore; how else to explain why she went off and danced with that other man?" asked Eli mournfully.

"Thinking about young women, and especially about those who dance or who kiss, is at the very least a great distraction, and more than likely to lead you into sin," said the Abbot. "In fact, you must realize that your sins are probably both deep and severe. We are all sinners here and must repent of our sins and expiate them by fasting, sleeplessness, and prayer."

"But what sins can I repent of?" asked Eli. "I swear no oaths. I acknowledge no God but that my father Solomon told me of. I remember my father with honor and attempt to carry out his work for the common good. I have even endeavored to help Marna's parents by following them, hoping to return them to a virtuous life with Sennet on the River Spitte. When I found them dead, I gave them a decent burial. I have taken nothing that did not belong to me, unless you count the necklace Horatio gave me from the body of Marna's mother—but I gave that to Marna. I have wronged no man. Once I was angry with an artist who spoke harshly and jabbed at me with a paintbrush, but I did not commit murder. I have not desired the property of any man nor stood between the understanding of any man and his wife. I have given no false testimony of anyone, but generally tried to speak well of all."

"But," said the Abbot, "have you not just said that you desired this girl you speak of?"

"Desired her," said Eli. "Oh yes! I had not thought of it that way until you mentioned it, and I still desire her now, but with sadness and despair because I believe she does not want me anymore. More than anything I can imagine, it seems to me, it is sad to desire where one is not desired, to yearn and long for one who does not share that longing, to want and to be wanted not. If living with sadness is what you mean by penance, then I thank you for having helped me understand the true meaning of sorrow."

"That is because desire for a woman is still a distraction to you," said the Abbot. "Until you have gotten her out of your mind, you will never know the peace that is at the heart of this community."

"Reverend Abbot," said Eli, "it may be as you say, and I do seek peace. But I think it will be hard to do, even to imagine that God could condemn such joy as I sought in loving Marna. It was good. It was caring and unselfish. And is it not love that God calls us to?"

"It does not seem to me," said the Abbot, "that you come here in the proper spirit to be a novice. You are telling me about God's purpose where you should be asking *me* what God wants of you. Father Theodoric, let him pray with the novices for a day or two and see how he adapts to monastic discipline. If he improves, you may allow him to be a postulant for half a year, and then perhaps become a novice. If he does not take to it well, give him a blessing, some clothing, and send him on his way."

"Which way?" asked Eli. "Not back into the sea, I hope?"

"Yes," said the Abbot. "Unless you can traverse the long interior passages to the west. We have tunnels through the rock that lead to the high lands at the foot of the Long-Eared Mountains. From there you may be able to find your way to the West again."

So Eli followed Father Theodoric to a chapel where three other young men were kneeling in a row on the floor, their arms folded so that their hands were hidden inside the sleeves of their habits. Their quietly smiling faces seemed placid and happy. They did not acknowledge Eli's presence. Father Theodoric showed him where to kneel, how to fold his arms, and whispered in his ear that he should follow the others to the refectory when it was time for supper.

Eli suddenly realized how long it had been since he had eaten anything at all. He tried to compose his mind to reject the world and the flesh, but hunger kept reminding him that he was composed of body as well as soul. The other three novices seemed to be staring fixedly at a large wooden cross which was fastened to the far wall of the chapel. Two large spikes were driven into the ends of the crossbeam and a third projected from the lower part of the vertical member. A double loop of rusted barbed wire had been wound around the upper part of the vertical beam and a long wooden spear with a rusted iron point stood at the foot of the rough wooden construction, leaning against the crossbeam. The wood was stained and splintered, and the whole place suggested torture and death.

Eli felt a great wave of sorrow and pity for the victim represented here by this grisly representation of pain, purposely caused and deliberately inflicted. There was no image of whoever had suffered on the wooden framework, no indication that it had been a man or a woman, old or young, although Eli assumed any person whose suffering was the focus of the silent attention of the monks must not have been female. He wondered if women and girls also contemplated this sacrifice of a man and why it should be so, and never the other way around. Could men not stand the idea of a holy woman who had been sacrificed, whose pain and suffering of whatever sort could be an example to men or to boys?

It was after considerable time spent turning over such unfamiliar ideas in his mind that Eli was startled out of his thoughts by the sound of a bell tolling somewhere in the passages of the hollowed rock. The three novices arose, bowed to the empty cross and then to each other, but did not speak. They bowed to Eli and then, they left the chapel in single file. Eli, his hunger now uppermost in his mind, followed after them.

PERFORMANCE

When it first appeared in the hazy south, the distant city of Lucro floated on a transparent ocean of mirage, purple above a brown and distant horizon. It was many days since the caravan of players, musicians, and dancers had left the ruined city of the ancient people. The Sorrel Plain seemed to grow more deserted and less clothed with tough yellow grass as they traveled to the south. They had crossed dry streambeds but found no water. The grassland gave way to cactus and then to the beginnings of a sand desert. They ate little and conserved their water both for themselves and for the mules.

And then one morning they saw irregular shapes far ahead, towers and domes, turrets and crenellated walls, tall flagstaffs and flapping banners. By midmorning they could see that it was a wondrous city indeed, ringed about with many tall buildings that bore sparkling colored roofs made of red and purple tiles, glistening in the desert sunlight.

"I have not been here for many years," said Pedrolino, "not since I was a boy acrobat in another company of performers. But it takes my breath away to see it, shining and perfect in the sun. You cannot imagine what it looks like on an early winter evening when the towers are bright with hundreds of thousands of lights! I remember that the crowds of Lucro liked my act and paid well to come and see it. We will do well here, Marna. Your dancing will be a great success with the audiences of Lucro."

And so it turned out to be. Myles contracted with the owners of a large indoor theater to become a small part of a variety program that was playing in the very center of the city. On their very first performance, Marna and Pedrolino were cheered at the end of their dance with the mandolin player, and were brought back for several bows. There were loud calls of *Bis!*, which meant that they should dance another piece. But they had not rehearsed anything that they could do without preparation, and the mandolin player had to have learned the proper music too.

So subsequent mornings were filled with practice and rehearsal. Myles entered into various business dealings with the theater owners and with the managers of an orchestra that played there. The orchestra took over the work of the one-man band who had been, along with the mandolin player, the musical accompaniment for the entire series of acts when the company performed in Berrymor. Myles said he had to let the one-man band go, but since his contract was not originally as generous as Marna's, he got very little notice of his termination. He took to playing for coins from passersby in the public squares of Lucro. Marna felt quite sorry for him, but she concluded that she had to look out for herself in the large and busy city.

The leader of another troupe of performers approached Myles with an offer to put on a joint production, and soon Marna found herself considered a rising star in a new world of very different people. Soon she was known as a principal dancer of a group of girls whose contracts Myles bought from another impresario. Myles was becoming more skilled in finance. He used the contracts of the performers he wished to engage as collateral for loans taken to finance the engagement of still other performers. As the spectacle he created increased in size, so did the audiences. People who had attended one performance returned at a later date to enjoy the novelty of the new programs Myles had been able to add to the larger show. It seemed that the more money he borrowed, the larger became the company and the more enthusiastic the audiences.

One of the new members of the company was a tall, black-haired dancer named Catarina Longfoot (a strange name, Marna thought, because although Catarina was tall, her feet were just the right size for a dancer).

"Have you been dancing for a long time, Catarina?" Marna asked during a rest period at their rehearsal.

"Only for the four years since I came here," she answered. "And I do not think I will do it for too much longer."

"But you are so good," said Marna. "You are the best in your company. In fact, I think you are really better than I, but I suppose Pedrolino couldn't lift you as easily as he can me."

"That may be a part of the reason that I could only be a lead dancer if I come upon a giant for a partner," said Catarina with a happy smile.

ROUND HEAD

NORTH EAST MOHRS

BERRYMOR

THE GREAT CANAL

THE FLUME

THE BLUE SWAMP

THE SORREL PLAIN

THE YELLOW-BROWN RIVER MOHR

THE DRY WHITE LAND

NORTH

LUCRO

"But part of it is luck. In your first performance, little Columbina, you were a novelty and the mandolin was a new sound in the theater and you received an enthusiastic applause on your first night. Myles and the managers built on that and you became the latest rage. After that, success created an expectation of further success, until you became a star. For now, whatever you do is wonderful because *you* do it—because you are a star, and audiences are more interested in the star than in her performance. But as my teacher, Donna Elizabetta, taught me, things can spiral down just as rapidly after one poor performance."

"Donna Elizabetta?" asked Marna. "Did you also come to Lucro from Casa Sapienza?" asked Marna.

"Yes," she answered. "I am one of the motherless who learned music and wisdom at Casa Sapienza. But I will leave the dancing troupe soon. Donna Elizabetta also taught me something else by means of a riddle which I think I have solved. I have met a most wonderful young man named Zeno who is almost a foot shorter than I am, but he isn't a bit unsure of himself. He knows that he is my match in everything we do—except when it comes to reaching the packages on the very top shelf at the market."

"Is it the riddle about the leader without a follower and the follower without a leader, and how one does not need to lead or follow?" asked Marna.

"Yes, that's the one," Catarina said.

"What does it mean to you?" asked Marna.

Catarina smiled. "I believe it means a man does not have to lift a greater weight than a woman, nor a woman do domestic work that a man does not do, but that both can lift and support each other all their lives through," she said.

"Perhaps you are right," said Marna. But she thought to herself that there was something else in the riddle that Catarina had not found. Nevertheless, she envied Catarina her certainty and the devotion of her *fidanzato*.

"But doesn't it make him feel inferior when he knows that he has to ask your help to do something that requires physical stature?" asked Marna.

"Not Zeno. He is very sure of himself," said Catarina. "He is such a wonderful man, so capable and so creative, that I know he is strong enough to carry me off with his mind and heart even though he isn't strong enough to lift me when I dance. He designs buildings. When he was in school he was one of those little boys in the class who did very well in mathematics and didn't do very well in sports. Some of the big, strong boys laughed at him, and the bullies picked on him. But now he is a man, and he works with a firm of architects who have built some of the tallest towers in Lucro. Although still young, his work is so good that he is soon going to become a partner in the firm, and then we are going to be married. I will stop dancing on the stage then and dance only with him. And then we will have a family."

"But what is it like?" asked Marna. "How can it be fun dancing with a man who is so much shorter than you?"

"Oh, it is wonderful!" answered Catarina. "To begin with, I am in love with him, so anything we do together is fun. But besides that, he really dances very well. He puts his cheek on my bosom and a smile on his face and we dance in the old-fashioned way. He leads the dance with lightness but with strength, and I follow and do whatever his strong arms lead me to do. He says that all the other young men are envious of him because he has so much of a girl in his arms."

"But if you leave the company," asked Marna, "won't you miss the applause and the cheering after a great performance?"

"Perhaps I will," said Catarina, "but applause is not the only worthwhile thing in life. Love is more valuable and can last much, much longer, and so is wisdom of the sort that Dottore Umberto and Donna Elizabetta pursue. But for now, we must dance because we are under a contract that says so; come, let's get on with our rehearsal." And the two returned to the stage and joined the other dancers.

In the days that followed, Marna went from success to success, but Myles made no alteration in the terms of her contract. He did, however, provide her with a place to live that was appropriate for a celebrity. In fact, all the most successful members of the company were given very expensive rooms to live in, and Myles disposed of the mules and the caravans. Marna was pleased to find that her new apartment was in one of the towers located in the neighborhood of the theater.

The apartment faced northeast to northwest, high above the city. Windows filled the entire curving outside walls from floor to ceiling. There were no curtains because the sun came from the other directions, and even at night there was no place within many miles across the Sorrel plain (eighty meters below) from which anyone could be in a position to look in. There were mirrors on the inside walls and a dancer's exercise bar where she could do her morning routine. In the bathroom there was a very large tub that rose up from a raised marble platform. The tub was equipped with pumps that made either hot or cold water swirl and foam around her when she had finished her preparation in the morning or performances at night.

At sunset the view to the northwest revealed distant mountains that were illuminated by the last pink rays of the setting sun when the whole plain below her was dark. She could not make out quite which mountains they were, but she guessed they were connected to the distant chain of peaks that Eli had traveled through with the Sons of Homer, the Long-Eared Mountains. She wondered if she could ever travel that way again and find her way back to Casa Sapienza, and perhaps see Maria and Margaretta again. How far would it be from here to the distant Valley of Spitte where Sennet would be peering through his telescope, searching the view both up and down the river for passing boats, or perhaps for her?

In the late mornings, Marna went to the theater and rehearsed with Pedrolino and the others. Now, when she went out into the streets, the doorkeepers at the tower bowed and hurried to hold the door for her. Strangers in the streets whispered to each other and pointed at her when they passed. As each night's performance succeeded the last, her fame and reputation grew. But after a while, the new and glamorous life began to change. The more she became the darling of the audiences at the theater, the less she seemed to be a member of the company. Pedrolino danced with her and lifted her in graceful leaps on the stage, but, it seemed, he took less interest in her when they were not on the stage together. Myles seemed to spend more time in consultation with the financial managers and less in planning new acts and more spectacular performances. Several times she had long conversations with Catarina about what the life of a dancer was like and what she had to look forward to. Catarina merely said that it was a good job as long as it lasted, but that she was ready to change it for a husband, a home, and a family.

Then, one night, as Marna sat alone wrapped in a satin quilt on the foot of her bed, she looked out into the dark distance at the northern stars, the Great Bear and Cassiopeia. Suddenly she knew she had to find a way out of Lucro and a way of returning to the West.

She spoke to Myles the following day.

"Myles," she said, "could you be persuaded to alter my contract? Perhaps to make it for less time in exchange for giving me less money?"

"I suspected that might be on your mind," he said. "I can tell that you are not dancing with the same enthusiasm you had when Pedrolino first picked you up. And you will not remain a star long if your heart is not in it. Let me think about it. We can discuss it again in a few days."

But the possibility of Marna leaving the company did not seem to meet with anybody's approval in the theater. The managers concentrated their attention on Myles and there was much talk of the terms of the dancer's contract.

And then, one morning after rehearsal, Myles came to the company to make an announcement.

"I am sad to say farewell to you all, but the time for me to make a change has arrived. I have spent much of my life in theater," he said, "too much I think, and so I have liquidated all my loans by selling my interest in the acting and dancing company to an investment company. They have the means to finance this group and several others, and they will arrange to put on performances in several theaters. Antoinette and I have taken the money they have paid me and will retire here in Lucro. We will live our lives in private here on the income from the sale."

A short man with a broad-brimmed hat stood beside Myles. He introduced himself as the secretary of the investment company, but did not give his name.

"First off," the secretary said, "no one should be anxious about his or her employment. We will honor all of your contracts, and we intend to pay bonuses for very good performances."

This announcement was met by happy murmurs of appreciation from some of the members of the troupe, but a few scowled and grumbled to each other. Marna did not know quite what to think. She wondered if the change boded well or ill for her. Myles came over to her and asked that she come to one of the seats on the side aisle of the theater so they could talk privately.

"Columbina," he said, using her stage name, "your contract was the most recent of all that I sold and, as a result, it had the longest to run at your present salary of two and a half scudi for each performance for a year. That and your current popularity made it a costly item for the new owners. When it comes time to rewrite your contract, you should ask for a large sum, for they have much invested in you."

"And who has that investment?" she asked.

"I do," said Myles. "And that is as it should be. I took the risk of putting you on the stage and the expense of getting us all to Lucro. I have paid for your lodging and your food for a long time now. So now my property—your contract, that is—has increased in value. It is only according to our agreement that I, who made the investment and took the risk, stand now to reap the profit."

"But Myles," she said, "I am not a mine of minerals or a basket of turnips that you should sell me without asking my permission!"

"Columbina," he answered, "that is the way these things are done. Your contract is now in their possession. If you do not want to dance, you will not be paid, and you will be put out of your apartment. But no one else in Lucro will employ you for the next ninety days, since you are contracted to this investment company."

"You may tell them that I will dance for a few more nights, because I will not desert the others in the company without a few days' notice."

"You must tell them yourself, Columbina," said Myles. "The secretary of the company of investors is named Mr. Bond. You can speak to him. His associates own your contract now."

WHAT IS TO BE DISCOVERED IN OLD BOOKS

Life in the community of Theodoric Yorb was peaceful but physically demanding. The novices and postulants were expected to spend six hours of each day in sleep, three more in eating and washing, six in prayer, and six in manual labor or in study. The remaining three hours of the twenty-four was for "recreation," during which time they were allowed to follow their own thoughts and speak if they were in the presence of the Master of Novices or the Abbot. The time allocated to study was to be divided between reading the Aphorisms of Theodoric Yorb (which had been copied into large leather-bound volumes in the library) and other texts that were judged to be suitable for forming the minds of the younger members of the order. The reading room was not really a library, since it contained only the writings of members of the order, and all the members were forbidden to read anything that had not been written by a member, or a canonized saint. Even this list of acceptable works for instruction and meditation was limited to some extent, for the earliest works of some members were not judged to be entirely appropriate for the minds of young postulants.

These books were restricted to the use of older, reliable members of the order who did research that had been assigned them by the Abbot. A modest shelf of a hundred or so such volumes was contained behind cabinet doors with wire-mesh panels in its doors. A golden z was tooled in the leather on the spine of each book in this collection. The letter stood for "Zingari," which was the name by which the members of the order who had written them were known.

Eli was set to study the First Aphorisms of Theodoric Yorb. These seemed to be a relatively simple list of commandments:

THE SIMPLE ARE CLOSE TO GOD.
STRIVE TO BE SIMPLE.
THE PURE KEEP THEIR IMAGINATION IN CHECK.
MEDITATE, BUT DO NOT IMAGINE.
TO DO NOTHING IS BETTER THAN TO DO THE WRONG THING.
BE FORGIVING OF YOUR BROTHER SO THAT HE WILL BE ABLE TO FORGIVE YOU.
REMEMBER THAT YOU KNOW MORE OF YOUR OWN SINS THAN THOSE OF ANY OTHER MAN.
BE WATCHFUL UNLESS THE EVIL SPIRIT TAKE YOU BY SURPRISE.
PEACE IS TO BE FOUND IN RENUNCIATION.

After studying a number of books that commented on the regrettable results that would come from ignoring these and many other instructions, Eli concluded that he agreed profoundly with many of the Aphorisms, but not completely with all of them. He especially believed that to imagine might be even better than to meditate—at least some of the time. He found his mind becoming curious about other possibilities. He realized that he was supposed to limit his inquisitiveness, but he wondered what the other members of the order might have written in those books marked with the z. He wondered why they were closed in the caged shelves.

Although novices such as Eli were expected to talk very little and ask few questions, they were required to speak to the Master of Novices and seek his instruction in various matters, in particular about their pursuit of spiritual perfection. He approached the Master one evening during the recreation time after dinner.

"Father Theodoric?" he queried. "Why are the z books kept apart? If they are not proper for the younger members of the order, why are they in the library at all?"

"Young Brother Eli," said Theodoric, "you should accept the way things are done here without question. Such obedience to our rules is the perfect freedom. But since you are still very new here, I will explain some things in part and some things entirely to you.

"The z books are works that were written by members of the order before they actually joined the community. They contain some good things, which are wholesome and true, while other things are only half-formed and immature, for the minds of the authors had not yet been reconciled to the Rule of the Order.

"But we are careful scholars here, and we preserve the written word of all of the members of the order, even though some of it may contain error that we wish to keep from the young novices such as yourself."

"But," asked Eli, "if these writers eventually came to see the truth of the Aphorisms, wouldn't their early writings lead us to follow them?"

"You have much yet to learn, Eli," answered the Master. "For now it would be better if you accepted what I say and concentrated on composing your mind to be in harmony with the deeper meaning of the Aphorisms."

But Eli was not really content with the discipline of such limited inquiry. He felt that *all* books should be open to him as they had been at Casa Sapienza, where Umberto had given him the use of everything that was in his library. Once an inquiring mind has tasted the full flavor of unlimited research and reading, it is quite impossible to confine it again to a restricted list of truths. He felt that if he could not read of the experiences of those early members of the order, he could never fully join it himself. In fact, he began to feel that he did not wish to be a member of any group that limited its members' access to any books. What freedom could there be in a rule that closed off part of the world as though it did not really exist? In short, he began to imagine.

Getting books out of the z shelf turned out to be easier than Eli had first imagined. He merely waited until most of the other monks were deep in study and then went to the closed bookcase, turned the latch, and opened the interdicted shelf.

The first few volumes he found were not particularly unsettling, or even interesting. One was the autobiography of a professional soccer player who had turned to religion after a successful career as a center forward. Another was a book about economics that contained many small graphs of increases in supply plotted together with decreases in demand. There was no indication of when or how the author had come to join the order.

But other books presented more intriguing themes. One was a slender volume on the origin of the universe. It was a brief treatise on astronomy that seemed to explain the existence of the sun, moon, and stars as being the result of chance discontinuities in an unimaginably gigantic cloud of dust and gas that had always existed and had neither beginning nor end. The author pun tuated his explanation with descriptions of the nature of matter and energy, time and dimension, which were in themselves the probability of coincident locations in a vast web of vibrations that extend to beyond infinity in all directions from all locations. The author seemed to feel that all things were related by attractions that were carried through an invisible and impalpable field to all other things, and thus, everything was caused by everything else, and yet nothing had a cause outside of itself. There were formulas and strange symbols in this book, but Eli could not understand them, so he put the book back on the caged shelf and decided to give it no further thought for the present.

But another volume had a different result.

It was a book of poems by a man known as Brother Cyril. The verses seemed to have been written long ago. Most were about ancient myths, tales of centaurs and hamadryads, of white oxen who drew the chariot of the sun across the heavens, and a childish bowman whose arrows never missed their mark. There was a set of sonnets written to "An Imaginary Lady," which Eli skipped his way through. But then he came upon this poem, the tenth and last of the series:

YOU SEARCHER OF THE UNIMAGINED DUSK
OF SOME VAST LIBRARY IN THE FUTURE YEARS,
STRIVING WITH FOOTNOTES TO MAKE QUICK THE HUSK
OF OUR DEAD TIME, AND ALL ITS BLOOD AND TEARS,
CHANCING ON THIS PAGE, AND RAVISHED STRAIGHT
BY SOME QUAINT BEAUTY OF MY ANTIQUE PHRASE,
FOR ITS SWEET SAKE MAKE KINDLIER ESTIMATE
OF THE HUGE BEASTLINESS OF THESE OUR DAYS.
FOR THOUGH WE DEALT IN LIES AND GOLD AND PAIN,
YET, BY MY POWER OF SONG, THERE WAS, I SWEAR,
ONE WOMAN GRACIOUS AS THE APRIL RAIN,
AND LOVELIER THAN THE SUMMER OF HER HAIR
ONE WOMAN TO LIVE IN BEAUTY I AVER,
AND, YEA BY GOD! ONE MAN TO WORSHIP HER!

Trying to compose himself in meditation later that day, Eli found that he had nearly memorized the poem in two readings, and it would not leave his mind. He had found the ancient words in a library just as the poet had predicted, and he had even experienced some trouble without footnotes to understand everything in his "antique phrase."

But he had been ravished straight, not so much by the poem itself as by the images it brought back from his own experiences. Brother Cyril may have written to an imaginary lady, but he brought to Eli's mind the very image of a real girl, as physical as his own body, although far more beautiful. His mind was filled with images of her hair and eyes, of the weight of her body as he lifted her from the river above the falls, of the feeling of her knee touching his on the deck of the *Polaris*, of the soft sweet fullness of her lips when they kissed in the dawn watch.

Marna!

Marna contemplating mushrooms with wise eyes in the woods below the Rock Tower. Marna's wild summer hair confined in braids before and behind her shoulders. Marna's face haloed by the yellow hood of the storm jacket, looking up at him, standing close on the deck of the schooner. Marna, who could live in beauty more surely than the poet could ever have imagined as she descended the great stair at Casa Sapienza in the dark green gown and Eli had seen her as though he had seen her never before.

At that moment he felt all countervailing thoughts swept before the one surety—that he could be the one man to worship her! There was innocence in the community and protection from the terrors of the untrammeled power of the Council of Berrymor. There had been salvation from wave and rock. But would such a saved and protected life be worth exchanging for a life that confronted every peril except her absence? Perhaps Pedrolino had taken her away. Perhaps even the handsome glassblower had a deep and distant power over her imagination now that she believed him dead. Nothing mattered but that he find her again, and forever!

The images of the chapel icons came to his mind, but they were no match for the remembered tilt of the girl's small chin, the perfect fullness of her lips, the challenging brown depths of her eyes. Whatever the exchange, he reasoned, she was worth it. He must go out from this place and find her.

ADVICE

Although Marna decided not to discuss the sale of her contract with the other members of the company, she felt that the secretary of the investment company paid very close attention to her performances, and even to her rehearsals in the following days. Several times he seemed on the verge of asking her to confer privately with him, but he merely watched and smiled pleasantly whenever he was present.

But Pedrolino and Catarina Longfoot seemed to know that something was wrong, and asked her about her feelings toward the new owners of the company. Eventually she told them both that she wanted to leave the company but did not know how to do so. Pedrolino said that he would guard her secret carefully, but Catarina, when she learned that Pedrolino also knew of her plans, said she felt they would not remain secret for long.

"You must know, Marna"—for the two girls shared the use of their given names—"a secret is something that is known by fewer than three people. If a third knows it, it will not stay a secret forever."

And indeed, an article appeared in one of the financial newspapers of Lucro only two days later. The reporter seemed to have guessed at the truth of the matter, although Pedrolino insisted he had never spoken to a newspaper man. The headline read:

STAR DANCER UNHAPPY OVER CONTRACT TERMS— WILL SHE QUIT COMPANY?

The article went on to say that shares in the Theater Investment Company had risen dramatically on the Lucro Security Exchange in the previous weeks when it had been announced that the company had purchased all the contracts of the actors and dancers of Art Comedy of Myles Gloriosus.

The secretary of the investment company summoned Marna to his office on the following morning.

"Miss Columbina," he began, "do you have any idea how much damage this public speculation about your intentions is going to cause? I am sure that the price of shares of our common stock will be down from one and a half to two scudi per share when trading opens on the Exchange this morning. Many thousands of unrealized value will be lost!"

"Sir," said Marna, "I don't know what unrealized value is. It doesn't sound as though it is really very valuable if it can disappear so quickly."

"Miss Columbina," he said, glaring at her, "we are going to call a meeting of the financial reporters today, and you are going to tell them that we are even now negotiating a new contract for the next season, and that you will dance for our company."

Marna looked at the little man, who was still wearing his broad-brimmed hat, and decided that he was a pitiful little bully. She also decided that she would quit dancing for him as soon as she could.

"You can tell the writers whatever you want," she said. "I will continue to dance for now, but I will sign no new contract. The old one is bad enough, but it still has many months to run."

And, after a short and wordless rehearsal with Pedrolino, she left the theater and walked through the shining streets of Lucro, deep in thought.

The theater and financial districts of the city were really one and the same, a fact that made Marna reflect that skillfully crafted illusion and growing financial success might be closely related. But farther toward the south end of the town, near the edge of the dry expanse of the Sorrel Plain, she came upon one of the smallest buildings she had ever seen in the gigantic and modern city. It was a little church built of worn golden stone with a ruddy brown tile roof. There had once been carvings around the doorway, but they had been smoothed to unrecognizable shapes by rain and windblown sand long ago. In front of the weathered wooden double doors, in the shade of the great metal and glass towers above and behind it, there was a little garden which consisted of a small circular fountain surrounded by a ring of white petunias and a set of four curved benches with a circle of clipped grass around them. It looked like a good spot to stop and think things out.

But almost as soon as she sat on the bench and began to contemplate the nearly unrecognizable sculpture of a fish that was spouting water into the air in the center of the fountain, the door of the church opened and a vaguely familiar figure emerged. He was clad in a blue denim coverall, and he carried a hoe and a cultivating hook in one hand and a watering can in the other. He looked intent on weeding the flower beds. But Marna knew she had seen him somewhere before.

He was a small man with a pale brown complexion. He had a small, neatly trimmed beard which was more gray than black, and while the same gray-black hair covered most of his head, it did not completely cover its crown. He wore gold-rimmed spectacles and looked rather more like a monkish scholar than a cultivator of the soil. He smiled at Marna and set to work pulling weeds from among the petunias. And then she knew where she had seen him before. He was the priest who had celebrated the Christmas service in Berrymor. No longer shrouded in the white and golden vestments he had worn then, he seemed more human and approachable.

"Hello, Father," she said. "Is that what I should call you?"

"You would delight me if you would," said the priest, looking up from his petunias. "I try to meet all people, both young and old, as I would greet my own children if I had any. May I call you daughter, or would you like me to use some other name?"

"Maybe Marna would be better," she answered. "But what are you doing here in Lucro? We were in your church in Berrymor at Christmas."

"Ah, yes," he said with a faint smile. "It was the bishop, bless his saintly heart. He decided to favor the people of Lucro with my care. You see, this great city has very few churches, and those that are here now are very small and were built a long time ago. The bishop consulted with God, I guess, and then told me that I should restore the church in Lucro. So here I am, restoring it." And with that he began poking ineffectually at the dirt around the petunias with the cultivating hook. The priest looked so gentle and almost frail as he attempted to improve the garden that Marna got up from the bench and set to work next to him with the hoe.

"Thank you very much," he said. "I am not very good at this sort of thing, I am afraid. But if I am to get the people of Lucro to come to church, I really must first make it look inviting."

"Do very many come?" asked Marna.

"Not really; at least, not yet," he said. "There have been some, though. I think there were twice as many at mass last Sunday as there were the week before."

"Twice as many?" said Marna. "But that's quite wonderful!"

"Perhaps," said the priest. "But twice three is still only six."

"Oh," said Marna, thinking what it would be like if there were only six people in the theater to see her dance. "That must be very discouraging."

"But we must never be discouraged," said the priest quite firmly. "We must always be sure that things are going to work out for the best, or at least the better, if we keep hoping properly."

The simple optimism in the priest's voice made Marna think again of how downhearted she had become.

"Oh, Father—how can we keep hoping when we have nothing to hope for?"

"But how can you be discouraged, my dear?" he answered, gently removing a cluster of dry weeds from between the flowers. "You are young and beautiful, you sound intelligent, and your costume would make me suppose that you are well favored by family and social position."

And quite suddenly Marna began to remember all at once how far she was from home at the Rock Tower, how her father and mother were dead, how she was far away from her friends at Casa Sapienza, and most of all, how Eli was gone, lost forever in the Great Northern Sea, loaded down with a long anchor chain. And she began to cry.

Until this moment, in the company of Occam and Carlo and Maria, of Myles and Pedrolino and Catarina, with the members of the dance company, or even alone in her tower apartment, she had shed no tears. But somehow the cheerful presence of this small bearded religious man gave her the feeling that it was safe here in the little neglected garden to blink her eyes and let the tears roll down her cheeks.

The priest said nothing for a while, but then he reached into a pocket inside his blue coveralls and produced a red bandanna handkerchief which he offered her.

"Perhaps you would like to come into the church and tell me what is making you so sad," said the priest. He then picked up the tools and, leaving the watering can at the front step, entered the church and left the door standing open.

Marna watched him go, and wiping her eyes on the bandanna, she followed him to the door, washed her hands with the watering can, dried them on the bandanna, and followed him inside.

The light was dim, and although the church was clean, it had a neglected and unused look. There was, however, one tiny red light glowing, suspended in the gloom at the far end of the shadowed nave. She sat in the next to rearmost pew and tried to make out the figures on a partially ruined painting on the wall to her left. There were figures of people and animals there and a few glints of gold leaf and dark colors of red and blue. But she could not see what the subject of the painting was. The whole interior seemed so melancholy that she felt like crying again.

A door opened and closed at a distance, off in a shadowy corner where Marna could not see, and then the priest returned. But now he was dressed in a black cassock. He looked at Marna, refused the return of the handkerchief, and then glanced around his church.

"It does look a bit discouraging," he said, sitting down in the pew beside her. "But I have time. Suppose, though, that first you tell me about you."

So Marna began the story of her life, beginning almost as early as she could first remember. The priest nodded gravely from time to time, but never interrupted her. He did scowl a bit when he heard about her parents' quest, and he stared briefly at the green stone she wore about her neck. He smiled at her description of Eli flying through the air into the river over her canoe. He seemed sympathetic about her concern for his wounded shoulder. He laughed at her descriptions of the three Sons of Homer, and his eyes opened wide in appreciation of her description of Casa Sapienza and the followers of the Red Priest.

But her account of Berrymor made him frown, and the description of Eli in chains being taken into the Watch boat caused him to make the sign of the cross and murmur something under his breath. When he learned of her life in Lucro and the sale of her contract, he folded his hands in a posture of prayer and turned his eyes up toward the dark and distant ceiling of the old church.

"There was once another Bishop of Berrymor whom I followed and who taught me. He granted clemency to a number of criminals because he believed that man should never take a life that God had created. He reduced their sentences to perpetual servitude in monasteries and hospitals, where they were allowed to do the cleaning of the drains when they were not kept in their cells. He himself was a former monk who had been called from a monastic community beyond the Northeast Coast. He was said to be a descendant of an old family of the former age when people migrated away to the West. But he was not popular with the monks of his monastery because he had been too worldly, and the Council thought him unsuitable to continue as bishop because he was too worldly wise and impractical. The Council made him retire when he became old, and appointed another who believed more firmly in law and order at any cost. He was sent away in a small sailing vessel."

"But what is he to me?" asked Marna with a hostile tone in her voice. "No one granted Eli's appeal or reduced his sentence."

"Ah, but what do we know?" said the priest. "There are three great virtues that we must practice," he said. "They are faith and hope and charity, which is love. They will help us find the way through the mazes of life. But these virtues are not things that are going to happen to us without our doing something about it. They are things that we do because we *choose* to do them. If we stop doing them, we dry up and become unhappy. All three are related and connected to each other, but it helps if we concentrate on doing them one at a time.

"Now it seems to me that you have kept faith with your grandfather and your parents and the friends you have met during your remarkable travels. And you must have at least some faith in God, or you would not be in this church today."

"But Father," said Marna, "I don't always believe that God is there at all."

"Of course not," said the priest. "But the virtue of faith is to work at it and pray that you will get better at believing in God. You have to *do* faith, just the way you do the steps of a dance that is very difficult to learn.

"I think most of us find it easier to love, even when we are not loved back. It seems you have loved many friends, but most of all, this young man Eli has been the object of your fondest love, although you didn't always feel that way before he vanished from your life."

"Is it a virtue to love someone who is gone—who has drowned in the Northern Sea?" asked Marna, starting to feel the tears in her eyes again. "I never even said I loved him when we were together. And I often scolded him for being so sure of himself. And how can I practice the virtue of love when I really only found out that I loved him after it was too late?"

"Ah, but things are not too late or too early for God," said the priest. "It only feels that way for us because we live in time, experiencing today and regretting yesterday and hoping for tomorrow. But God created time, too, as well as love and loveliness. So our task is to love as God loves, outside of time. Now this requires hope, and it is quite a task to practice the virtue of hope!"

"But what can I hope *for*?" she asked.

"I do not know," said the priest. "I wonder what the old Bishop would say to you. Perhaps Eli escaped from the chains. Perhaps the Watch deposited him on shore. Perhaps a passing boat found him in the sea and saved him. Perhaps you will meet another young man and he will beguile you away from your sorrow over Eli. But you must hope that something better is to come, and that love and faith will have their reward. And I must hope that there will be twice as many people here next Sunday as there were last week. Do you know that if I was able to double this congregation every week for just six weeks, they would not all be able to fit inside the church? In sixteen weeks they would outnumber the entire city. In less than a year, doubling every week would give me a congregation larger than all the people in the world. Now I can't believe that I could do that, but I can hope that the first few steps could be taken this week or next.

"So perhaps you can hope when you say your prayers at night, that somewhere, somehow, God intends for you to find love and faithfulness with someone—perhaps even with Eli."

Marna had not said prayers at night for many years. But that night she tried to focus her mind on the words of the kindly priest as she looked down from the tower apartment and wondered where she would be living by the end of the six-week miracle of a growing congregation that he was praying for. She could not see the tiny and ancient church from the high windows of her apartment, but she knew that below her, in the shadows, it was there.

42 PURCHASED FOR DELIVERY

Marna dressed in a gray exercise suit when she went to the theater for rehearsal. She locked her apartment behind her and gave the key to the concierge at the great front portal of the tower building when she left for her morning run, past the little church with the petunias in the front garden. As she jogged her way around the park-fringed edges of the city along streets that led her to the theater, she wondered what the name of the slight and kindly man she had spoken to yesterday might be. She had called him Father, but she did not know what given name he might have.

But other events came upon her so rapidly that she scarcely had time to think of the priest for several days to come. When she arrived at the theater, she met Catarina Longfoot in the dressing room.

"Marna," she said, "whatever you said to Mr. Bond, he hasn't taken it well. He just announced that he was putting your contract up for sale and that you wouldn't be dancing with the company any longer."

"But can he do that?" gasped Marna. And then she thought that perhaps this change might be for the better. She would leave the company and go to the priest for help. If she had no other way of supporting herself in Lucro, perhaps she could become a nun. Being a nun certainly sounded very different from being a dancer, but perhaps it was not so very different after all. As a dancer, she had always tried to make each motion perfect. Didn't nuns try to be perfect all the time?

Mr. Bond arrived in the theater at ten o'clock and presented Marna with a little leather bag containing a handful of coins, her salary for part of the thirty-day period of cancellation called for in her contract.

"We have just repossessed your apartment and your clothing," he commented in a dry, businesslike tone. "Sorry to inconvenience you, but business is business, you know. There is a bag of your personal items with the concierge. The auction of the remaining sixty days of your contract is scheduled for two o'clock this afternoon. I assume someone will buy it and then you can arrange with him for sleeping quarters."

And with that he turned away and strode out of the theater.

Marna reflected that she had felt more lost when the balloon carried her over the wilderness and resolved to concentrate on practicing the virtue of hope. She returned to the entry of the apartment tower and received the sack of her belongings from the man at the desk. It contained her sailor's clothing, the dress she had purchased with her first salary advance, some clean underwear, her hairbrush, toot brush, a tortoiseshell box containing a cake of very good soap, the recorder she had been given at Casa Sapienza, along with the "dancing dress" tied in its proper knot along with its pretty shoulder clasp from Donna Elizabetta. There was also her pocketknife with the many tools and blades folded into its red handle and the straight razor that Occam had given her. With this small bundle of possessions she felt a little less poor. After all, she had three changes of clothing. Finding the knife and razor made her feel capable and resourceful, and she knew that she was attractive in the brown dress with the black lace. Shoes were another problem. She was wearing running shoes, and the deck shoes she had worn with her sailing clothes certainly didn't go with the dress.

Nevertheless, Marna arranged with the concierge to use the servants' bathroom near the service entrance of the great tower and changed into her dress, packing everything else into the tote bag. She brushed out her hair and put it up in a Grecian knot, high up on the back of her head. Then she set out for the theater to witness the auction of her contract.

Before she returned to the theater, however, Marna found her way to the finest shoe shop in Lucro and there she spent an hour comparing pumps, slippers, and sandals, finally selecting a slender pair of tan shoes that seemed somewhere between the sort designed for walking and for dancing. They were made of very fine leather, lined with kid, and sewed together with the tiniest stitching Marna had ever seen. They had delicate straps across the instep and small golden buckles.

The lady in the shoe shop assured her that they were the latest model in the store and would be stunning with her pretty dress. The price was twelve scudi, almost half of everything she had. But Marna reasoned that if she had to face the world alone again, it would perhaps be better to face it looking like a success rather than as a penniless orphan who had been abandoned in the richest city in the world. Being well shod was a proclamation of one's position that everyone who was attentive could see.

The auction was a relatively brief affair. Her costumes were sold first, and these seemed to generate more interest than the contract of the dancer herself. The news of Marna's lack of cooperation with Mr. Bond and the investment company seemed to have made most of the theater people uneasy about taking her on.

But when Marna walked across the stage and smiled at the little audience of businessmen, she was thinking of the salary she needed to live in Lucro, so she did her best to appear both lively and charming. An obese man wearing a velvet jacket and a lavender necktie opened the bidding at eight scudi, less than the price of a fashionable pair of handmade shoes, an amount so low for a well-known dancer's contract that some of the others laughed when the auctioneer announced it.

This first bid was followed by a long silence while the auctioneer asked for a higher offer.

"Ten!" he called out. "Ten! Do I hear twenty? Gentlemen, this contract is for the services of Columbina, lately the prima donna of the Gloriosus Company!"

Marna saw a hand flicker for an instant in the rear rows of seats.

"Twenty!" said the auctioneer. "Twenty! Do I hear thirty?"

The man with the lavender necktie shrugged and wriggled his nose.

"Twenty," said the auctioneer with a little less enthusiasm.

Marna noticed that the man in the back of the room was staring hard at her. He had a bushy black beard and red cheeks. She felt there was something slightly familiar about the face. Two other men, also with bushy black beards, were sitting with him, and they bent their heads together to confer every time the bid changed.

"Thirty!" said the auctioneer with some relief. "Thirty! But come now gentlemen, who will offer me thirty-five scudi for this talented girl?" The man with the black beard nodded slightly in agreement. The man with the lavender tie studied his fingernails, keeping his hands in his lap. No one else seemed interested.

"Going once for thirty-five scudi!" intoned the auctioneer. "Going once—going twice. Sold! To the three gentlemen in the rear for thirty-five scudi! And a fine bargain they have, too!"

And so, Marna thought, she had been sold, or at least her services for two months had been sold, for the price of three pairs of shoes. Marna came down the side stairs from the stage and walked up the aisle toward the three black-bearded men in the back row.

"And what theater do you represent?" she asked.

The tallest of the three looked at her closely and then at his companions.

"Arnold, you were quite right," he said. "It is the very same girl. I never forget a face."

Marna also felt that she had seen the speaker before, as well as Arnold and his other companion, but she could not remember where. Verity? Berrymor?

"We three, Aelred, Ali, and I, do not actually represent a theater at all," said Arnold. "We are merchants who buy what we can when it is cheap and sell it where or when it is dear. We think we can get a very good price for your contract in another part of the country."

"You see," said Aelred, "we met you some time ago at the house of Lucindar, the glassblower. Then on our next trip, you were not there when we were arranging to buy his merchandise. We bought much of his glass on credit and at interest on our last trip to the West. Thus, we owe him a good sum. But he is lonely and he told us when we were there that you ran away with his second-best balloon, a green and yellow one that was worth more scudi than we have paid for your contract."

"And, Miss Columbina," said Ali, the tallest man, "Lucindar loves dance, besides being lonely, and he also wants to catch the thief who stole his balloon. Taken altogether, I think we should be able to turn a good profit on this transaction. Perhaps as much as a hundred scudi."

"Of course," said the second, "we deserve a good profit since we accept all the risk."

"There is always the risk that you might not honor your contract for Lucindar and he might refuse to buy up your rights, leaving us out of pocket for the whole thirty-five scudi as well as your keep until we can deliver you to him. I don't imagine by the look of you that you eat a great deal, but we have to deliver you in good health if we expect to get anything at all for you."

The three merchants looked at Marna with questioning eyes.

"Now," added Arnold, "the next question is whether you want to be left here without money or possibility of employment in Lucro, trying to find shelter for the night, or whether you will come with us and be delivered to Lucindar in exchange for the price of your contract? Not a bad exchange, eh? And tell us, by the way, your true name. We know that Columbina is your stage name. Who are you, really?"

Marna was about to refuse indignantly. She knew that even if men like Myles and Pedrolino were unlikely to afford her much protection, she could seek refuge with Catarina, who would probably be able to find a place for her to stay for a few nights. And then she thought of the priest whose name she did not know. Surely he would give her a safe place to stay?

And then she felt a strong new sense of security knowing that these alternatives were even possible. And with that feeling of safety she felt her old sense of adventure and daring return. Why not? Lucindar's glassworks was close to her own river, the Spitte, and her own canoe might still be there at the riverside landing up the backwater where she had left it. And perhaps dancing for Lucindar would be an adventure, too. He was, after all, not at all unattractive with his broad brown mustache, white teeth, and flashing eyes. He was quite a lot older than Marna, but not really old by any means. And there was something intriguing about knowing that a man would have to pay a good deal of money for her contract just to keep her from dancing for someone else, and all of this without anyone having extracted a promise from her that she would do much of anything in return.

"I will not tell you my name, or anything else until I please, but if you treat me with dignity and respect, I will come with you," she said, "provided we go soon directly to the West. And I must have my own mount to ride and my own tent alone when we stop for the night. Although I will not tell you my name, I will assure you that I have many and powerful friends in this country and in the West, and I will deposit news of this agreement with them before we depart. If anything happens to me on this journey, it will go very hard with those who brought it about. If I am falsely stolen away by those who have contracted to protect me, they will surely never be able to trade again in this whole land south of the Long-Eared Mountains, and you will be sought by the watchmen of the eastern cities and swiftly caught and brought to harsh justice.

"So now go and make arrangements for our departure, and I will arrange my affairs here and meet you at the little garden in front of the small church at the foot of the great tower this afternoon."

The three merchants looked at each other and nodded. "It will be a good bargain for all four of us," said Aelred. "And for Lucindar too," added Ali.

Marna started out of the theater with her tote bag in her hand, feeling freer than she had ever felt in Lucro. At the stage door she found Pedrolino who was deep in conversation with a new dancer, a fragile redheaded girl who was looking intently into his eyes.

"Good-bye, Pedrolino," she called. "I wish you success in all your new ventures with your new company. Good success to you in whatever you undertake, or whomever you lift up from now on."

The little redheaded girl smiled and Pedrolino looked up from her face just long enough to murmur "Good-bye" in Marna's direction.

At the church, Marna found the priest sitting quietly inside, next to an empty confessional box, reading from a small but thick prayer book. She explained her new situation and asked if he knew how to get a letter to Dottore Umberto who lived at Casa Sapienza, far up the valley of the Black River, almost as far as the falls below the Long-Eared Mountains.

"I do not know how to go there myself," he said, "and of course I could not go there unless the bishop sent me. And this bishop only asks me to work here in Lucro where everyone is rich, even though he knows I would prefer to work with and among the poor. But bishops usually get their way and often have ways of getting information passed about. I suspect that he could arrange to convey a letter to Casa Sapienza if you were to write one."

So Marna went with the priest into an office in the rear of the church where there was an old oak desk with a brass-nibbed pen and a little jar of green ink with a hinged pewter top. Explaining her plans took a great deal of time, and it took even more to copy out her thoughts on paper. The tale was long, and Marna's account was written in formal language addressed very respectfully to Dottore Umberto. She gave them word of the tragedy that had overtaken Eli in Berrymor and how certain she was that he was innocent of the crime for which he had been condemned. She told of her new career, of her success in Lucro, of meeting Catarina Longfoot in the theater, and finally, of the collapse of her good fortune and the sale of her contract to merchants who were to take her through the Trackless Wastes of West to the house of a man she knew, Lucindar, who was said to want to purchase her dancing contract. She asked Umberto to keep her in mind and to inquire of his friends about the honesty and reputation of Arnold, Aelred, and Ali. She disclosed her intention of going back to the Rock Tower after she had determined if Lucindar's interest was honest and could be expected to be lasting. Finally, she sent wishes for fond embraces to Maria and Margaretta in hopes that they would all gather again someday to make music together. Then she sealed up the letter with some green wax that was on the priest's desk and gave it to him. After changing into her sailor's clothes again, she bid him good-bye with a kiss on the cheek which she found to be, rather to her surprise, at the same level as her own.

"Good-bye, Marna, and may God bless your way and bring you through all mazes and perils to find the reward of hope at length." And he put his hand on her head and made a sign on her forehead with his thumb.

As she left the small, ancient building and went out to meet the three merchants, Marna realized she had again forgotten to ask the pastor of the little church for his name. She knew him only as Father. Since she had never called him anything else, she decided it would have to do.

TO THE WEST

"Father Abbot," said Eli, standing in the pose prescribed for novices, slightly bowing as he spoke, arms folded, hands in sleeves. "I feel that there is great wisdom to be found in the order; indeed, I feel I have absorbed a great many wise things while being here even for so short a time. But, while thanking you for rescuing me from death in the sea, I feel I must seek your permission to return to the world, for there is much that I must still do there."

"I feared as much," said the Abbot. "But you have scarcely yet become truly aware of your own limitation and sinfulness. For some it takes years of concentration and meditation before we really know how evil our inner selves can be."

Eli bowed again but did not answer. He reflected that this was perhaps the principal reason for leaving now, before he too could come to a decision that a life outside the monastery would somehow be wrong—that the pursuit of Marna might be wrong, a conclusion he did not wish to reach.

"I suspect that you have been reading forbidden books," said the Abbot, "and perhaps even allowing thoughts of things other than spiritual perfection and penitence to creep into your mind. Is this so?"

"There is so much in my mind, Reverend Father," said Eli. "I have thought of apple orchards on hillsides in October and the hot sweet smell of strawberries ripening in the sun in May. I have mentally rejoiced in the flavor of goat's milk cheese on toasted oatcakes and the bursting of sweet corn kernels I have bitten off the cob, hot, running with butter in August. Sometimes I think of the joy called up by the music of Father Vivaldi and the sense of mastery I feel when I look at all the stars in the sky and know that I can name at least several dozen of them. Sometimes I cannot keep my mind away from the happy sting of the wind on my face when the boat is close hauled and well heeled over. I mentally rejoice in looking over a well-printed title page of a book that I have never opened before and the handsome letters invite me to follow some learned mind into adventures I cannot yet imagine. But most of all, Reverend Father, my mind is full of the pursuit of the single greatest adventure that I think a man can undertake: to pursue and win the love of a lady whose perfection stirs mind and heart both night and day."

"It had occurred to me that such thoughts might be at the bottom of it," said Theodoric. "I am afraid you are a hard case. But I think, perhaps, in another few months your mind could be subdued and your will trained to conform to the Rule of the Order."

"But that is just the reason I wish to leave this good and holy place," said Eli. "I wish to preserve my mind, unsubdued and unconformed, so that I can put my full energy into finding and winning my prize, Marna of the Rock Tower."

At the name of the girl the elderly monk crossed himself and cast his eyes upward as though searching for some escape in the heavens.

"Perhaps," he said, "perhaps God wills it that some are left to propagate the race, although I doubt that is what you consider your prime purpose now. Very well then, with our blessing we send you out of the monastery. You will be given a pilgrim's robe, sandals, a begging bowl and a staff, and then conducted to the Northwestern Portal from which no monk ever can return. Thence through the ancient tunnel you must, if you can, find your way into the high valleys, for that is the only way out of our retreat except if you were to be let down into the sea again in a basket."

"Many thanks, Reverend Father," said Eli. "I have learned from my brief life here and go away much richer than I came."

And so Eli found himself dressed as a pilgrim, walking down a long, dark tunnel, picking his way toward a dimly lit exit in the distance, carrying a bowl and a staff, lacking money or even the tools of a multibladed knife like the one Marna used to carry.

He emerged in an upland meadow with the lofty masses of the Long-Eared Mountains in front of his right hand, displaying hanging fields of ice and fissured snow that were even then melting into rivulets, plunging down the lower slopes and ravines in icy cascades. Ahead, due west, the meadows were fresh with new grasses and a scattering of little blue flowers.

Eli walked through a land of tilled fields and passed an occasional farm. At one of these he approached the rear yard where there was a small well house and some rusted farm machinery, a mowing machine with a shaft for harnessing a horse, a hay rake and a harrow. Eli stepped up to the back porch of the house and, carefully putting down his staff so that he would not appear threatening, he knocked at the door. He stood there for a long time, his begging bowl in his hands, waiting for someone to answer.

After a few minutes he knocked again and then backed away from the door to peer up toward the upstairs windows of the farmhouse. There appeared to be no one present at first, but then he thought he saw a motion at a window. Was there someone there, or did he imagine it? He waited for a bit. There—he was sure he saw something move. A face had appeared in the upper right-hand window of the house, a narrow face with bright eyes and unkempt hair. It appeared for an instant and then moved quickly away from the window.

"Halloo!" called Eli. "Anybody home?"

No sound came from the house, but the face reappeared in a ground floor window and then vanished again. Eli decided to wait. He was hungry, and it seemed a long way to another farm. He began to hum one of the chants that the monks used. After what seemed a long time, the back door opened and a bright-eyed, disheveled little man peered at him, keeping his body out of sight behind the doorjamb. He said nothing.

"Good day, sir," said Eli. "I am a mendicant traveler in need of a cup of water, a crust of bread, and instruction about where I wish to go. Can you help me?"

"But you look like one of *them*," said the unkempt little man. "You're not religious, are you? Your robe looks religious, but you don't sound that way."

"Well, I am not religious enough to adjust easily to the life of the followers of Theodoric Yorb," said Eli, "but what would be wrong with me if I were?"

The little man shivered and looked anxiously in all directions. "Ah, what indeed!" he said.

"But tell me about it," said Eli, "and perhaps we could have some water and bread while I learn from you."

The little man moved from behind the doorjamb and pushed the door open with a flicker of a smile.

"Come in," he said. "There is bread and soup. I think you look harmless, but it is always hard to tell."

Eli entered the low-ceilinged kitchen and sniffed a series of mingled smells: tomatoes, garlic, bacon, and beans. The aroma seemed to emanate from a black iron pot, suspended from a crane in the fireplace.

"Sit down," said the man, "and I will fetch you some water." He went back outside and returned with an incongruously shiny steel pail full of water. It must have been very cold, for the pail was frosted on the outside. He poured two tall earthenware mugs of water and set them on the table. "Come, sit down," he said as he rummaged in a cupboard, emerging with a crusty loaf of bread that looked nourishing.

The water was indeed cold, and very refreshing. Eli looked hopefully in the direction of the pot in the fireplace.

"Tell me, who are you, and how do you come to be walking through this high country?" asked the man.

"I am Eli, son of Solomon," he answered. "I have just left a holy place, a monastery where they saved my life, but where I think they wanted to possess my spirit in return."

"Monasteries are perhaps the best of religious things," said the little man. "They don't often start wars or put people to death for their beliefs. It is fear of those who do that makes me uneasy in the presence of people who wear religious clothing."

"But who would want to start a war or kill people if he were religious?" asked Eli. "Do you really know of such people? And who are you—how have you come by such ideas?"

"My name is Nessuno," he replied. "I am one of the last left in this part of the country where there was a small but terrible war a number of years ago. Many people hereabouts were religious, and most were kind to one another. But not everyone believed exactly the same things about their religions; they knew they had different beliefs. One group called themselves the church of Man Who is Made for God; another, the Church of God's Care for Man; and the third was known as the Congregation of Man, Nature, the Stars, and the Almighty.

"All believed in love and forgiveness, but there were some who felt that it was hard to be forgiven for one's sins. Some of the others believed that men and women didn't commit many sins at all. I cannot remember which group believed which things, but they were all known by shortened titles of their long names—the Previes, the Posties, and the Evers—and they all got on pretty well together." Nessuno paused for a moment, as if remembering his guest. "Would you like some soup?" he asked.

"Oh, I surely would," said Eli.

Nessuno took two enamelware bowls from the cupboard as well as large spoons and a ladle. From under the lid of the kettle he produced two large servings of vegetables and barley, swimming among the beans, pasta, and a few flavorful trimmings of bacon.

Nessuno continued: "There were scholars among these groups, men expert in reading and interpreting old ideas from religious texts. They were mostly nice fellows in their own right. They studied the past and present of their religions and ensured they had everything right. They seemed harmless enough, but they did sharpen the differences among the three groups, especially among the three kinds of clergymen." Nessuno took a mouthful of soup and a bite of bread, smiling at Eli's enthusiastic appreciation of the meal.

"Then, once, not too long ago," Nessuno said, "a perfectly decent man who wanted to be chosen as the Tribune of the People asked all the members of his faith to choose him so that the right and good ideas of their faith could become the guiding principles of the government. One of the other groups immediately began to say that another man, the old Tribune, was closer in faith to their position, although he always said he was in favor of all religions. But the third group, the smallest, became very anxious at the disagreements among the candidates. You see, they lived near here in the High Valleys at the southeastern end of the Long-Eared Mountains, and they were all very close to each other. They said that they would withdraw from the Tribunate and form a new little country of their own, where everybody would believe in the same church.

"But neither of the other religious groups seemed to want their country to be divided into smaller pieces. There were also some arguments about how to choose the Tribune. People wrote books about their positions and others said the books weren't true. And then a bishop of one of the religions said that "Truth must prevail and Error has no Rights," so his followers went and seized all the books written by the other religion and burned them in a great bonfire in the central square of their village."

Eli was horrified at the idea of such destruction.

"I can't remember which group said that error had no rights. Many felt that way, but no one had ever done anything about it before that time. Perhaps it was the Previes or the Evers. Anyway, the Posties had among them a number of young students who were very idealistic, and they said they would rather die than allow anyone to burn their books—or any books, for that matter. So they went into the Other Valleys to the south and brought back swords and spears. Then at a Christmas celebration, they rushed upon the Tribune, who was of one of the other religions, and ran three spears through his body. They left him dead outside of the cathedral.

"That was when the war started," said Nessuno. "There were some who thought this was a terrible thing and were very sorry that it happened, but others said that the people who did it were just plain bad people, and it was appropriate to kill them to avenge what they did to the Tribune. Others said that one of the groups was just as bad as the next, and that they were joyful when they killed their countrymen, raped their women, stabbed little children with their spears. But I do not think so. I think that when leaders—the people who have power—owe their position to the differences in religion, sooner or later, the result will always be a bloody crusade. People will always think they are doing God's will when they imprison, maim, or kill people of some other religion that they feel is inferior to theirs because someone in religious authority has told them so. I think that is the way it always happens.

"So this land near the foot of the chain of the Long-Eared Mountains is only populated now by a very few descendants of the survivors. For many years there were too many women and not enough men to marry them. My father, for example, died in the fighting, and when I was little, my mother and three aunts used to argue bitterly over who would marry the only single man left in the village, but he was a priest and didn't feel he should marry anyone at all. Nevertheless, all of my aunts argued with each other about who should have the right to try to make him abandon his vow and marry them. Without enough people, the country became very poor and also very suspicious of strangers who looked religious because of their clothing, even those dressed as unarmed monks, because they might be part of some savage movement that kills in the name of God. Or they might be seeking vengeance for some dreadful act that was inspired by some leader of another religious group," Nessuno concluded.

"It must be a sad land," said Eli, "to always live with hatred and fear in your memory."

"Oh, I do not hate so much," said Nessuno. "All of these things happened when I was a little boy, and now I am old. But I am suspicious and can never really trust anyone. Not even you. You may not have observed this, but under the table, I'm holding a weapon. In an instant, I could wield it with such force that I could crush your head before you knew what was happening."

Eli shifted slightly in his seat and measured the distance to the door with a glance. "And all of this from the pursuit of truth and religion," Eli mused aloud.

"Not really," countered Nessuno. "Many people believe in a religion that is good for both God and man. But people who believe devoutly and uncritically are easily led by political leaders who can convince them that there is evil in the hearts of those who do not share their beliefs. Sometimes these are religious leaders, sometimes military or political—but they all sharpen the religious differences among people. Then comes a time when *they* come to be seen as not the same sort of creature as *us*. Perhaps not really quite the same sort of human being, and then, later, as not being worthy of the same sort of life. Perhaps eventually no more difficult to kill without a pang of conscience than a mosquito, a frog, or a chicken."

Eli had finished his soup by this time, and the discussion had taken away the rest of his appetite.

"I must go across this land," Eli said. "Do you know the way to the West? Am I far from the famous Casa Sapienza, where the scholar Umberto and his sister Donna Elizabetta live?"

"Never heard of them," said Nessuno. "Perhaps they live farther up the High Valleys. But if you go on to the southwest from here, in a few days you will reach the Black River, where there is a ferry that will take you to the other side. Thence, you can go north of the city of Verity and, if you can find them, there are said to be ways to cross the Trackless Wastes of West. Beyond that it is rumored there is an even greater river, but I do not know its name."

"It must be the Spitte," said Eli. "Then to the east there must be the White Land, where it is very dry. But since I do not know where to search for what I seek, wherever she may be, north or east, south or west, I must go back by the way I came into this country."

And so, accepting a loaf of dry bread as provision from Nessuno, Eli set out again across the grain of the country toward the West.

Eli's strength was magnified by his resolution and desire; his time in the monastery had been a healthy interlude. He was strong and able, and walked swiftly when he did not actually run. He kept his bearings on the southernmost of the Long-Eared peaks and followed the setting sun to the west each day. Later he could not remember what he ate, and indeed he ate very little and slept seldom. He found some mushrooms of a sort that

Marna had taught him to trust. He gathered wild herbs in the meadows and along the stream banks and chewed them.

In three days he reached a shallow cove on the edge of the Black River, swam its broad current, and turned to the north on the farther side. A day and a half later he came around a curve in the river valley and saw the balanced arches of Casa Sapienza on the breast of the hill ahead of him. He was exhausted, his sandals had holes worn in them, and his stomach was tied in a knot of hunger, but he still had the strength to climb the hill swiftly and pull the bell chain at the entrance. Margaretta opened the door and gasped at the sight of the sunburned and tattered pilgrim that stood in the portal.

"It is Eli!" she cried. "Maria, Donna Elizabetta, Padrone! It is Eli—and he is not dead!"

FAMILIAR FACES, FATEFUL NEWS

The normal gaiety of the measured life at Casa Sapienza had been crushed when Marna's letter had reached Dottore Umberto. Maria and Margaretta had dissolved in tears when they heard the news. They wept not only for Eli but also for Marna, whom they felt was destined to be his bride. But now, on the following day, there had appeared at the front portico this weatherworn and dirty wraith, seemingly returned from the depths of the sea to which the news in the letter had consigned him. Donna Elizabetta took the young man in hand and in short order had him restored to at least a semblance of his former self. Eli was famished and seemed capable of eating anything set before him and still be ready for more.

Marna's letter had an opposite effect on Eli. The news that Marna had taken to dancing for paying audiences was in itself disturbing, but to learn that she was delivering herself to the glassblower to perform for him filled him with a mixture of rage and depression. How could she show another man what Eli himself had never seen?

"It is hard to remain true to one you have been told has died," explained Donna Elizabetta.

"But so soon?" asked Eli.

"It is not so soon," she answered. "Where have you been all this while? She had to support herself, and dancing was her talent. Why did you not come to rescue her sooner yourself?"

"But I was in the monastery, in the community of Theodoric Yorb. They told me that thinking of Marna would lead me to sin."

"And it took you more than three months to determine that you should leave?"

"They seemed very sure of themselves, and they said that was what God wanted of me."

"Eli," said Umberto, "what God wants of you can never be determined by anyone other than yourself. Nor can they determine sin or virtue. Your own conscience is the seat of sin and virtue. Even if you do all sorts of seemingly good things for reasons you know are selfish, or use another person as a thing rather than love that person as a sacred other being, you will be wrong in your own conscience. But if you pursue the good of another, you will be pursuing virtue."

"Then I must pursue Marna and prevent her from allowing herself to fall into the hands of that Lucindar!"

"Perhaps," said Umberto. "It might be so, unless Marna truly wants to be with Lucindar. Perhaps you just want her selfishly for yourself."

"Of course I want her for myself," said Eli. "But how can I know if that is just selfishness? She seemed to want to be with me when we were on the schooner. How can she have changed so much? The argument over that silly boy with the lavender pants and the mask couldn't have been that important to her."

"Follow your heart, Eli," said Donna Elizabetta, who had listened silently to the discussion.

"You must go and find her," said Margaretta. "She does not even know you are alive and looking for her."

"And if this Lucindar is as attractive as you are afraid he is," added Maria with a giggle, "perhaps you should send him here where one of us may be able to solace his loss of one girl with the possibility of choosing between two others. And we are, you know, older than Marna and perhaps better able to tame and guide such a man as the mustachioed glassblower."

The affectionate and often teasing encouragement of the two sisters had an even more noticeable effect on Eli's spirits. He soon inquired of Umberto about the snow depth in the passes that crossed the Long-Eared Mountains at this spring season of the year. Searches of the various wardrobes and cupboards of the great house produced a pair of hiking boots that fit him quite well. Eventually, with further help from Margaretta and Maria, he was outfitted and lightly equipped for cross-country travel with a rucksack of dried food and a rolled and folded sleeping bag.

The night before he started his journey, Eli talked late in the library with Umberto.

"Eli, my young friend," said Umberto. "I am older now. I will not be able to keep this place as a center of learning and of refuge forever. I wonder who could take it over and continue it in the pattern which my sister and I have formed from the traditions left us by our ancestors. I have heard of a young architect in the South who might be able to do so. He has the ability, but I do not know if he has the vision. Vision is an odd thing. I think I have seen more since I lost the sight of one eye than when I had the use of both. Sometimes adversity, such as you are experiencing now, may help you learn even more than health and satiety."

"How did you injure your eye, Padrone?" asked Eli.

"When I was a very small boy I traveled up into the Long-Eared Mountains where there was a stone carver. He made wonderful things of rock crystal. When I visited him he showed me lenses he had made from the purest quartz that can be found in the veins of the rocks far up the valleys. He made a telescope with these lenses and told me that I would learn many wonderful things if I looked through it. And this was true." The old scholar paused and fingered the velvet patch that covered his right eye. "But once I stared on the surface of the sun just at the end of a total eclipse, and the sight of the streaming corona lines around the dark disc was so wonderful that I could not resist looking too long, and when I turned away, that eye was blind."

"But Padrone," Eli said, "you see more with one eye than most men do with two."

The next morning, Eli left the great house almost as abruptly as he had arrived, promising that he would return again someday with Marna. Going up the valley past the great cataract, he was soon beyond the stream valleys where he had first encountered the statues of green stone. When he passed the representation of the graceful maiden with the jug and the goat boy with the flute, he was reminded of Horace's poems about the youths and maidens who would dance in the spring. He became more determined than ever that Marna would dance with him, and no one else. Not Pedrolino, not Lucindar—but only because she would know that he was the only one who valued her, would always be true to her, would love her and keep her in an open hand so that whatever happened, she would always want to return to him. *Fairer than the April rain ... more gracious than the summer of her hair ...* As the words of the poem came back to him, he resolved more surely that he was the one man to pursue and find and win her.

At the steeply rising slabs of shale and basalt that led to the grave cairn of Marna's parents, he experienced greater cold, but he found the wind was at his back, and he reached and passed the high notch in the mountains without trouble. Beyond, the way was all downhill across the lesser ridges and through the bowl-shaped valleys that he had traversed the previous year. He followed the setting sun to the west, and after a great while and much hardship from sleeping in the open, he came at last to a stone wall running across his path in the wilderness. He knew at last that he was back in his own country.

The Sons of Homer were at the great gray barn tending half a dozen gray and white kids that their goats had borne in the early spring. They welcomed Eli warmly, and shared their own tales of a rough passage across the Northern Sea. They told of how Old Gormley, guided by Reuben's revisions of Solomon's charts, had brought them to shore from his ketch in a small and leaking dinghy at a gravelly beach on the northwest coast of the land. Then, he had embarked again, leaving them behind near a colony of sea lions. From there they had made a difficult winter crossing of the northernmost Branch of Spitte and found their way eventually back to the Cove, to the dock of Stanley and Staley, and eventually, to their own last cleared field. They had shared the tales of their adventures on the lake and rivers beyond the Long-Eared Mountains with the two storekeepers, and the goatherds were able to tell Eli that his skiff was waiting for him beside the house by the water. Eli wanted to learn more of their northern adventures, but he had more pressing concerns farther south along the other branches of the Valley of Spitte.

"I think perhaps she will wait for you," said Hamlet. "In matters of love it takes a long time to settle a lady's mind. It is possible that you will not be too late."

"Go on!" said Horatio. "The prize is to be won. Press on, young Eli, press on!"

"Love does not linger," said Horace. "It is like the morning dew and is as like to light upon a thistle as a rose."

Eli hastened down the pasturelands to the Cove and found Stanley and Staley in the process of giving his boat a coat of new anti-fouling paint below the waterline.

"Just in time," said Staley. "We can launch her this afternoon. It is good to get the boat into the water while these soft copper paints are still tacky."

"But it will get paint all over us while we are moving her," said Stanley.

"That's why we have gloves and are wearing our old clothes, Brother," responded Staley.

So Eli was soon on the water again, equipped with a new oar that Staley had made to match the one he'd had when he first sculled into the Cove. There was also a leeboard that fit over the gunwale of the skiff and functioned like a keel but could be detached and put in the bottom of the boat when he came into shallow water. Both sailing and rowing with the current, he made rapid progress to the south until he reached the Branching of Spitte. Here he circled carefully with the current, near the shore, and went three-quarters of the way around the basin that centered in the whirlpool until he reached the East Branch and set off upstream into a rising easterly wind.

When the wind was against him, he set up the leeboard and tacked back and forth across the river, but even so, sometimes he had to row to make progress against the current in the East Branch. The rowing was not hard against the wind, but the signs of a storm were rising unmistakably in the western sky that faced him. Huge towers of cloud appeared blue-black against the sun-filled sky, and he knew that he would have to make shore before long to avoid being caught out on the water in a squall like the one Marna had taught him about on the Black Lake.

He moored the skiff to a pair of shoreside trees, and putting a dark green poncho over his shoulders, he continued along the riverbank as darkness gathered and the first few raindrops spattered on the back of his neck.

45 THE TREE

Arnold, Aelred, and Ali were quite true to the bargain they had made with Marna (whom they still called Columbina). Mounted on four mules with two others carrying packs of merchandise, they started west from Lucro and took the narrow trail that led them up into the White Land, which they crossed by night marches to avoid the heat of the day in that dry climate. They crossed south of Hat Mountain and rode easily along the side of the Upper Mohr and the shore of the Black Lake. A few days later they met with merchants from the city of Verity with whom they bargained for several hours in the evening after setting up an encampment of tents. The emissaries of Verity were in need of colored-glass goblets for their library table service for the enbibliated, and the three merchants had only a single pair of golden yellow ones to offer.

But after much haggling they executed a contract to return with a large collection of colored glass; goblets in a variety of colors for the guild hall, red and green collars for the navigational markers in the harbor, and panes of colored glass for the windows of the library. Marna remained silent through all these negotiations. She had no desire to return to the city of the consistently true and false speakers of the guilds.

Thence they proceeded northwest into the Trackless Wastes of West, where the merchants found their way by following secret signs, blazes, and guideposts that led them to the West. There were old logging traces running among the tangled trees, and although all looked similar, the three merchants seemed to always have a way of determining which path to choose.

The terrain was hilly, and from the crests it was often possible to discern two bulky prominences that Marna decided must be the Broad

Hump and Toe Top Mountain, although they looked altogether different when they were seen from the different angle of passing between them, moving slowly to the northwest. But then, from the height of a minor hill where they paused to survey the woodland ahead, Aelred pointed at something above the distant horizon.

"There he is. Look—to the left of the blue hill."

The others followed his pointing arm and saw a tiny round object just above the distant hills beyond. It was one of Lucindar's balloons, sent up to guide merchants to his glassworks.

It was still another day's journey before they reached their destination—the little house and the barn set beside the small pastures on a wooded ridge above the valley of the East Branch of the Spitte. Just knowing that she was near her own river again raised Marna's spirits, and she was looking forward to meeting Lucindar again.

Ali rode ahead to meet the glassblower and discuss the purchase of Marna's contract with him. The others made another camp in the woods and waited for him to come back.

"Now, at last we know your name," announced Ali upon his return. "Lucindar tells us that you are Marna and that he is acquainted with your grandfather, Sennet of the Rock Tower above the River Spitte."

"Well and good," said Arnold. "But does he want the girl—or rather, her contract?"

"He says he does, and he sends her a message," continued Ali. "If her dancing pleases him, he will consider giving her the contract to keep or sell to whomever she chooses."

The idea of being the mistress of her own life again appealed to Marna, but the idea of being put on trial for Lucindar's approval didn't seem proper at all. She was not sure how she should react to his proposal.

They followed the sign of the lofty balloon the next morning and came to the clearing around the house by midday.

"So!" said Lucindar with a broad smile. "So now you have learned how to dance. Not just learned to dance, but to dance so well that your contract was bid for at the great theater of Lucro. Now that I own your contract, you will dance for me, will you not?"

Marna was never quite sure why she refused. She did not really think that Lucindar was a bad man, or that he meant her any harm. In fact, she liked him and found his request exciting. And she loved to dance in the pretty pleated dancing dress not only because she knew it was pretty, but also because it reminded her of Maria and Margaretta and her friends at Casa

Sapienza. But the idea of Lucindar owning her contract, owning any part of her, had begun to bother her. She wanted above all else to be free of constraint and directed by her own decisions.

She shook her head. "No," she said. "I dance when I will, but not at anyone's command. You may own a contract, but you do not own me."

Lucindar looked very disappointed. "You will dance for me, here in this house, sooner or later; I think I can be sure of that."

In spite of Marna's unwillingness, Lucindar entered into a long negotiation with the three merchants. He had very little money to offer them, but he did have a great deal of blown glass, of all the colors of the spectrum.Some they packed into straw-filled crates which they lashed to the pack frames of the mules. Part of the bargain was for more goblets and blue and silver paperweights that Lucindar contracted to prepare before their next journey to the West. Paperweights seemed to be in great demand in Lucro. Eventually all four men were satisfied with the arrangements, and they concluded their affairs with a supper of roast lamb which Lucindar cooked on skewers over a stone fireplace outside the house.

Although the supper was a merry affair, Marna became more tense as the evening wore on and it became obvious that the three merchants were ready to leave and start for the valley of the Black River again. When they departed, she helped with the washing up and said very little to Lucindar. He too was largely silent, although he smiled a lot and hummed an unfamiliar melody as he moved about the house. Marna soon went upstairs to the tiny blue bedroom she had occupied before. Lucindar settled himself in the living room below where he could observe the stairs and carefully watched her departure.

Marna wasn't really frightened, but she still made sure to fasten the door behind her with a wooden turnbutton on the inside. As the storm that had been brewing all day began to approach, she realized that leaving the house of the glassblower might not be as easy this time as it had been when she was carried off in his balloon. Finally she heard the *click* of the locks on the doors below, as though Lucindar had locked them both inside the house. Then his heavy tread came up the stairs and there was a rattle of the tumblers as a key turned in the lock of her room. The latch slid home and she was firmly locked in.

"Tomorrow we will talk again of what is owed and what is owned. You have a debt to settle here for making off with my balloon."

"I did nothing of the sort," said Marna through the closed door. "It was you who told me to get into it." But she began to feel less sure of his good intentions when he chuckled from the other side of the door.

"This door can be locked and must be unlocked from both sides," he said. "We should come to an agreement to be agreeable to each other. We will discuss it again tomorrow. Sweet dreams, pretty dancer of mine." And with that he went back down the stairs.

Marna tried the door very quietly, but it was firmly closed. The drop from the window was not too great, but it was more than she wanted to attempt in the middle of a stormy night. She thought of calling out, but there was no one to hear, no help for many miles around.

The storm only increased as the night wore on. Locked in the little bedroom, Marna decided to make the best of the bad situation and get some rest. Wondering what might happen tomorrow, she sat down on the edge of the bed, undid her braids, and pulled off her shoes.

And then she saw her nightgown. It was hanging on a wooden peg on the back of the locked door where she must have left it those many months ago, before the unplanned flight in the balloon. She remembered that other stormy night as being so much more pleasant than this one, but the old nightgown with its ruffled hem, white with tiny pale-blue and green flowers printed on the soft cotton flannel, was familiar and comforting. She undressed, took the chain with the green stone from her neck, and hung it on the peg. She slipped the familiar garment over her head and climbed into the bed. She pulled the covers around her shoulders and wiggled her toes under the pink and white quilt that was folded at the foot of the bed.

She was warm enough, and with the covers close about her ears, the howling of the wind and the distant rumbles of thunder didn't bother her. She fell asleep soon but woke again when she heard the stairs creak once or twice during the night. Eventually she heard Lucindar's bedroom door close across the hall. But it was hard to get back to sleep. Flashes of lightning would suddenly appear from the inky black of the rainy night and then wink out into invisibility again.

The thunder followed after a pause of some time. Marna tried to count the seconds to learn how far away the lightning had struck. In each second the sound would travel more than a thousand feet, about four seconds to the mile. At first the flashes and the rumbles were too distant and she could not estimate which flash went with the distant booms, until there was a more brilliant illumination of the windowpanes and the crash followed just an instant later. The rain seemed to beat more heavily on the roof after that and the thunder rumbled more distantly for an instant.

And then it came. The deafening explosion shook the house, and light brighter than the day instantaneously threw all the details of the little room into total clarity. As the darkness burst back upon Marna there was a second noise, a wrenching, cracking burst of explosive sound that seemed to be coming down from the darkened sky above the house.

"The tree!" she cried. "*The tree!*"

The whole house lurched and shuddered as the mighty trunk, riven by the lightning, split in half and fell in two pieces across the very center of the house. The door to Marna's room was torn away and a shower of bricks from the shattered chimney burst into the room. Rain and wind gusted in and a subsiding thrashing of branches settled slowly among the remains of the broken timbers, plaster, lath, and clapboards of the whole middle of the house and where the hall to Lucindar's bedroom had been just moments before.

Marna's only thought was escape. Escape from the house, from Lucindar if he were still alive, escape from that terrible tree. She wrenched up the sash of the dormer window and wriggled through the small opening onto the slippery wet pine shingles of the steeply pitched roof. As she was about to lose her hold on the sill, she leaped off into the dark, into the air, into the muddy bed of myrtle below where she rolled over and over in the wet leaves.

Shaken but not much hurt, she struggled to her feet and looked back at the house. In the blackness she saw blue and yellow flames licking up from the kitchen where the gas lines that connected to the glassblower's fuel supply connected also to the house's heater and stove.

"Lucindar!" she called. "Lucindar! Get out! Get out!"

But no sound came from the crushed remnants of the house. Only the flames flashed higher in the pelting rain, and suddenly she saw that the barn was also on fire. The glass furnaces were always alight, and the gas pouring from broken tubes and pipes ignited in sheets of flame.

Barefoot and soaking wet, Marna ran. Away from the house and tree, past the now-burning barn toward the broad path that led to the cleared field, she ran in terror of the awful things behind her. The flames leapt higher for a moment until in an instant, a huge explosion sent an immense orange fireball rolling up into the storm-filled sky. The light of the flame cast her shadow onto the bushes beyond as she rushed toward the dark mouth of the trail ahead that led she knew not where.

THE THIRD MEETING

46

In the gathering darkness, Eli, wrapped in his dark green poncho, picked his way along the shore of the river. Several times he was startled by the fluttering explosion of a grouse flushed from the undergrowth by his approach. The river seemed to be running faster and deeper, as though it had received new sources farther upstream. Distant flashes of lightning cast weird shadows through the trees.

After more than an hour of this halting progress he had come upon a more cleared area of the riverbank, and a little dock built on a pile of stones where a turn in the riverbed had created a small backwater. On a rack, gleaming in the intermittent light, was the smooth rounded shape of a canoe. *Marna's own craft!* The sight of the fragile boat in which he had first seen the girl raised his spirits, even though it meant that she could not yet have returned by this route to the Rock Tower. He quickened his pace, but the rain also increased, and the lightning flashes seemed to be coming closer together and with greater intensity.

He had just started up a muddy trail to the east that seemed to lead from the dock upward, out of the valley of the river, when a close lightning bolt blinded him for an instant. Doggedly he went on in the darkness until another deafening crash and brilliant blue-white light surrounded him with a shock wave that almost threw him to the ground. Looking up, he saw a huge flaming tree beyond him slowly separate into two giant torches that toppled deliberately in opposite directions. There were a series of sharp reports and crashes as the limbs descended and then burst into flame.

Over the roar of the storm he heard a high-pitched scream in the distance—an animal or a human being?

He ran onward through the woods, through wet brush, his face whipped by laurel branches, thorn bushes catching at his wet trousers. He mounted the next rise and found himself looking down at the remains of a small house, its entire midsection crushed under the mighty trunk of a flaming tree. In the blue and yellow light of the fire he could see the figure of a man pounding at the windowpanes of the room at the end of the house. At that very moment the glass broke under the impact of his fist and, dragging a limp right arm beside him, the man hurled himself through the jagged panes onto the pine needles that covered the ground outside. As he did so, he emitted a loud cry of pain.

"Come—come away from the house!" shouted Eli as he approached.

The man tried to struggle to his feet, using his one good arm. Eli put his own arms around the man's waist and pulled him away from the house.

"But Marna!" groaned the wounded man. "Locked in! Upstairs, in back!"

Eli was around the house in an instant, but looking up at the shattered chimney beside the broken ridgepole, the fire only revealed the blackness of an open dormer window and a flickering of flame. At that moment a streak of flame flashed across the space between the house and the glassworks beyond it, and flames burst out of the windows of the farther building. Beyond the barn, for a brief instant, he caught sight of a small figure in white running away from the scene of the fire. A slight figure of a girl, barefoot, with tangled hair flying behind her, fleeing into the darkness of the pelting rain.

And then the whole barn disappeared in a huge ball of flame that roiled up into the blackness of the storm with the thud and roar of a shock wave that knocked him from his feet and crushed his head and shoulders against the stones of the terraced wall. Unconsciousness closed in upon him for an instant.

Eli awoke to the man's face peering down at him. He seemed anxious, and his dark eyes were fierce as he looked down at Eli. "I cannot climb," said the man. "My right arm is broken. She will burn!"

"No," said Eli, "she is gone—gone beyond the barn. I saw her, somewhere in the fields!"

And with that he pulled himself erect again and staggered toward the remains of the flaming glassworks. Blood from the cut beside his eye blurred his vision, and his shoulder was painful where he had been injured long before. Nonetheless, skirting the burning hulk of the furnaces, he began to run up the path toward the summit of the hill.

"Marna!" he shouted. "Marna! Come back! It's me, Eli—come back, come back!"

And from a shadowy gap in the bushes at the edge of the clearing, the figure of a girl appeared before him, hesitated for a moment, and then, arms raised, ran toward him through the rainy dark.

"Oh God!" she cried. "God! Make it be. I cannot hope again but this one time!"

"Marna," he said into her wet hair as he wrapped his arms and the folds of his poncho around her shivering figure. "Don't ever go away from me again. Not ever."

"I never will!" she said with her lips pressed against his bloody cheek. "Eli, I never will!

47 THE PASSING OF GORMLEY

Many other things happened in the Valley of Spitte thereafter. Lucindar's broken arm was set by Aelred, who, along with Arnold and Ali, had been attracted by the huge explosion. The glassblower inspected the smoking wreckage of his wor shop and house and decided to go to the land beyond the Trackless Wastes of West with Arnold, Ali, and Aelred. He had a large financial credit for the glass the merchants had already packed to take back to Verity and Lucro, and he felt he could restart his enterprise in a less-remote location in the East. It seemed likely that there would be a market for his skills in that other country. The fire had destroyed his copy of Marna's contract, which, in the light of her feelings had been proved to be worthless anyway. But he brightened up somewhat when Eli told him that there were other musical young women who might assuage his loneliness beyond the Long-Eared Mountains.

There was nothing left in the charred ruins of the glassworks or the house, although Marna and Eli did find the razor that Occam had given to Marna. The case was stained, but the blade was as keen as ever. Marna gave it to Eli with a laugh. "You will need this as soon as the place where you slashed your face heals up. Just don't cut your throat; it looks like a dangerous implement for an amateur!"

Marna and Eli brought the two boats down the river to the Rock Tower, much to the joy of Sennet, who saw them coming from a long way off with his telescope. Although they'd been away for little more than a year, to Sennet it had seemed much longer, and he appeared to have aged far more than a year's worth.

And indeed it was not very long after this that both Sennet and then Solomon died, full of years and honor for their good and useful lives spent in guiding and protecting sailors on the river and the sea. So, of all the senior gener ation, only Gormley, the oldest of all, was left alive. He was then so old that it was even credible when people said that he knew some of the first settlers when he himself was young. There were tavern jokes that he was as old as the last of the Wall Builders, but this could not have been true.

And then, later on, after a time of work on the buoys and range markers on the upper river, after correcting the charts, Eli and Marna interrupted their first ripe autumn together when they received word from Reuben that Old Gormley was back in Salem and wanted to speak with the two young people. He was said to be ill and wished them to come to him soon. They went down the Spitte on the ketch *Mercy* with Reuben, who seemed to have become stand-in master of the vessel while Gormley was incapacitated. When they arrived they found the old man lodged above Solomon's chart shop.

"You have traveled a long distance and lived a great deal in a short span of years," he said. "But have you learned anything?"

"I think I have learned to trust myself," said Eli.

"Rubbish!" said Gormley. "You would do better to trust Marna when she tells you to reef your sails."

"I guess I have learned that, too," said Eli after a pause. "I know, and I will."

"And you," he queried Marna brusquely, "what answers to the mystery of life have you learned while over there beyond the Long-Eared Mountains?"

"I think I have learned the answer to a riddle that a wise woman told me at Casa Sapienza," she said. "What leader needs no follower, what follower needs no leader, and who needs to neither lead nor follow?"

"Ha! Who is that?" said Gormley.

Marna told him Catarina's solution to the three questions—that a man does not have to lift a greater weight than a woman, nor a woman do domestic work that a man does not do, but that both can lift and support each other all their lives through.

"Pfaugh!" said Gormley. "Half an answer at best! Learn this, young people: With faith you need no follower; with hope you need no leader;

with love you need not feel compelled to either lead or follow!"

"You are right," said Marna. "I should have learned that from the little black priest in Lucro."

Gormley looked hard at Marna.

"So, you met him too when you traveled. One can learn much from traveling. But I think you have reason to stay home for a while now, in the Valley of Spitte," he said. He was silent for a few minutes before he spoke again. "I will leave my boat to Reuben who can exercise command. If you are to undertake another great adventure, ask him the way you should travel."

Within a day, Gormley passed away in great peace. He told no one his age, but everyone was sure he was much more than a hundred years old. His final wish had been to bequeath to Eli and to Marna the sea chest with mementos of his many voyages, and to give a commission to Reuben to take title of the old ketch, *Mercy*, that had been his vessel for the later years of his life.

Marna and Eli carefully unpacked the old sailor's chest. It contained a few papers concerning ownership of the ketch, and some maps and clothing. The maps were largely corrected versions of the charts of Solomon of Salem. There was an old-fashioned blue jacket with high lapels and a double row of gilded brass buttons. They found a sextant, a bearing compass, and a suit of yellow oilskin foul-weather clothing. At the bottom of the chest, they came upon a garment of heavy silk brocade, cream colored with red and blue appliquéd flowers and geometrical designs done in orange and pale green. It was trimmed with gold lace and had a scarlet satin lining. Beneath it was an oddly shaped, flattened object, embroidered with golden gallooning. Two broad fringed and decorated tapes hung from the back, and in front there was a band of embroidery decorated with sixteen small triangles of polished green stone, bound in shiny wire. A place for a seventeenth stone seemed to have been torn away and was missing. The interior was like a flattened envelope and was lined with scarlet silk.

"What is it? It is so beautiful; could it have belonged to this rough old sailor?" asked Marna.

"It must have belonged to him at one time," said Eli. "I think it is a ceremonial hat, designed to make a man look tall—a symbol of authority. Could it be the mitre of a bishop?"

Then there were summers of sailing the river and correcting the charts that Eli prepared for his brothers' publication under the old imprint of Solomon of Salem. These were seasons of love and longing, but eventually, there came a time for the wedding of the two grown river children. Their union was a party such as the valley had not seen since the days of the first settlers. The celebration was in the late warm days of autumn, and boats full of guests from both up and down the river came and moored beneath the tower. In the evenings they were decorated with blue and white paper lanterns, and music from mandolins and recorders filled the night.

Stanley and Staley came from the north in a brightly painted barge and brought the three Sons of Homer with them. Even Amalthea was on board. Reuben sailed up from Salem with several more of Eli's brothers in his crew. The mariners of the river assembled in great number to honor the young couple, for they were to become not only man and wife, but also the Keepers of the River Markers and the guardians of the Rock Tower itself.

Their marriage was witnessed by Reuben, because he was now the captain of a ship, and in that capacity had presided over weddings in the past, and had the legal authority to do so. He dressed in Gormley's double-breasted dark blue jacket with the gilt buttons and high lapels. But he spoke gently to the young couple, and advised them never to speak harshly to one another for any reason, for the rest of their lives, and to be faithful in all conditions of weather or storm, on sea and on land, until death should dissolve their union.

The party went on until the guests left, and they saw the stars begin to fade in the morning sky over the distant lands to the east.

Then Eli and Marna took each other's hands and ascended the several flights of stairs to the large room at the top of the Rock Tower where they had furnished their bridal bedroom. They had placed a broad iron and brass bedstead, covered with woven white linens, to face the northwestern balcony windows. Between the tall glass doors there was an ancient was stand with a large pink and white pottery basin and a small mirror on the wall. The floor of the room was of smooth worn flagstones, cool to bare feet but covered beside the bed and in front of the washstand with oval rugs of braided white cotton.

Marna filled a white china ewer with hot water and poured it in the basin. Eli brushed up a great lather on his face and used the razor of the Barber of Berrymor to shave closely, until his cheeks were as smooth as Marna's own. She looked again at the faint red lines of the scars on his cheek, shin, and shoulder, and traced the marks on his skin more gently than when she had healed the first of the wounds he had received. And then the grown-up river children led each other to the broad, white-covered bed and surrendered to each other all the sweetness and desire they had looked forward to for so long.

And through the long night, beyond the northwestern windows
of the bridal room, there circled all the northern stars:
Alcaid, Mizar, Alioth, Kochab, Thuban,
the other companions
of Cassiopeia,
and Polaris
itself.

FINIS

ALCAID

URSA MAJOR

MIZAR

ALIOTH

ALCOR

MEGREZ

KOCHAB

THUBAN

URSA
MINOR

POLARIS

CASSIOPEIA

ABOUT THE AUTHOR

David D. Hume served as headmaster of a boys' school for many years. Along the way, he has also become a painter, a sailor, a boatbuilder, and a writer of travel books about Italy. Still a teacher of young and old, his *Beyond the Long-Eared Mountains* contains a rollicking good yarn, lots of good advice on how to anchor, how to predict approaching stormy weather, when to reef the sails, and when to avoid wild mushrooms. The book abounds in menus of Italian cooking, and some theological advice for young and old alike.

Photo by Adam Hume